Early Praise for *The*

Haunting and compelling. A story that will stay with you long after you finish it. A story of survival and triumph. A 19th century tale of three women who find their way to freedom, and along the way their paths are woven into a very twisted and surprising ending.

Alex Smith- NFL Quarterback

"Brilliantly written! It's a vivid, twisted tale of a dark time and culture as three women struggle toward freedom."

Javier Soto- Good Morning Arizona (CBS TV3)

It's a great story! You'll love Peri, a 19th century "she-ro," fearless and determined, haunted by a dark past forced upon her family. Only by discovering the "Treasure of Cedar Creek" can she find peace. The reader's emotions plunge and soar, intertwined in the lives of three young women who survive unthinkable horrors that rip a family apart - but bind them together in a quest to escape.

Tracie Potts- NBC News

I loved The Treasure of Cedar Creek! The characters in the book are so vividly described and so genuine that you can't help but empathize with them. The book reads like a journal in many ways, making you feel like you're reliving actual historical events. As the story builds, you can't put the book down; ... It's an intricate story with just the right amount of twists and turns. I highly recommend The Treasure of Cedar Creek.

Mike Parsons, Morning Show Host
B98.7, Salt Lake City, Utah

The Treasure of Cedar Creek

Brenda Stanley

The Treasure of Cedar Creek

Copyright 2018 – Brenda Stanley
ISBN # 978-1-943789764

Taylor and Seale Publishing, LLC.
Daytona Beach, Florida 32118
Phone: 1-386-760-8987
www.taylorandseale.com

For my daughters and granddaughters.

"A woman is like a tea bag—you never know how strong she is until she gets in hot water."

—Eleanor Roosevelt

The Treasure of Cedar Creek

Chapter 1

Emma

October 7, 1896

This isn't my story. I'm telling this for the lost souls. I've been told that I am safe now, but my heart still pounds when I hear footsteps coming to the door or even the rustle of the aspen leaves in the breeze. I'm not sure I'll ever feel safe again. He's still out there and as long as he is, I know that he will be searching for me. I have something that he feels is his and he will kill me to get it back. I know his rage and have felt his violence. He may call himself a man of God, but what was done in the name of the Lord is nothing less than cold-blooded killing. It may have stopped for now, but I hear whispers in the wind and murmurs in the water of the stream, and it is his voice letting me know he's still there and watching me. So much evil. So much pain. I spend my time watching and waiting because in my heart I know it isn't over.

My name is Emma Elizabeth Dixon. I was named after my father's mother Emma and my mother's sister Elizabeth. I never knew either of these women. What I know was told to me by my mother as she sat by the fire and talked about her past life in Missouri. In fact, I've never met any family outside of my own. I often feel we were dropped like a spot of ink on paper when we landed in the tiny town of Challis, Idaho. We knew no one and nothing about the area, except that it was ripe for the word of the Lord.

Father brought us here when he heard the mines were fruitful. We were already on our way to California when he changed routes and headed to our new home in Idaho. Father wasn't a miner and had no intentions to be. He was a man of God; a minister, and he wanted to make his mark on the world. Finding fresh and unenlightened souls is what he was prospecting for and the rugged, simple, and often orphaned young men of the mines were exactly who he was hoping to save. I wonder now if he's watching us from heaven and wishing he had tried to save us.

I spend my days in this cabin hiding and thinking, and when I want to block out the sinister memories, I think back to before it all turned dark and murky. I think back to when Father was still alive, and to when I believed that being a god-fearing Christian gave me the armor I needed to survive whatever I faced in life. Now I wonder if it was my lack of faith or just God's plan. I guess until it's over, I'll never know.

I often think of when I was young. One day in particular is still vivid in my mind. It's been almost eight years, and not until now do I realize the significance of that day. I was only twelve years old and my life was simple and happy. How could I have ever imagined the turn it would take and that I would be where I am now?

It was a hot day for May in Challis, but we were shaded by the barn and watching as father prepared to cull a newborn foal.

"It has to be done, Peri," said father, as my younger sister held his leg, tears pouring from her eyes.

It wasn't that anyone wanted to see this done, but Peri was particularly fond of animals and even cried when Mother butchered chickens.

My brother Paul, Peri's twin, went to her and put his blond head to hers. "Don't cry. Come in the house with me and we'll finish the puzzle," he said, trying to comfort her and remove her from the barn.

It was a newborn colt that was causing the scene. Although father was the town's minister, he, like the other men who worked in the area, kept a few cows and other livestock, including a half dozen Appaloosa horses that he bred. He had bought them from a Nez Perce Indian man in Northern Idaho as we passed through the area. Father had tried to convert him to our beliefs, but instead the Indian converted father on the distinct and extraordinary markings of the Appaloosa, their stamina, their sure and resilient hooves, and most importantly, the potential they had for profit.

"It's not fair!" Peri wailed. "There's nothing wrong with him. He's beautiful. Why are you going to kill him?" Peri was fiery and stubborn, and as I watched her counter every response Father made, I witnessed a ten-year-girl turn a grown man from thinking he was in control.

The colt stayed close to his mother; his wobbly legs trying to keep from trembling and collapsing underneath him. He was obviously unaware of the magnitude of the debate that was taking place as he struggled to stay upright. His ears twitched when Peri cried out again, pleading with Father to spare him.

Father bent down and with Paul standing by, put an arm around her shoulders, tried to explain the importance of the horses having good genes and being able to see the identifiable spots that signaled a worthy Appaloosa.

"It takes a lot of work and money to raise a foal. This one won't sell, so it will end up costing me money. It's what we have to do to make a living. If I kept all the foals that won't sell, I wouldn't be able to buy us the things we need, like flour or beans," he tried to reason with her.

"I don't need flour or beans. I don't need anything if it means you have to kill him," she spat back. "Please, Father!" she begged. "I'll do anything."

Father stood and heaved a long and laborious sigh. He looked at Paul, who shrugged. He lifted Peri's chin and looked down into her red and swollen eyes. "You'll have to clean out the stalls and find other chores to pay me what it costs to keep it. And if you don't keep up and this turns into work for me, I won't give you another chance."

Peri's eyes widened with excitement and triumph. She hopped up and down, with her hands clasped together. "Do you mean it? I will! I will!" she shouted. She hugged him and then turned to Paul. "My own horse!" she exclaimed and hugged him too. She went to the fence and started talking to the colt as though explaining the careful details of what had just occurred and what she was expected to do.

Father watched her for a moment, then rolled his eyes, and with tired defeat gave a huff. He went to the next stall and began to gather up some loose rope.

Paul went to Peri and stood at the stall watching the pardoned foal. "What do you plan to name him?" he asked.

Peri raised her eyebrows and contemplated the question.

"What about Spotless?" I yelled, trying to pop her bubble, by reminding her the foal was missing the desired dappled coat.

She gave me an annoyed smirk and then dismissed me and turned back to Paul.

He smiled at me, actually finding humor in my suggestion. He looked at the colt, turned to Peri and said, "What about Chance?" He gave a nod to the foal. "After all, you gave him a second chance."

Peri clasped her hands together in joy. "I love it!" she exclaimed. "It's perfect."

Paul smiled, genuinely happy for her. They were twins, but their bond seemed even closer than one would expect. I often felt like an outsider because they had each other and it seemed that is all they needed. They obviously weren't identical twins, but Peri refused to wear girls' clothes unless Mother made her wear them at church or when we went to town with the twins being the same size and with the same coloring, they were often mistaken as such. It would have horrified me to be confused for a boy, but Peri seemed to revel in it. We had little in common except for our gender, and even then we looked like opposites.

I climbed down from my perch on the fence and walked to father. "Why does she get her own horse?" I whined. I didn't want a horse. I didn't enjoy riding the way Peri and Paul did, but I felt slighted and needed to point that out.

He pulled at the bow in my hair. "If you want to clean out the stalls, I'll give you a horse too," he chided me.

I huffed seeing he knew my ploy. I had no reason to resent my sister but I envied her strong will and confident nature. Even at such a young age she had a sense of self and refused to let anyone try to alter that. She loved Paul and our parents, and while I felt she barely put up with me, I knew that if anyone ever tried to hurt me, she would be the first to step between. And when father died just three years later, it was Peri who stood and comforted me at the gravesite. She was stoic and squeezed my hand as we watched our mother begin her fall into darkness.

I shouldn't blame mother for the result of what she did. She had little choice. She knew that without Father, our family had no means to survive. We were helpless and that is how we found ourselves at the mercy of a man who claimed to be our savoir. Mother made the decision to marry him because she thought it would save us both physically and spiritually. We left Challis and traveled to a place he described as God's earthly home. And it wasn't until we arrived that we learned what our mother's decision meant for the rest of our lives.

Deon Heff was the prophet and the man my mother believed would save us. He claimed he had been called by God, just as his father before him. He was responsible for the two hundred souls living in the community of Cedar Creek several miles north of Bear Lake, Idaho. He came to the mines in Challis to do business, and when he saw my mother, widowed, and in need, he offered her a life of service to God, a life of never wondering where her next meal would come from.

Peri hated the idea and made it known. Paul stayed silent. He felt he had let us down by not being able to step up as the man of the house, and when Deon told him he had arranged for him to stay in Challis to look over our home and land, he agreed. I silently wondered how Mother loved my father and yet could marry so soon. However, Deon was so kind and generous, I quickly found myself clearing the path for her to marry him.

Chapter 2

About twenty miles southwest of Montpelier, Idaho
August 20, 1896

The sun was just beginning to peek above the horizon giving Peri enough light to see where she needed to go. Her horse kept trying to grab bites of tall grass as they walked along the narrow path through the steep canyon.

Grace was wrapped in a shawl, reins in hand at the helm of the old wagon. In the back, Emma still slept, her belly bulging from under the blanket. It was a single trail and the wagon heaved and twisted over rocks and gopher holes. When the branches of the cottonwood trees reached out and tangled Grace's hair or poked at her face she whined, but Peri just kept riding. She had had no intention of bringing Emma, and therefore the large and slow wagon was a hindrance, and she fully intended to punish Grace with it.

"It wasn't my idea to take this route," Peri reminded Grace. "You were the one that didn't want to stay on the main trail through the willow grove."

Grace huffed. "We'd all be dead if we had entered the grove. The demon is strong and would have killed us all."

Peri shook her head. "There is no demon," Peri said, knowing exactly how that folktale got started.

"Yes, there is. I know a girl who saw it. The demon lives in the tops of trees. He knows when young women are there and swoops down and picks them up by their hair. Anyone who leaves the compound is in danger," she said and pulled the shawl tighter.

Peri rolled her eyes. She had agreed to help Grace escape, but had never met her. It was Grace's brother Marty that had Peri's devotion.

The escape was successful so far, but Peri hadn't planned on Emma and a wagon. Emma was her sister, but she had no use for her and hadn't intended to save her or even see her. It was Grace she had come to rescue, and now she not only had one more person to fend for, but also one who was pregnant. The wagon made it difficult to navigate thin trails and brushy country. It made the long trip slower, more erratic, and the stakes higher. The Elders of The Kingdom of Glory compound didn't take lightly to losing what was theirs. Stealing two of the prophet's wives, and more importantly a future child destined to carry on the prophet's blood, would have the entire colony out for vengeance.

Her mother had brought them to Cedar Creek. Emma and Periwinkle. Peri found it hard to be angry with her mother, especially since she was dead, but even at eighteen years of age, she couldn't forgive her for giving her that name. She went by Peri and was the very contradiction of the sweet flower she was named after. She cut her long blond hair so short that, until she hit puberty, people thought she was a boy. And even then, she was mistaken because of the way she dressed and her ability to ride a horse and shoot a gun.

Her mother tried to teach her the ways of the home, but Peri had no interest in anything that happened inside the walls of a house. She could mend but she couldn't sew. She could cook, but only on a campfire. She wore her twin brother's clothes, refusing to wear the long gingham dresses the other girls and women wore.

Up until age fourteen, she hoped to just keep being a boy. However, that summer as she watched the other young men strip off their shirts and lift large bales of hay, something stirred in her that was overwhelming, and when it came to the idea of being with a man, she knew inside she was unmistakably female.

When she moved with her mother to the compound, she was required to wear long billowy dresses and grow her hair into long braids that were customary with the women. It felt awkward. She was also forbidden to associate with any boys, to ride horses, hunt, fish, or do any of the things she enjoyed. The compound for Peri was no less than hell. Once she escaped, she went back to her pants, chopped hair, and the activities she loved. Now it was a matter of survival. They didn't allow women to work in the mines and that was all she knew. Peri learned the swagger of men and how to talk in a low voice. In fact, she rarely spoke. Mainly she watched and did whatever it took to keep her place in the world secure. The past year it had become harder to hide her breasts, hips, and feminine features that had eluded her before.

She swallowed the last piece of bread she had torn from the loaf for her breakfast. They had plenty of food and water to take them to the next town where they could replenish their supplies. Peri had stopped in Montpelier on her way down to Cedar Creek. She figured they could get there before anyone gathered a posse and catch up to them. She felt pretty confident that the worst of it was over and now she just had to stay the course and reach the meeting place and Marty.

"Why are you mad at me?" Grace asked as she sat holding the reins of the wagon. "Is it because we had to go around Willow Grove? Or because of Emma?"

Peri ignored her questions. She hadn't planned to divert their route around the main trail, but it also didn't bother her. She had her own reasons for not wanting to travel through that area. And Grace's silly delusions about a ghost in the trees was worth the diversion just to shut her up. However, Peri was beginning to realize nothing seemed to help with that.

Grace continued, unaffected by Peri's irritation with her. "Why aren't you happy that I brought Emma? I didn't know she was your sister. Why don't you want her to come with us?"

Peri didn't want to talk and she certainly didn't want to discuss her feelings with someone she didn't know.

Grace looked into the bed of the wagon. "She's sleeping now but the pains are getting worse." She motioned at Emma, who lay in a large woolen blanket. "I know you were only planning on rescuing me, but she needs it more. I thought this could be a great way for me to repay you."

Repay me? Peri thought. She wasn't doing this for Grace but for Marty. He was the reason she dragged this load of helpless and exhausted women across a windy and desolate valley. No one knew her reason, not even Marty himself. She loved him and he had no idea of the feelings of his friend and hunting buddy. Peri wasn't sure if he even thought of her as female, but she believed with her whole heart that bringing his younger sister to him and away from the compound was sure to keep him close to her. Peri knew the trail and the compound. She had escaped from it before, and was Marty's only hope of rescuing his sister.

Peri gave Grace a disgusted grunt, and spurred her horse to move ahead and out of earshot. The plan was to meet up with Marty at the railroad stop in Pocatello. He had planned to travel with her, but became ill the night they were to leave. This disappointed Peri, but his kiss on her cheek was enough to keep her smiling for miles.

They were making good time and expected to arrive the day they had planned. The problem was Emma. She hadn't planned to rescue her, and Peri worried about what to do with her after they arrived in Pocatello. Grace would be sent to Oregon on the train and Peri and Marty would go back to their life in the small mining town of Challis. It had been Peri and Emma's childhood home before they moved to Cedar Creek. Peri shook her head remembering her own escape from the compound and Emma's resistance then. She was the reason Peri had lost the rest of her family. She was the reason Peri felt the heart piercing pain of loss.

Peri had just squatted, pants around her ankles, and the stream beginning to hit the dirt, when the dry grass crunched behind her. She spun to find the back-lit silhouettes of two men watching her.

"Don't let me interrupt you," one said, amused at her vulnerable state. He stepped closer giving shade to Peri's eyes. He was bulky and wore a white shirt buttoned to his neck and a brown hat that showed the sweat stains around the brim. He had a long beard, large blue eyes and small yellow teeth.

Peri yanked her pants up and stumbled back. She put her hand to her gun and then realized the other man's gun was already pointed at her.

"That would be stupid," he said. He was older with the same white shirt and a dark bandana across his face. She saw that he was in charge by the way he stood, surveying the area and the situation. "Well, my oh my, Miss Periwinkle. You almost fooled me. You've taken this being a boy thing to an extreme don't you think?" the man said, pulling down the bandana and revealing a long gray beard and knowing smirk.

Peri looked at him more closely and then realized it was the prophet, Deon Heff, the very man she was saving Grace and Emma from, and now he held her prisoner. Her heart sank. It had been four years since she had seen him, and he looked even older and more evil.

"I'm going to need you to walk to where the rest of your little rebels are waiting, so we can get you all back to where you belong," Deon said.

Peri folded her arms and tried to sound stern. "We're not going with you."

The other man, Gordy Thornock, one of Deon's Elders, stood straight. "What makes you think you have a choice? Those women belong to the prophet. Emma is carrying the prophet's child and Grace has been chosen."

Peri dug her heels in. "He's no prophet. He's a filthy old man."

Deon grinned and huffed. "Child, why are you so angry against our heavenly father? Why are you forsaking the calling of the Lord? It was He who called your mother to me, just as he has with Emma and now Grace."

"Grace is a child," Peri spat. "She doesn't want to be with you and neither does Emma. You brainwashed her just like you did Mother."

Deon took a step toward Peri. "Didn't I take you into my home? Didn't I provide you with everything you needed when you had nothing?"

"My mother's dead because of you," Peri sneered.

Deon lowered his head. "You know that isn't true. What happened to your mother was a result of her loss of faith. Luckily we were sealed for time and all eternity. Isn't that what you want? To be with your mother in the Celestial Kingdom?"

Peri shook her head.

Gordy stepped toward Peri. "Give me the gun. Slowly."

Peri hesitated.

Deon motioned with his own gun, his prophet-like demeanor gone. "Do it," he ordered.

Reluctantly, she removed the gun from its holster on her hip and tossed it to him. Gordy picked it up and looked at the pearl handle and elegant engraving with her initials. "Where'd you get this? Did you steal it?"

Peri ignored him, but inside she boiled that his disgusting hands were touching one of the few things she still had, given to her by her father.

"Now, come on," Deon directed.

They walked into the valley where two horses waited, tied to a tree. Peri fumed at being found so easily, at the warm wetness of urine down the leg of her pants. The men mounted the horses and, with guns pointed, followed as Peri walked to the wagon. Another man on a horse stood guard as Emma and Grace huddled in the wagon, clinging to each other with red wet eyes.

When Emma saw that is was Deon under the bandana, she gasped and whispered his name.

"Surprised, Emma darling? I bet you thought I was dead," he said with a lilt. "Sorry to disappoint you."

She slowly slid back into the wagon bed with eyes filled with terror and dread.

Deon ordered Peri to stand by the wagon. The man who had stayed with the women was Rolly Wilson, the man Peri had been promised to. He gave her a slant-eyed sneer. "I say we shoot her here and leave her for the vultures," he said when he recognized who they had captured.

"That would be a waste of a good woman. She'll come around and see the error in her ways. She'll be sealed to you and give you many children," Deon said.

Peri scoffed.

"Who says I still want her? Look at her," said Rolly with disgust.

"Brother Wilson, remember that the Lord wants us to forgive," countered Deon. "I'm sure that she'll repent and be a faithful wife." He smiled at Peri. "Just like her Mama."

"I'm not my mother. She was weak minded and you lied to her. I know better," Peri yelled.

Deon sat up in the saddle. "Your mother was my help mate. She loved serving me and the Lord."

A soft moan came from the wagon and they turned to see Emma in a ball, holding her stomach. Grace looked up with panic in her eyes. Peri cringed. This couldn't be a worse time.

Deon looked pleased. "This is God's way of letting us all know that he guided us to you at the right time. Just in time. A precious new life will be added to our family." He turned to the large man. "Brother Thornock, I need you to ride quickly back to Cedar Creek and tell the Spirit Keepers to prepare for the birth. We will follow."

Gordy nodded then spurred his horse and turned to the south. A small dust cloud lingered as Peri watched the man and horse disappear over the sage covered hill.

Deon smiled back at the women. "Brother Wilson, you take Sister Periwinkle with you on your horse and ride ahead. I'll follow the wagon."

"I've got my own horse," Peri said, motioning to her large red gelding.

Rolly walked his horse over to Peri, and put his arm out to lift her on. "Do you really think we're stupid enough to let you ride alone? Get on!" he ordered.

She glared at him, so he reached down and took a handful of hair on top of Peri's head and pulled, almost lifting her off the ground. Peri shrieked and reached up to claw at his hand in an effort to squirm out of his clutch.

Emma gave another loud groan from the back of the wagon. Rolly looked over to her. With the distraction, Peri raised her right leg, pulled a knife from her boot, and swung up stabbing Rolly in the side. He screamed in pain and released his grip on Peri's hair. She stumbled to the ground as Rolly's horse spooked and lunged to the side. Rolly slumped over, holding the wound and Peri saw blood already soaking through his white shirt. The horse spun, with Rolly grasping the horn of the saddle, trying to stay on. Peri looked up to see Deon with his gun aimed at her.

A blast echoed throughout the valley. Peri flinched waiting for the red-hot lead of the bullet to hit her. When the sound faded, she opened her eyes and looked up to see Grace trying to regain her balance from the seat of the wagon; a pistol hung by her side. Deon lay in a lump on the ground. Grace stared blankly at what she had done.

Rolly's horse had spooked from the blast and run. Peri watched the hunched and dying outline of her former betrothed, as the horse made its way from the clearing, up the hill and then disappear into the junipers.

"God damn," Peri said, standing up and steadying herself. She walked cautiously over to where Deon lay. She studied him, making sure he was really dead, then looked up at Grace and shook her head. "Where'd you get the gun? Nice aim, but now we have a dead prophet on our hands, plus an injured elder riding back to tell them where we are."

"I didn't mean to kill him," said Grace, frantically. "I just didn't want him to kill you."

Peri took a deep breath and sighed. "Better him than me," she said bluntly. This had become a nightmare and Peri wondered if her reason for agreeing to this was really going to pay off. She debated in her head whether they should run or if she should track down Rolly and finish him off before he had a chance to expose them. "Give me the gun," she ordered.

Grace handed it to her.

Peri studied it. "Where'd you get this?" she asked.

"I stole it from . . . Uncle Deon."

"You shot the prophet with his own gun?" Peri laughed. "That's just great."

Emma moaned loudly as she pulled herself up to look over the edge of the wagon. "Please, help me. It's coming!"

"Lay down," Peri ordered. She turned to Grace. "Take her to the next town and find a doctor, fast. I think we're about two hours from Montpelier. Stay on the trail and keep the horse at a steady pace."

Grace's face turned to fear. "Wait. What about you? You have to come with us."

"I will," Peri said, drained. "But I have to bury Deon first, then I'll catch up."

Grace hesitated a moment. It was obvious that she was terrified of going on without Peri, but she nodded. "You're right. We have to give him a decent burial."

Peri huffed, "Bullshit. He doesn't deserve anything."

Grace flinched each time Peri swore, as if God was about to come down on her at any moment. That type of language was never heard among the women at the compound.

Peri cleared her throat and looked around for a good spot. "I'm hiding the body. If Rolly doesn't die on the way back to

Cedar Creek, he'll have a posse out searching for us, and we can't have them finding this. We'll have a hard enough time without a body to prove what we did. I'll be burying this gun too."

Grace nodded, then her breathing became faster and she started to weep. "I killed the prophet. I'm surely going to hell now." Her voice shook along with her shoulders.

Peri grunted. "You killed an evil dog, who was planning to rape you. He's no prophet. You did the world a favor." She looked over at Emma whose face was contorted in pain. She turned back to Grace and motioned to the ruts cut into the red dirt on the trail. "You need to hurry. I won't take long and I'll catch up. Don't tell them who you are or where you came from. Tell them you were traveling from Missouri and became lost. Make up names."

Emma's weak voice called for Peri. Peri looked over the wagon. Emma's face was covered in beads of sweat. She looked at Peri and tried to smile. "Thank you for coming back and for saving us," she said, her voice breathy and feeble.

Peri raised her eyebrows and scoffed at her sister, "We're not out of this yet."

When the wagon was out of sight, Peri tied a rope around Deon's ankles and dragged the body of the prophet behind her horse, over the rocks, sage brush, and dirt until they were off the trail and far enough away that the stench from the body, when it began to rot, wouldn't be apparent. She dismounted and pulled a small shovel from a scabbard tied to her saddle. She looked at it and shook her head. It was one of the few items she had kept from her brother. She never thought she'd had much use for it, but because it was his, she kept it close. Now it served a purpose that was fitting, considering how her brother had died.

As Peri struggled to dig in the hard clay of the southern Idaho desert, she cursed the man who had taken so much from her.

When she had a hole that was just deep enough to cover him, she had Chance move forward and drag the dead prophet into place. As his heavy, limp body tumbled into the shallow grave, several coins slid to the ground. She picked them up and then decided to search his pockets for more. She hadn't killed him, but she wished she had, and stealing was hardly going to change her fate if she got caught. More coins, a short bladed knife, and a small and thin leather case tied with a string.

Peri took the case and untied it. When she unfolded the leather flaps, she saw that it was a ledger with dates and numbers. She quickly recognized the flowing and elegant penmanship of her mother. It made her stomach clench knowing it was hers. She wondered why Deon had it and what it meant. She quickly leafed through it, to see if anything related back to names or things she remembered from the compound, but none of it made sense. She would study it later, knowing she was running short on time. She tied it back up and shoved it in her pocket along with the other items she'd taken off the prophet's body, and went back to the gruesome task of burying him.

Peri knew that even though she buried the evidence, there would be a posse of men looking for them and regardless of what they could prove, they would be persistent in trying to learn what happened to the leader of their church. Peri had seen what they were capable of. They preached of God and heaven, but what she had witnessed made her chest tighten with fear and her face flush with anger. She knew it meant nothing to them to kill her and the others, and do it in the name of the Lord and feel it was His will.

When the last of Deon was covered, she gave the grave a couple of good stomps. It was a sorry looking grave, and that gave her pleasure. Damn him to hell, she thought. Then it dawned on her that if there was such a place, she would likely be there too and that made her skin prickle, but she shrugged at the situation and, as with most of her life, she knew worrying about it wouldn't solve anything.

She took the reins of Chance, her beloved horse, and felt relieved that at least one of the gifts from her father was still safe in her possession. She already missed the ivory handled gun with her engraved initials, but knew there was no way of getting it back without risking everything. She had already put her life and that of others in jeopardy, but that was to save them from a predator.

Peri had been through enough to know that no matter how sentimental something was, objects were never worth the price of life. However, she was willing to risk hers for a few hours more to go to the river, strip off her stale and dusty clothes, and wash the urine and other burdens she had accrued from her most recent journey on the trail. She took one last look at the grave and surveyed her work. After a moment, she shrugged her approval of the job. It certainly wasn't what she expected to be doing when she agreed to rescue Grace. She didn't expect to find Emma, and now she would not only be hunted for the girl and woman she'd taken from the Kingdom of Glory church, but for the murder of their prophet.

Chapter 3

Montpelier, Idaho
August 20, 1896

The weather was typical for an August day in Montpelier, Idaho, but the tone of the town was still tense and guarded after the events of the previous week. Many of the people in the town witnessed the robbery, but it wasn't until the next day was it confirmed that the brazen gang who stole thousands at gunpoint at their local bank was led by the known outlaw, Butch Cassidy. The search was called off when Sheriff Ben Griffin and his men chased the outlaws up the canyon, and eventually lost them near Snyder Basin. They had captured one of the members of the Wild Bunch, Bob Meeks, who claimed he was only asked to watch the horses and didn't know about the impending robbery. He sat in the small jail facing trial.

Montpelier was located in the southeast part of the state and was home to a few thousand people who had settled in the area to farm or work on the railroad. Most were Scandinavian and had come to America because of their conversion to the Mormon Church. In teams of wagons, they made their way across the country and found the land in Idaho rich and ready to be farmed. There was a main street with shops, a restaurant, and two hotels. Dirt roads spider webbed, leading to small homes and pastures that dotted the entire valley.

It had been just over ten years since Ben Griffin became sheriff. It wasn't the reason he came out west, but he was satisfied with the decision to take the job and make Idaho home. Ben was from Virginia. He was a union soldier in the civil war and when he returned home, he found nothing left. His wife and baby daughter he had never met, had died during an outbreak of influenza. When he returned to the small brick home he had shared with his wife, he found someone living there, and that complete stranger was the one who gave him the sad news about his family. Ben sold the house and decided to leave his life and memories behind and like so many others, head west.

Ben was only twenty years old when he took a job as a deputy in a small town near Salt Lake City and a year later he fell in love with a determined young school teacher named Jessica. They were married and with that she was fired from her job. The laws stated that no women school teachers could be married. This devastated Jessica. It was her dream to teach and Ben couldn't stand to see her sad, so they made a plan that would give them what they wanted. They decided to hide their marriage and move so no one would know.

Jessica took a position in Montpelier as the teacher in a small one room school, and a month later, Ben applied and accepted a position as a deputy. They were both able to continue to do the jobs they loved. They found separate places to live and in public went about as two people simply living and working in the area. This gave Jessica time to pursue her dream of working with children until they decided to have some of their own. Living apart was inconvenient and often frustrating, but both knew it wasn't forever and their secret meetings and romantic hidden interludes kept their love and desire for each other strong.

They both enjoyed the quiet life of a small town. The people were friendly, and for Ben, the idea of being in a land that was virtually undiscovered was also a draw. The sheriff was an older man, who took to Ben quickly, and because the other deputies were also farmers, he gave Ben hope of seeing the position of sheriff in his future.

The town was made up of mostly Mormon settlers sent by Brigham Young to farm the land and develop the area. Ben wasn't a fan of the puffed up so-called prophet and when Young had the name of the town changed from Belmont to Montpelier, after the capital in his home state of Vermont, Ben found him even more pompous. Over the years, Ben kept his feelings about Young to himself, knowing the unequivocal love many of the people of his community felt for their spiritual leader, and besides, those with a fear of god were more likely to obey the law.

It was a hot and exceptionally windy evening when the young girl driving the open wagon came frantically into town. Ben was on the steps of the dry goods shop, talking to a trapper, when he saw the distressed expression of the girl and the foaming sweat of the horse.

He caught her eye and she called out to him. "I need help. I need to find a doctor!"

Without hesitation, Ben ran to the wagon. "What's the problem?" he asked. Then he noticed the woman lying in the back, covered in a thick blanket. "I'll take you," he said, climbing in and grabbing the reins.

Grace's voice broke. "We tried to get here before the baby came, but it happened. I don't know if she's okay. I'm so scared." She burst into tears.

Ben slapped the reins to get the horse to move.

When they arrived at the doctor's home, Grace saw an older lady in the garden. The woman looked up and walked quickly toward the wagon.

"What is it, Ben?" she asked.

Dorothea had arrived in Montpelier after her husband died on the trip from New York to California. He was looking for a quick fortune in gold and Dorothea left the city and a comfortable life for the harsh and unforgiving trek across the country.

Before Ben could answer, she saw the situation and signaled him to carry Emma in. With red eyes, Grace followed with the baby, still wet and bloody, wrapped in a thin cotton cloth. Inside, Ben laid Emma on a bed in a back room.

"Did she deliver the afterbirth?" Dorothea asked Ben.

Ben shrugged and looked back at Grace who started to cry again.

"I know you're scared, but you need to tell me what happened so I can help her," Dorothea said calmly.

Grace nodded and took a deep breath. "I heard them coming, so I had to hurry. I don't know when it happened, but when I got through the canyon and could hide, I saw the baby in her arms. I just kept going. I didn't know if either of them would live."

With a furrowed brow, Ben stepped toward Grace. "Heard who coming? Who was following you and why?"

Dorothea looked to Ben. She saw his instincts kicking in and he needed answers. "I'll take care of the woman and the baby." She took the child from Grace and walked into the room and closed the door.

~*~

Grace felt a chill go over her, as she stood alone with Ben and his question still hung between them. "I don't," she said. "I can't lie."

"Then don't," said Ben firmly.

"It's just that I don't want to make things worse," said Grace. She wiped her eyes and took an exhausted breath. "Peri told me not to tell anyone anything or it could be bad."

"Who's Peri?" asked Ben.

"She's with us but had to do something." Each word was measured and stiff. "She'll be here soon."

"What could be bad?" he asked.

"It'll be bad if they find us," Grace flinched, as if wishing she could wind her words back in.

Ben shook his head. "Who's looking for you?"

"We were with a group and we got separated."

Ben didn't accept that. "Then why are you running away from someone?"

The door to the bedroom opened slowly and Dorothea stepped out and shut the door behind her. Her face was pained.

"Is Emma dead?" asked Grace in a panic.

Dorothea gave a small smile and shook her head. "No. She'll be fine. Both she and the baby are resting." She gave Ben a concerned glance. She turned to Grace and took her by the shoulders. In a hushed whisper she asked, "What happened out there? That poor woman is delirious. She keeps mumbling things about death and going to hell."

Grace felt her chest tighten. She started to blurt all the horrific details of the escape, the capture, and the killing, but tears overtook her.

Dorothea held Grace. "People say odd things when they have the fever. You're all exhausted." She stroked Grace's hair, "How long have you been traveling?"

Without thinking, Grace blurted out, "About three days."

"Only three days?" asked Ben surprised. "I thought you said you were with a party traveling through. You didn't start in Missouri?"

Grace licked her lips and looked at the floor. "Um," is all she could muster, as she searched for the right words to keep them safe and their situation a secret.

From behind the closed door of the bedroom, Emma cried out, "Please don't take my baby!"

Grace rushed to the room and cracked open the door. In the slim gap of sunlight, she saw Emma sitting up, clutching the baby to her with eyes wide and frantic. Grace stepped into the room and closed the door. She went to Emma and held her, trying to rouse her from her fright.

Emma was drenched in cold sweat and tears. She sank into Grace. "Don't let them take my baby," Emma whispered with dread. "They'll take the baby."

Grace looked over to the sleeping bundle nestled in Emma's arms. "We're safe here. We're not going back. No one can take your baby now."

"But they'll come after us again. They'll want him. He's perfect. They'll find us and hang us for the murder," she cried, "and they'll take my baby."

At the word murder, Grace took a swift shot back at the door. It was closed and she turned back to Emma. "No one is going to find us. Don't talk about what happened. We need to keep it all a secret."

Emma rubbed her eyes and peered around the dark room. "Where's Peri?"

"She hasn't made it here yet," said Grace, gloomily.

Emma lowered her eyes to the baby. "Now that I'm with you, she won't want to be here."

Grace hugged Emma. "That's not so. You're her sister. She loves you."

Emma gave a huff. "She doesn't love me and I don't blame her. If it weren't for the baby, I'd go back and turn myself in for all of it. I deserve it for what I did."

Grace took Emma's face in her hands. "What did you do? Why is Peri so mad at you that she didn't want to save you from that place?"

A knock came at the door, and both women jumped.

"You all right in there?" Dorothea asked.

"We're fine. I'll be out in a moment," Grace called back. She turned her attentions to Emma. She lifted an eyebrow as if to ask again.

Emma swallowed and turned away in tears. "I should have listened to her. I thought I was doing the right thing. Now Paul and Mother are dead. Peri is right to hate me. I don't want her forgiveness because I don't deserve it."

Chapter 4

Emma

October 7, 1896

When we first met Uncle Deon in November of 1891, we all thought he was our savior. To even say that word now makes me shiver with how he hid behind it and was able to play out his evil intentions. We had no idea how terribly misguided we were, and if we'd even had a clue, I don't think we could have imagined how horrifying our lives were to become.

When Father died, we were left with so little. We had two horses, a house the bank was taking away, and the clothes on our backs. Mother hid the family china and some other heirlooms, but everything else we sold. My brother Paul was young but he still had to go to work in the mines just to keep us from starving. When the wind turned cold and the top of Twin Peaks was dusted white, we thought we would freeze to death in the unforgiving Idaho winter.

Uncle Deon was kind and offered us a new life in the Cache Valley where we wouldn't have to worry about a roof over our heads or where our next meal was coming from. He proposed to Mother and she agreed to move with him to his homestead in Northern Utah. Peri and I went with her, and Paul would be sent for after he helped Uncle Deon take care of some business in Mackay, the town just south of our home in Challis. This, of course, was never really the plan.

We rode with Uncle Deon in the wagon, and two other men accompanied us on horseback. They called him Uncle Deon, and he called them each Brother. We soon learned that everyone at the compound called him Uncle Deon, even his wives. All the men addressed each other as Brother and all the women were called Sister. At first, this seemed odd, but soon this open acceptance as family was comforting, especially when you were lost and looking for the solace of home.

When Mother married Uncle Deon, it was done in what was called a sacred sealing. We weren't allowed to attend, and it wasn't until my own sealing that I knew what happened at these ceremonies. As soon as this took place, we moved into the main house where Uncle Deon lived. Peri and I lived in one wing of the house and Mother was in another. It wasn't long before we started seeing less of her, and when we did, she looked drained and gaunt.

"She's doing the Lord's work," is what other women on the compound told us.

It wasn't long before we realized those women were also sealed to the prophet. Mother was his sixth wife. It was hard to imagine that she would allow herself to be married to a man that was married to others, but the lessons we were taught about the principle of plural marriage were so persistent and vehement, I started to believe my very salvation depended on it. I needed to believe that there was more than just this life, that happier days were coming, and that my family would be back with me and the way they used to be. The covenants we made would allow us to live in a glorious kingdom with all our loved ones and to live forever, for eternity, in happiness. This promise was so appealing, I did whatever I could to attain it.

I missed my father, and even though Mother was still alive, it felt like I had lost her too. Peri was placed in the young women's quarters after several outbursts and rants against our situation. The Elders felt she needed to find the truth, so they isolated her from us. We were told she would be invited back when she accepted the Lord into her life and was willing to follow his teachings. When we were told that the prophet had a revelation from God that I would be his next spirit wife, I was surprised when Peri cornered me behind one of the out buildings and demanded I leave with her and abandon our life on the compound.

"Leave? How?" I asked.

"Paul will be coming to get us and we'll escape back to our home in Idaho."

I wanted to shake her and make her see the whole picture of what that meant, but I knew she'd never listen. When Eliza, the prophet's first wife saw us talking, we had to end our conversation and go our separate ways.

"You know where to be," Peri whispered. She turned, gave Eliza a glare, and then stomped off to her assigned area.

"She's trouble," Eliza hissed. "Let her go."

I wasn't sure if Eliza knew Peri's plan of escape or if she was simply urging me to avoid her dissention. Either way, my heart was breaking because I knew I was facing a life and an afterlife without my sister.

That night Mother came to my room. She was trying not to wake me, so I kept still. I felt her kneel beside my bed and slide something under my pillow. She placed a hand softly on my head. Her hand seemed so small. I heard her sniff and then pad gingerly out of the room. I don't know why I didn't speak to her or ask her what she was doing. And I had no idea it was the last time I would feel my mother's touch. Tears rolled down my face and onto my pillow and I still felt the dampness when I woke the next morning.

Before I could wipe the sleep from my eyes, I heard commotion in the hallways of the house. It then became quiet and after a little while I heard a knock at my door. The red eyes and sullen faces of the sister wives was all I needed to see to know that my life had shattered. They didn't say how, but I knew that my mother's death was not an accident. I asked if Peri had been told. Their faces distorted into anguish as they explained how my sister had found our mother and the angry outcries and blame Peri threw at anyone who came near her.

"She's in the Spirit Keeper's house and she has locked us all out," Amanda, the second of Rolly Wilson's wives, said. She had been assigned to Peri when the prophet had a vision that Peri would be sealed to Rolly. I was surprised that Amanda was still trying to fulfill her duty.

"There's no way in hell I'm marrying that old bastard," Peri yelled when she heard the news. "If he even tries to touch me, I'll kick him in the nuts."

Amanda, like the other sister wives, was horrified by the language, but she knew that this was a calling from God, so she continued to try to bring Peri into the fold. Her persistence just made Peri worse. She continued to curse at Amanda and even took to throwing rocks at her to shoo her away.

When Amanda went looking for her charge that morning, she found the door of the Spirit Keeper's house ajar. She entered the sacred house tentatively and found Peri slumped on the floor with Mother's body in her arms. There was no blood and no sign of conflict. Peri was staring out at nothing and mumbling to herself. It scared Amanda. She described Peri's state as possessed.

My heart broke and tears rushed from my eyes. How could I live without both my parents? I fell to my knees and sobbed. Why was God doing this? Had I not been faithful and done everything I was commanded?

My sister wives rubbed my back and wept, and eventually this did nothing but annoy me. I shooed the women from my room so I could get dressed and pray for guidance, and for my mother's soul. That is when I remembered the gift from Mother that she had left for me the night before.

I lifted the pillow and found a small leather case secured with a braided leather tie and when I opened it, there was my mother's handwriting in perfectly straight lines. Seeing her sweeping and beautiful cursive letters was like having her with me and I felt my chest tighten. I ran a finger across the words. On other pages were handwritten diagrams with markers and descriptions of our destiny and the treasure she left behind. I tried for a moment to read and interpret what she had written, but most of it was complex and rambling. I placed the folder in my garment drawer and steadied myself as the realization of what I was about to face hit me.

As I walked across the courtyard to the Spirit Keeper's house, I was aware of eyes on me. Eliza was at the door and gave me a disappointed shake of the head as I approached. Then she walked away, leaving me to face the horror alone.

"They did this to her," Peri growled at me as I knelt beside her. She had let me in when I knocked on the door, but threatened to kill me if anyone else came in. She had placed Mother's body by her side and wrapped it in several of the cotton sheets used in the Spirit Keeper's house. "You did this to her."

I flinched back at her stabbing words, but knew it was her anguish speaking. I ignored her. "What happened?" I reached toward the sheet to try and get a glimpse, but she slapped my hand away.

"She knew this was all wrong. She hated herself for bringing us here. She wanted to leave, but couldn't leave you behind," said Peri. Her voice was low and her words measured.

I knew that Peri was hurting and I didn't want to argue, but I also knew the love and devotion Mother had for the gospel. She was chosen to be a Spirit Keeper which was the most sacred and trusted position a woman could hold. What Peri said was wrong, but nothing I said or did changed her mind. I stood. I wanted to cry. I wanted to gather up my mother and hold her and beg her to tell me what had brought her to this, but I knew that she was at peace now. "You will need to let them prepare her for the funeral. You can see her again when we have the viewing."

Peri looked at me with heated eyes. "Paul will be here tonight, and I'm leaving." She looked at the white covered body of our mother. "I've said my goodbyes. There is nothing keeping me here."

I nodded.

"And don't come. I don't want you with us," Peri said. She shook her fist at me. "I don't ever want to see you again." Her voice cracked, but her resolve was firm.

I wasn't planning on going with them, but the hatred she spewed at me was more painful than if she had plunged a knife deep into my heart. All I could do was turn and run.

That night I let her go both from The Kingdom of Glory and my life. My love for her was still strong, and I knew there was nothing I could do to bring her back. The tasks surrounding Mother's funeral kept me busy the next day, and it wasn't until the viewing that evening that I learned of Peri's successful escape. The early morning assembly of the Elders decided they needed to stay for the funeral, so they sent two prospects off to find her. They readily accepted the assignment in the hope of earning the good graces of the prophet and the elders.

The church rarely accepted men. The prophet felt most were not worthy of the blessings and gifts of being a member, and it took an exceptional show of devotion for that to happen. It took even greater loyalty and service to be assigned wives, but that didn't stop some from accepting the challenge. Most had been driven out from other groups and were looking for a new home and family. They often proclaimed their allegiance to Uncle Deon along with their disappointment with the manifesto given by the leaders of the Mormon Church, rejecting the practice of plural marriage.

The manifesto was a constant concern for us. With the laws of the land turning against our families, we wondered what the future held and how long we had until the coming of the last days. It was this knowledge that we would be together for all eternity that kept us strong, and when my time came to become the prophet's seventh wife, I accepted it with humble gratitude and obedience. I would join Mother some day in heaven, not only as her daughter, but sister wife.

Chapter 5

Southwest of Montpelier, Idaho
August 21, 1896

Sam wasn't a loner, but he liked to ride alone. He enjoyed the open range and being with nothing but his own thoughts. It wasn't that he didn't like other people, but sounds in the wilderness called to him and he needed to answer back. This couldn't be done unless he was able to hear voices in the breeze or murmurs in the streams.

Sam had lived in Montpelier his entire life, but he never felt like he was home. He shot a gun faster and with more accuracy than anyone in town, and his hunting skills with a bow and arrow were the talk in the trading posts and saloons all over the valley. But even with the respect and admiration he received, he was still unable to achieve the one thing he wanted most in his world and that was to belong.

When Sam rode over the ridge and to the river, he was in search of a band of bank robbers. He wasn't expecting to find a woman, and certainly not a naked one. He pulled back on the reins and the horse slid to a stop.

~*~

When the dust settled, there stood Peri, hands and arms awkwardly trying to cover the important areas. She wasn't sure if this was one of the men sent from the compound or if it was just a terrible fluke that she was happened upon while naked. After all, she had been caught with her britches down just hours before.

"What in hell?" she asked. It wasn't a question as much as a statement of her frustration in being caught off guard yet again.

~*~

Sam tried to look away, but wasn't sure if he should pull his gun for protection or leave the woman in privacy. It was rare, but wasn't completely unheard of for a woman to turn to crime, and since he was searching for bank robbers, he wanted to leave no stone unturned. This robbery and these particular bank robbers would put him in the history books if he captured this bunch. This was a robbery, according to everyone who witnessed it that was carried out by none other than Butch Cassidy himself. The notorious outlaw and his gang held up the Montpelier bank and took over sixteen thousand in gold, silver, and currency.

Deputy Clyde was up the street talking with attorney Elmer Bagley and admiring his new bicycle when he saw the commotion. Deputy Clyde borrowed the bike and tried to pursue the robbers, but was quickly left in the dust. He returned to town and along with the Sheriff formed a posse to track the men.

Sam was fairly sure this naked and vulnerable woman wasn't part of the gang, and after two days of riding in the hot dusty Idaho summer, she was a sight for sore eyes, so he enjoyed the diversion. He knew who was leading the robbers, but it didn't mean the gang couldn't include a woman, and this one didn't look like the typical ladies in town. She was lean, and wore her blond hair short. If it weren't for her obvious breasts and the curve of her hips, he would have mistaken her for a boy.

"Turn around so I can get dressed," Peri yelled at him. Her blue eyes were fierce with both anger and distress.

Sam hesitated, then turned and looked away. "Who are you? And why are you out here all alone?" he called to her. He looked down at his dark and weathered hands. He was only in his early twenties and yet his hands conveyed the life of someone much older.

The girl walked to the river bank and pulled on a chemise she had draped over a large rock. The rest of her clothes, still wet from the washing, were laid out in the sun to dry.

"I was traveling with my family to California and I got separated. I'm meeting them in Pocatello," the girl said.

"They just left you behind?" asked Sam, genuinely surprised.

The girl walked to her horse and pulled a blanket that was rolled and tied behind the saddle. She tossed it around her and then stood defiant. "They didn't just leave me. They had to get to Pocatello on a certain day, and I'll be able to catch up."

Sam turned back around and realized he had left himself vulnerable when he saw that she had made it to her horse and pulled out the blanket. It could have been a gun and made him an easy target. This fact made him less skeptical, but no less intrigued. "Where are you from?"

"Why?" she asked. "Where are you from?" she shot back.

Her brashness caught Sam off guard and he smiled.

"Aren't you scared about being out here all alone?" he asked.

She straightened her shoulders. "I can take care of myself."

Sam gave a smirk. "Really? So, where do you hide your gun when you're naked? Being alone, especially without clothes, isn't a good way to take care of yourself."

Her face flushed from her obvious vulnerability.

"Do you need help getting somewhere?" asked Sam.

She scoffed. "I told you I can take care of myself. Can you just leave me alone so I can let my clothes dry and be on my way?"

With that, Sam tipped his hat, turned his horse and rode up the hill and out of view.

~*~

Peri had noticed how white the man's teeth looked against his dark skin and figured he was an Indian. This normally would worry her, but he was dressed in the same clothes the other men wore and didn't seem like the type of Indian she had been warned of.

She sighed with relief, but still stood contemplating the dark and handsome young man, that had seen more of her than any man ever had. Without a gun or even clothes, he could have killed her, raped her, and no one would ever know. Oddly, she never felt in danger, in fact, she got the sense that he actually cared about her well-being. He was a stranger in the middle of the Idaho desert and that brief meeting had her pondering over who he was and picturing his face over and over again in her mind.

When she was fully dressed she wondered what he would have done if he had thought she was a man. It was the first time since she had taken her brother's identity that she was pleased to have been exposed as a woman. It was also the first time she had thought about any other man than Marty. This made her realize she had been on the trail too long. She brushed off the dust from her pants and the saddle, took a deep breath to clear her mind, and then turned Chance to continue their journey.

It was early evening when Peri reached the town of Montpelier, and she kept her hat down low. A group of boys were chasing each other in an alley and she asked them where she could find a doctor. She figured they were less likely to ask questions.

One of the boys, with unevenly cut hair and dried snot in his nose, pointed her to the home on the outskirts of town. He looked her up and down, and made Peri avoid his gaze.

"Go on now," she muttered and turned the horse toward the hills.

When she reached the house, she tied Chance to a post, and cautiously knocked on the door.

The door opened and a woman stood stern, with eyebrows knitted. She studied Peri with skepticism. "Can I help you?"

Peri cleared her throat, "I'm looking for two women. One is pregnant. I was told this is where I might find the doctor."

Before the woman could answer, Grace came rushing through and pulled the door fully open. "You made it," she squealed as she threw her arms around Peri. "Emma had the baby," she continued to chatter. "She had it before we got here and I thought they were both going to die. When I came into town, I wasn't even sure if they were both alive." She took a quick breath in a fitful panic, then tried to continue.

Peri held up a hand to silence her and led her away from the house, out of earshot. "Has anyone else come asking about you?"

"No," Grace said without a pause. She turned to where the woman stood on the porch, watching them. "This is Peri. I thought she was a boy but she isn't," she called to her. Then she turned to Peri. "That's Dorothea. Her husband was the doctor, but he died so Dorothea does all the doctoring here, just like the women on the compound."

Peri looked at Grace horrified. Why was she discussing the compound, and with such ease and candor? Didn't she remember sneaking out in the darkness, hiding from the men, and all the other perils they had been through?

She took Grace firmly by the arm and walked her further away, out of earshot of Dorothea. "What have you told them? They don't need to know anything about us. We need to pack up and leave as soon as we can. Where's Emma?"

Grace turned to Dorothea who remained standing by the open door, arms crossed and studying them. "She's in the bedroom."

Peri nodded and walked to Dorothea. "Thank you for your help. I wish we could repay you, but we need to get on the trail soon."

Dorothea shifted to where she blocked the entrance to the house. "That is fine, but Emma and the baby aren't up to traveling yet." She looked Peri up and down. "Who are you running from? And why are you dressed like a man?"

Peri was fuming and trying to keep her cool.

"Don't worry," Grace chirped. "Dorothea is a Christian woman. She isn't going to tell anyone we're here." She leaned closer and whispered, "The sheriff also knows we're here but I didn't tell him anything about . . ." she raised her eyebrows twice.

Peri felt her stomach sink. She agreed to rescue this girl as a favor for the man she loved, but she had no idea what a prattling little idiot she was. Peri took a deep breath and looked again to Dorothea.

Dorothea gave her a small smile then turned to Grace. "You go check on Emma and the baby. I need to discuss some things with your friend here."

Grace frowned. "Did I do something wrong?" She turned to Peri. "I swear I didn't say anything about anything. I said exactly what you told me to. I—"

"Go," Peri said, cutting her off. There was no more time now that their cover had been jeopardized.

When the door of the bedroom was closed, Dorothea motioned for Peri to follow her into the other room. "You're all obviously being chased. You might as well tell me what you did and who is looking for you."

Peri started to lie, but then scrunched her lips and scratched her forehead. "We've done nothing wrong. I'm taking them from Cedar Creek to Pocatello."

Dorothea let out a hollow breath. "Cedar Creek?" she said putting her hand to her chest. "When Grace said the compound, I thought it was something to do with the army or the law." She paced the floor. She looked at Peri oddly, "I've heard things, but I've never seen anyone from there. Are you from Cedar Creek?"

Peri felt very uncomfortable continuing this conversation, and knew that the more she talked the more she risked. This was no longer just an escape from Cedar Creek, this was an escape from a murder conviction and hanging. She could throw Grace to the wolves, and at that moment Peri considered the thought, but it wouldn't help her with her quest to keep Marty, if not bestowed, at least dedicated to her.

And that is why she needed to get Grace, and now Emma and the baby, wrapped up and back on the road to make the meeting with Marty in Pocatello. They had a two day window of their five day trek. That was part of the plan, just in case something slowed their journey. Peri sighed at the incredible bad luck she had had every time she encountered anything regarding the compound and her past life. Even though she loved Marty dearly, it took her months to agree to help him in the rescue of his sister. The thought of going back and facing that prison, going in disguise right to the very place her life had been shattered, was something she never dreamed of considering, but

Marty's tall, lean build and soft blue eyes made it impossible for her to say no.

Peri shook her head at Dorothea. "I left when I was fifteen. I haven't been back since. It's been over two years. No one can know that we came through here. They will take Emma and Grace back to the compound. The baby too."

"What about you?" Dorothea asked.

"They'd sooner kill me. They have no use for me."

Dorothea stepped closer to her. "Grace said that Emma is your sister?"

Peri nodded, almost disappointed.

"And you haven't seen her since you left? What about the rest of your family? Where are they?"

Peri huffed. "In the ground."

Dorothea put her hand to her neck. "I'm so sorry, dear. Well, at least you have Emma back with you now. And a new nephew. That is a blessing."

Peri took a deep breath and closed her eyes. Her anger toward Emma had not subsided in the four years since Peri escaped the compound. Even though she had hardly said five words to Emma during their journey, she had no intention of doing any more than what she had already been through. She blamed Emma for what had happened to her mother and especially the terrible tragedy that had befallen her brother. Peri felt she had already done far more than anyone in her shoes would have, and now that Emma and the baby were safe, Peri was ready to leave them behind once again.

Chapter 6

Montpelier, Idaho
August 22, 1896

Peri lay awake most of the night, envisioning the meeting with Marty at the train station. Would he embrace her? Kiss her with joy and appreciation for rescuing his sister? She smiled to herself with the whimsy. It was a musing she had often, and in only a few days, it would be played out for real. It was the beginning of something new, she hoped. How could it not be? She had risked everything for him. He had to know how she felt, and Peri was pretty sure he was of the same mindset.

They had spent so much time together, talking, hunting, riding, and making plans. He told her his innermost dreams about owning his own ranch and raising a passel of boys to help with the family business. She saw herself riding alongside him as they brought the cattle in from the range. She dreamed of them settling down after a long day of working the steers, to the solitude of their bedroom, with a fireplace crackling and his bare chest hovering over her. Her heart expanded in her chest at the thought of him wanting her. Tomorrow would be a long ride, and tonight sleep escaped her as she contemplated the prospect at the end of the trail.

When she woke the next morning, she was surprised that she had slept at all. The stir of the house made her realize it was later than she had hoped. It was her intent to be on the trail just after sunrise, and that had already eluded her. She hopped from the makeshift mattress of quilts and clothes, and pulled on her pants and jacket. When she stepped from the room, she saw Grace sitting at the large wooden dining table with a man. He was older with a large dark mustache and eyes that were deep set but kind. He looked up at her and cocked his head.

Peri smoothed her hair and stood tall. It was her defense when she was feeling awkward and vulnerable. She cleared her throat and Grace turned and leapt from her seat.

"Here she is!" she announced to the man. "This is Peri."

Peri nodded and the man stood up. He was tall and dressed in a leather vest and chaps. He had dark hair that was matted from the hat that hung on the corner of his chair.

"Do you have a last name?" he asked, in a low, sturdy voice.

Peri looked at Grace, who shrugged her shoulders. "I told him I wasn't sure and Emma is still sleeping."

"Why? Who are you?" Peri asked.

"I'm the sheriff. My name is Ben Griffin." He took a step toward her. "There are a lot of different explanations I've heard as to why you three ladies are here in Montpelier. I'd like to hear what your version is."

Peri took a deep breath wishing she had stayed awake all night and hustled her little band out before dawn. "We were traveling with a group and we took a different trail and got lost. When Emma went into labor we had to get her to a town."

Grace nodded as if she were fascinated with Peri's tale. "Yep, that's what I said. Just like you did."

Peri rolled her eyes. One more day with this brainless fool and she would have fulfilled her mission and be with the one who would make her life and future complete. The joy in seeing Marty was only lessened by the knowledge that she still had to endure Grace. "We've done nothing to warrant a problem with the sheriff," Peri said sternly.

"Dorothea says you're taking these women from Cedar Creek to Pocatello. Is that correct?" he asked.

Peri nodded, but held her defiant stance.

"I was here when the other two came into town," said Ben. "Why weren't you with them? Where've you been?"

"I assure you, we are simply traveling through," Peri said, trying to avoid his question. "We're going to leave here within the hour to meet up with our group."

"Emma and the baby can't travel," Dorothea reminded her as she stood in the doorway behind Peri.

Peri turned, startled.

Dorothea lifted a defiant eyebrow. "Her fever is still high and the baby isn't feeding well. They need time to gain their strength before they travel." Dorothea nodded as if to punctuate her statement and then walked past Peri and crossed to the kitchen area where she placed two dirty dishes into the wash tub.

Peri huffed in frustration. "We can't stay or we'll miss them. We only have until Saturday afternoon. If we don't start today, we'll never make it, and they'll leave without us."

"Why so desperate to get there?" asked Ben.

"We need to get to Pocatello. We're supposed to meet there and then Grace will take the train," Peri said, not caring that she was giving away much more than she had planned.

Peri knew that her agitation gave Ben suspicion that there was more to her story. It only made sense that he would be unwilling to let her leave without learning more about who they all were and where they were going. Three women traveling alone was in itself unusual, but Peri's elusiveness and adamancy in leaving, even when one of her group was unfit to travel, made the whole situation suspect.

Ben looked toward Dorothea. "When do you expect you'll be able to make a decision on this?"

Dorothea thought for a moment. "As soon as both are able to travel." She turned to Peri. "You're all safe here until they're ready to leave."

Ben turned back to Peri. "That decides it. You can leave after your friend and her baby are well. You can stay here at Dorothea's until then."

"Peri and Emma are sisters," Grace piped up. When Peri shot her a look, she sat down and looked at the floor.

Peri couldn't believe that Emma once again was holding her back. Even with the unforeseen birth, she blamed Emma. She shook her head and walked back to the small room, slamming the door behind her. She sat on the floor and tried not to cry. The trip to Pocatello took at least two days with minimal stopping. If they didn't leave soon, there was no possibility of making the meeting with Marty in Pocatello. And if that was the case, she would be responsible for getting Grace to Oregon on her own, and that was not going to happen. She was determined to make the meeting with Marty, see him send Grace off to her new home in Oregon, and then she and Marty would ride back to Challis to begin their new life together.

A soft knock came at the door. "Peri?" asked Grace.

She was the last person, besides Emma, that Peri wanted to face right now. "Go away," she snapped.

The door cracked open.

Peri turned, red faced and fierce. "Get the hell away from me."

Terrified, Grace cringed. "I just wanted to say that it's okay if we don't make it on time. We can go later after Emma is okay. I don't mind."

Peri threw her head back and gave a forced and hollow laugh. "Do you think I give a shit about what you want?"

Grace looked behind her as if worried the others heard Peri's language. She stepped into the room and shut the door. "But I thought I was the reason you came and rescued us."

Peri huffed. "I didn't do this for you. I did this for—I did it for the money."

Grace raised an eyebrow. "My brother's giving you money to rescue me?"

"Yes, and if I don't get you to the drop off point on time, I lose the money," Peri lied. There was no money, but the last thing she wanted was for Grace to know of her feelings for Marty, and she wanted it to be real clear that she cared nothing for her or how she felt. "Plus, did you forget about the dead prophet I had to bury? I'm pretty sure we have people looking for us."

Grace began to speak and then her brow furrowed and she turned toward the door. Peri heard it too and stood up quietly. It was a man's voice; loud and urgent. She tip-toed to the door and slowly opened it, just enough to catch a glimpse of the strange and frantic visitor.

It was an older man. Shorter than Ben, and he stood with his head bent back as he spoke. His mustache was long and white and trailed down along his jaw.

"He says he's a marshal out of Cedar Creek, but I don't know him. He's looking for help finding some people. He says they killed a woman in their town and then took off with two of the prophet's wives." The stocky little man leaned in for emphasis. "They're part of the Kingdom of Glory group." He stepped back and lifted his eyebrows for emphasis. "Their prophet and two other men tracked the women down, but their prophet was shot and killed and another man is stabbed in the gut and almost dead. He barely made it back to tell what happened."

"Did they give you a description of who they're looking for?" Ben asked.

The man removed his hat and scratched at the long thin tuft of hair. "They said it was a woman dressed like a man and that she kidnapped two of their women."

Ben took a quick glance back to the bedroom door.

Peri leaned away from her viewpoint. "Shit," she whispered.

"What is it?" asked Grace.

Peri shushed her.

Ben turned back and put his hand on the old man's shoulder. "Tell the marshal to wait for me at my office. I'll be back there shortly." He walked the man out the front door and onto the porch.

Peri gathered her saddlebags, her large knapsack, and the journal. "We have to go. Now."

Grace went out to the kitchen and Peri whispered urgently to her. "Not that way. Get back here!"

"I have to get something. I'll be right there," she whispered, looking cautiously at the door. When she stepped back into the room, Peri glared at her.

"What the hell are you doing? You stay with me and do what I say!" Peri said as she shoved Grace toward the open window.

Ben returned inside, he went to the room to see what Peri might know about this murder and kidnapping. It all seemed too coincidental along with her evasive answers. But when he opened the door, the room was empty and the cotton drape fluttered from the open window.

~*~

As Peri untied Chance, and watched the front of the house, she turned to Grace and threatened, "Keep your mouth shut or I'll turn you in for murder."

Grace nodded. Her eyes large.

Peri had no time to saddle the horse, so they both mounted on bareback and slipped through the back alley of the home and over a ridge that hid them from view. Leaving Emma behind was not her plan, but Peri had no misgivings, and actually nudged Chance into a full gallop at the thought of it.

Chapter 7

Thirty-three miles southeast of Pocatello, Idaho
August 23, 1896

Peri had an almost empty jug of water and only a few stale pieces of bread in the packs she had managed to take with them. Her stomach ached from hunger now that the fear of being caught had subsided. Even if they were being pursued, they had gone off the trail and into a long valley of cottonwood trees and juniper bushes that kept them from sight. There was no reason for anyone, except the Elders of Cedar Creek, to chase them, and Peri hoped they had slipped away with enough time before they were considered suspects.

They were on day three of what she calculated to be a five day trip. With no money, few supplies, and a frantic getaway, she knew it would take longer than she originally planned, but was confident she would reach the meeting point in Pocatello on time.

The long stretch of trees and brush gave Peri hope that water was close by. They might survive the rest of the journey without food, but in the heat of the Idaho desert, they wouldn't last long without water. With Grace's body leaning against her back and making her clothes stick to her skin with sweat, the ride was even more intolerable. She was just about to stop and give her legs and butt a rest, when she noticed a large covered wagon in the distance. A thin trail of smoke drifted upward, just visible in the early evening sky. It was a single camp, but there were no obvious people, just several animals including two oxen, a cow, and a large black mule with a white face.

"What is it?" asked Grace. Her voice startled Peri. The girl had been quiet for hours.

"It's a camp, but I can't see anyone."

"What if it's Indians?" Grace asked.

Peri ignored her and walked the horse out of the cottonwoods and toward the camp.

"What are you doing?" Grace whined. "What if they . . .?"

"Shut up," Peri snapped. "We have no food and thanks to you, we have no water."

Grace lowered her eyes apologetically. Peri was still furious after learning Grace had used most of their water to wash her face that morning.

"We've got to do something," Peri grumbled.

A woman stepped out of the wagon and shook out a large cloth. She seemed to sense something and looked up. When she saw Peri and Grace she froze. Slowly, she said something into the wagon and then stepped down the stairs, studying them.

Peri sat up straight and continued to direct the horse toward the camp. Then a tall man struggled through the small door of the wagon. Peri stopped the horse.

"This isn't good," Grace whimpered.

A young man stepped out and all three stood watching Peri and Grace. Then the woman raised an arm to wave them in.

Peri hesitated.

"It's a trap," Grace said. "They're going to rob us."

Peri turned back at her. "Rob us? We have nothing for them to take." She nudged Chance forward.

As they got closer, Peri saw that the woman was older with long gray hair, and deeply creased, weathered skin. She guessed the man to be her husband. He was of similar age and had a hand on her shoulder. He was stooped and weathered, but gave them a welcoming smile. The younger man was taller than both, but stood warily behind them, barely peeking out.

Peri tried to smile and put up a hand in greeting.

When they got within speaking distance, the woman called out. "You look like you've had a rough trip. Bring your wife inside."

Peri realized their perception and Grace gave a muffled giggle that irritated her further. "I told you to shut up," Peri snapped back at Grace.

When they got to the wagon, the woman looked at Peri closely, realized her mistake and gave a hearty apology. "I'm sorry dear, my old eyes just don't work anymore."

Peri shrugged. The woman was genuine, unlike those she was used to. She looked hard-working and authentic. Grace slid down from the horse and then Peri dismounted. "We have almost no food or water. We're on our way to Pocatello, so we don't need much. We'd sure be obliged if you could help us."

The man nodded and smiled. "I'm James Guthrie. This is my wife Tildie. And this is Cooper," he said motioning to the young man, who stood and looked off in the distance, mumbling.

The woman smiled and took Peri by the arm and led her to the wagon. "It's getting dark and you can't travel at night. Have a meal with us and in the morning we can get you what you need for your journey."

Peri looked at the horizon, wondering if they couldn't push on a couple more hours until dark. But what then? At least here they had shelter, food, and a fire. "Thank you," she said to the woman, and looked back at Grace who stood timidly at Chance's side.

The young man stood facing the wagon and shaking his hand near his ear.

The older man noticed Peri staring. "He's harmless."

Peri nodded and followed the woman inside.

"Why's he doing that?" Grace asked, motioning to his hand flapping.

James took a deep breath. "We're not sure. He's only been with us about a year. We rescued him from a freak show. They were using him like a trained animal. He's actually quite smart in his own way."

Grace perked up. "I was rescued too, but not from a freak show." Then she contemplated what she said. "Kind of a freak show," she whispered to herself.

"Where are you ladies headed? And why only one horse?" James asked.

"We're going to Pocatello to take the train to Oregon. We didn't have a lot of time to plan when we left," said Grace. Then she noticed Peri glaring at her. "I didn't say anything, really," she said and looked at the ground.

Peri pulled two blankets and a tarpaulin from her large knapsack. James reached out and offered to help her string up a makeshift tent.

"It's called a prairie chicken in other places," Cooper said loudly to no one. "It's a sage grouse here. It's called a greater prairie chicken. A pinnate grouse in Missouri."

"Yes, that's correct," said James, smiling at Cooper. "We're having sage grouse for dinner."

"It lives in sage brush," Cooper continued, not really speaking to anyone. "Artemisia. That is what it's called."

Peri looked at Grace, who raised her eyebrows. "Whatever it is, I'm starving," she said.

Darkness fell quickly making Peri glad she was convinced to stop and camp. The smell of the stew embraced them in tempting wafts as they sat by the fire.

"While we wait for our dinner to cook, why don't you let me read your future?" Tildie asked Peri. She pulled a thin board from under the wagon and placed it between them. She then took a deck of brightly decorated cards out of a carved wooden box.

Peri gave her a skeptical eye roll.

"You don't believe in the mystical world?" asked Tildie.

Grace scooted closer and looked at the cards. She stood up and backed away. "Those are witches' cards. Why do you have witches' cards?"

James and Tildie both laughed. Tildie picked up the cards and motioned to Grace. "I'm not a witch and these are just tools that allow me to help you with what is happening in your life and what might happen."

Grace shook her head. "They bring about evil forces. Why would you want to do that?"

Tildie looked annoyed, then grinned. "They aren't evil because I'm not evil. Don't you want to know what your future might hold?"

Grace shook her head. "We believe it's witchcraft. It's against what our Lord teaches. They kill witches to keep the evil away. Aren't you afraid they'll find you?"

Peri scoffed. "Don't drag me into your beliefs," she said, shooing Grace away. "No one is going to kill her over some cards. Go sit over there if you don't want to watch." She turned to Tildie. "So, what does my future hold?"

Tildie shuffled the cards and spread the deck over the table. "Pick three. Make sure you take your time and let the cards speak to you."

Peri snickered then placed her hand over the cards and with an overly dramatic wave picked one from the spread and handed it to Tildie.

Tildie smiled and placed the card in front of her.

Twice more Peri gave her card picking performance.

With a pout Grace slumped against the wagon, but she watched closely.

Tildie laid out the other two cards and then gathered up the rest of the deck and placed it back in the wooden box. "The three cards represent your past, present, and future." She turned the middle card over. "This is where you are currently." The card showed a large angelic looking being and a naked couple standing with hands held. Tildie looked up at Peri and smiled. "This is the lovers' card. You are currently in love or wanting a relationship that consumes your thoughts and deeds."

Peri scoffed, but inwardly her heart flipped, and she worried that it was apparent.

Tildie continued without acknowledging Peri's unquestionable skepticism. "Deep love is the strongest force of all. This doesn't mean that the relationship is a sexual one. Sometimes the Lovers can represent the force itself that draws two people together. It can mean ideas, events, or even other people. Something has happened recently that has put you in a situation that opens you up to deep love."

Peri rolled her eyes again and gave a shrug.

Tildie turned over the card to the left of the center card. It showed a figure draped in black with three overturned gold cups in front of him and two gold cups behind that are upright. She hesitated with brows furrowed and then looked up at Peri with concern. "This card represents your past. It is called The Five of Cups. What it shows is great loss and it refers to that time when the pain of a loss is the greatest. But it also shows that the man is only looking at the cups that have fallen over. He still has the two cups that are standing. This means healing needs to take place before the good in life can be seen again."

Could Tildie see the sorrow in Peri's eyes? The woman took a deep breath. "Does this make sense?" she asked.

Peri was looking at the ground and snapped to with the question. "Make sense?" she said, trying to act flippant. "It's all hocus pocus, right?"

Tildie raised an eyebrow. "You don't have to tell me what it means to you. But I do hope you'll think about what it might mean in your life. We don't spend enough time thinking about how our actions affect everything and everyone around us."

Grace stirred. "Is that card her future?" she asked, pointing to the final card.

Tildie placed her hand on top of it. "This card represents the future, but it doesn't mean this is what has to happen. It's just a look at what could happen."

"In other words, it means nothing," said Peri.

"I didn't say that. It means a lot if you let it," Tildie said. She turned the card over. It showed a large angel with people rising up toward it. "The Judgement Card. Interesting."

"Why?" Peri asked, eagerly. She sat back and tried to act unaffected.

"All the cards relate to each other somehow. The Judgement Card can mean different things, but when I look at the other cards it's telling me that you have lost someone close to you that you loved deeply and you blame yourself somehow for what happened. This card also shows the angel as salvation and being reborn. It shows that you can start new and be free of guilt. It can also mean you have a calling. Something you must do to make things right."

Grace gasped and looked at Peri.

Peri threw her a threatening glare. "It means nothing," she grumbled and turned toward the fire. "When are we going to eat?"

Tildie took the cards and placed them in the box with the others. "I didn't mean to upset you, dear. You're right. It means nothing," she smiled at Peri. "Unless you let it." She stood up and stirred the big pot. "Oh, this is just about right. James, can you bring out the bowls?" she called to her husband who had gone into the wagon.

Peri looked out to where the moon hung low in the sky. The stars were bright and the sky above them seemed unusually expansive. She was irritated at what Tildie's reading had stirred in her. She had become proficient at hiding her emotions, even with herself, and this had created a fissure in her well hardened countenance.

As she awaited the meal, she felt good about her decision to stop for the night. Along with the need of food and sleep, she was actually enjoying the break that James and Tildie gave her from the incessant irritation of her charge.

Grace went to the back of the wagon to pee, but as she rounded the corner, she yelled out, "Hold it!"

Peri heard the click of a gun being cocked.

"Peri!" Grace yelled.

Peri jumped up and ran with Tildie to the back of the wagon. James followed.

In the light of a flickering lantern stood Grace with a large pistol pointed at Cooper, who stood at the horse, the open saddlebags on the ground, with their contents spread about, the journal in one hand and a lantern in the other.

"Where'd you get a gun?" Peri yelled at Grace. She looked at Cooper. "What are you doing with my stuff?" she demanded.

She went to him and ripped the journal from his hands. He flinched back.

James held his hand out to Grace. "Put the gun down. He wasn't robbing you. He's only curious. Please, I promise he wasn't doing anything to hurt you."

Peri turned to Grace. "Lower the gun," she ordered. "And give it to me." She walked over and snatched it away. She looked at it wondering where she had hidden it the entire ride and where it had come from.

Cooper started flapping again. "It's a mine," he said.

"It's not yours," Grace yelled. "That's Peri's!"

Tildie stepped in, "No. He's saying that the papers are a mine." She looked at Peri, "Does that make sense?"

"It's a mine," Cooper said again. "It's a mine map. It has aliquot parts. It's a placer claim."

James went to Cooper and without touching the boy tried to comfort him. He leaned close to him and spoke softly.

Peri's forehead scrunched in question. She turned to James as if hoping he would interpret. "Why does he think it's a mine? What does he know about mines and maps? How does he know all this stuff?"

James looked back. "He knows about a lot of things and remembers everything he sees. We don't know why."

"It's a silver mine," Cooper announced.

Peri heard silver and the hairs on her neck stood up. She worried what he might give away of her mother's secret.

"It says A and G," Cooper continued. His eyes were closed and he spoke to no one, just into the night. "That is silver. AG is silver. It is a silver map." He rocked back and forth, quietly repeating, "It is a silver mine."

"AG is silver?" asked Peri looking at the writing in the journal. "How can that be?" she said to James.

James went to Cooper. "How is A and G silver? A and G don't spell silver."

Cooper rocked. "It is science. AG is silver. It is called the periodic table. That is what they call it. And AG is silver," he continued in his rambling monotone.

James and Tildie both stood staring at Peri who was glad she held the gun.

"Are you treasure hunters?" Tildie asked with a lilt of humor.

"No," answered Peri flatly. "I don't know what he's talking about. It's an old journal that my mother wrote while she was going insane. It means nothing. There is no silver mine." She shoved it safely into her coat. "I think your stew is burning," she said to Tildie, in hopes of changing the subject.

Tildie nodded and she and James directed Cooper back toward the fire. Peri scooped up the rest of her belongings and shoved them back into the saddlebags. She looked at Grace as she thrust the gun into the back of her pants.

When they returned to the fire, Tildie was scooping up thick, steaming stew into wooden bowls. She handed one to Peri. The smell was heavenly and made her irritation with what had just happened subside. "Thank you," she said taking a seat. Cooper was sitting across the fire with his back to the flames. He was already eating from his bowl and seemed unaffected.

Tildie handed a bowl to Grace and then went into the wagon with James. They returned with four large cups and a jug.

"Have some drink," Tildie said, pouring a cup and offering it to Peri.

Peri took a drink and gave a sour face that made James chuckle.

"Not used to wine?" he asked.

"Wine?" said Grace, with concern. When a cup was handed to her, she refused. "I can't drink wine. It's against the Word of Wisdom. Our church doesn't allow liquor."

With that Peri took a long guzzle and then held the cup up to Grace. "Cheers to the prophet!"

Grace gasped.

"If you still believe in all that shit after what you've seen, you're a bigger imbecile than that boy," Peri said, motioning to Cooper.

"He's not an imbecile. He doesn't act or think like us, but he's not an imbecile," said James, defensively.

"He's not your son," Peri quipped.

James looked at Cooper. "I know he's not my son, but I care for him like a son. He's a good person."

Peri shrugged. "Well, there's something wrong with him."

"Because he isn't just like you?" asked James. "There's nothing wrong with him. He's just like the rest of us all trying to make it in this life."

Peri felt a pang of guilt, but wasn't about to let on. She took a long drink and noticed Grace doing the same. "The road to hell is getting easier?" she asked.

Grace looked at her. "With what I've already done, I don't think I'm going to heaven."

Peri smirked, "Then you might as well enjoy the journey." She laid back against a large log that was used as both a seat and a table. Her body was weary and her brain started to fog. The exhaustion from the travel and angst of their circumstances mixed with the wine, had Peri unable to keep her eyes or her mind focused. The voices all sounded like water in a stream as it spilled over the stones in a soft babble. The gentle veil of sleep was welcomed and conceded. The deep weight of slumber came quickly and soundly and Peri's usual caution left just as swiftly.

Chapter 8

Thirty three miles southeast of Pocatello, Idaho
August 23, 1896

It was Chance's hoof pawing on the dry dirt that brought Peri out of her stupor. The horse was hungry, it was hours past his normal feeding time, and his patience was gone. When Peri sat up, her head throbbed so violently, that she laid back down and moaned. She began to peer out from raw and hazy eyes and saw there was nothing good about what she was waking up to. The sun blinded her, and as she propped herself up with a weak arm, she saw that the wagon and everything else was gone.

"Shit!"

"Shit?" murmured Grace. "That's all you have to say?"

Peri tried to rotate around and found Grace sitting cross legged behind her and looking out over the empty valley. "What happened? Where are they?" asked Peri.

"Gone."

Peri rubbed her eyes and tried to focus. Grace was right. Everything was gone. Grace and Peri were left with a jug of water, two blankets and the horse. Peri stumbled up to standing. "The bags. The saddlebags!"

"Gone," chirped Grace.

Peri patted her coat and dove her hands inside searching. "The journal's gone."

"So is the gun," Grace announced.

Peri felt around to the waist of her pants. "Shit! Shit!" She walked in a circle kicking at the ground and stomping until her aching head forced her back to the ground. "What the hell happened? Did you see it happen?"

"No, I was out just like you."

"How did they rob us and leave without us waking up?" Peri said, not expecting an answer.

Grace gave a loud snort. "You were the one drinking that wine. That is how they did it. They used the devil to get away with it. I knew it was the wrong thing to do. I told you . . ."

"Don't you dare blame this on me," Peri growled.

Grace looked around theatrically. "Well let's just see who else around here was drinking that wine and saying how I was an imbecile for trying to stay true to my god."

"You're no saint," said Peri. "You act innocent and pure, but I saw you kill your precious prophet and I think you enjoyed it. If I weren't trying to get you to that train, I'd leave your ass right here."

"Go ahead!" yelled Grace. "Ride after them and get it all back." Grace stood up and starting walking. "I'll get myself to the train."

Peri stared out over the horizon contemplating what to do. As much as she wanted to kill Grace and bury her along the side of the trail, she knew that her only option was to get her to Pocatello. They had no food, no way to protect themselves, and she only had a few hours left to complete her task and see Marty. That thought is what would get her through this. It was the only thing that had kept her going, and now being with him and starting a new life was in sight.

She untied Chance from the tree and strode over to Grace. "Get on," she ordered.

"No. You go get your little book, and the Sheriff's gun, and I'll keep walking. You can catch up and still get your money from my brother. Then everything will be perfect for you."

Peri stopped and took a deep breath trying to calm herself. She felt the tingle of hair on her neck as she processed what Grace said. "What?" she called.

Grace kept walking, not looking back.

Peri pulled Chance to a trot and caught up to Grace. "The sheriff's gun? Did you say that was the sheriff's gun?"

Grace looked at her as she continued walking and sighed impatiently at Peri's slowness to grasp what had happened.

Peri jumped off Chance and ran to Grace. She grabbed her arm and spun her around. "How? When did you steal it?"

Grace rolled her eyes. "He left it in the holster hanging on the chair in the kitchen." She shrugged as though the sheriff was asking for it.

"They'll be after us for sure now!" said Peri.

"For what? That witch and her family have the gun now. They probably did us a favor by stealing it."

Peri's rage boiled over. "You stupid little bitch!" she yelled and shoved Grace to the ground. "You have us facing murder charges and then you steal the sheriff's gun." Peri pounced on top of her and slapped her so hard, her hand throbbed. "You idiot!"

Grace screamed in pain and tried to roll over to hide her face, but Peri was like a windmill as her arms and hands flailed at Grace's head. Then Grace stopped moving and Peri sat up, wondering if she had killed her. Without warning, Grace exploded and punched Peri so hard she saw black and was on her back in the dirt when she came to.

When she saw Grace straddled on top of her, she tried to escape, but Grace held her by the neck. Peri felt blood run from her nose.

"Don't you ever hit me again," said Grace, cold and detached.

"Get off me," said Peri in a choked gurgle.

Grace ignored her. "I swore no one would ever hit me again. You do, and I'll kill you. Just like I did him. He'll never hit me again. Never again."

Peri kept silent and watched as Grace slowly stood up and walked, dazed and wavering. She pushed herself up cautiously, still watching Grace, guarded and wondering what to expect. She had never seen her show any emotion other than naiveté and folly. Her show of fury not only surprised Peri, but also jolted her. Grace had spent years at the compound and Peri could only imagine what horrors she had seen and endured. She was sure this is what sparked the immense wrath that she had just witnessed and the exhausted stupor that ensued.

Peri mounted Chance and followed Grace as she meandered along the trail. "Please just get on the horse so we can get there on time."

Grace shook her head and walked on.

Peri rode the horse past Grace and blocked her path. "I'm sorry. Okay? I'm sorry I hit you. I shouldn't have done that."

Grace stopped and with weary, red eyes stared up at Peri. She stayed silent a moment and then seemed to come back into herself. "I'm sorry you lost your journal or map thing."

Peri scoffed. "It's worthless. There are a bunch of pages missing. They were torn out. They think they stole a treasure map, but all they got was a bunch of directions to nowhere."

"Then why were you so upset that it's gone?" Grace asked.

Peri was silent. She knew why, but she had no intention of letting Grace see any sort of sentimentality, especially with how Peri was feeling at the moment. "I'm not. But I wish we still had that gun."

Grace nodded. She walked over to the horse and Peri gave her a hand up. "I don't know why you continue to help me," she mused, as she settled into her spot. "I've caused you so many problems. I'm a liar, a cheat, and a . . . ." She took a deep breath. "I might as well say it. I'm a murderer. I am. You'd be better off to just leave me on the side of the trail."

"And lose the bounty?" Peri said with a smirk.

Grace gave a good natured huff and then hugged Peri from behind. "I'm not near as afraid of going back now."

Peri straightened in the saddle and against Grace's embrace. She wondered why Grace was fearful of leaving the compound, but figured any type of change could make her anxious.

"I'm glad you're going to be with me," Grace continued.

Peri took a deep breath. She had no plans to spend any more time with Grace than the next few hours of their ride to the train in Pocatello. From there the plan was to see her off and then return to Challis with Marty and resume their life together. It would be Marty and her, not Marty, Grace, and her. She shrugged off Grace's comment to her creating things in her head and not knowing the real plan. She considered telling her, but decided that Marty would already have that taken care of. Marty. She saw his face in her mind and that brought her thoughts back around to what this journey was all about. It had been a terrible struggle, but in the end it would be her dream come true. Her future with the man she loved.

Chapter 9

The Story of Dakota
Montpelier, Idaho
1885

Casper was a big man in both size and spirit. He was a hunter and trapper and even though significantly successful, his stories were monumental. His bright green eyes shone as his long mustache twitched with the details of each stalk and kill. His pelts sold well at the trading post near the Fort Hall Indian land.

In the fall of 1876 he met Kimani, a dark eyed and soft spoken Shoshone woman that Casper was drawn to every time he stopped at the trading post to sell his bounty. He finally convinced her to join him on his hunts and in life, and it wasn't long after that Kimani gave birth to a baby boy they named Dakota after her grandmother's tribe from Nebraska. The family journeyed the Idaho wilderness and camped in the forests as Casper harvested what they needed for both trade and survival.

Most of the stores and businesses accepted them. The women in the town sought Kimani's Indian beading and crafts as valuable trading items. There were some that opposed the union of white and red, but most kept their sentiments to themselves and ignored them. Kimani never spoke even though her English was proficient. She stayed in the wagon and waited as Casper did his business. Casper often took his son along, and Dakota gave no indication he knew anything about the circumstances of his parents or the views that some people held of him. He was so engaging and precocious, the store owners often gave him small bits of Johnny cake or popcorn along with a tousle of his thick black hair.

The summer after Dakota's third birthday, Kimani became pregnant with their second child, and Casper realized that instead of their migrant life, they needed the more secure and stable life of a home. He built a small cabin in the hills behind the town of Montpelier, where the mountains and streams surrounding the two room home were filled with wildlife and fish. The setting seemed idyllic to Casper, but the idea of having the family living so close to their town, made the people who once greeted them so kindly, wonder just how immersed into their community they wanted to be.

That winter as the snow settled heavily on the home and Casper had to work for an hour just to free the door, Kimani went into labor almost ten weeks early. Casper had helped deliver their first child, but the urgency and earliness of this labor had him frantic. He contemplated trying to take her to town, but the distance and amount of snow made the trip impossible. He stoked the fire and put Dakota in the loft with some corn husk dolls Kimani had made that fall.

In the silence of the isolated cabin came a weak and watery cry. Kimani had stopped her groans of pain and lay still on the fur covered cot. Casper wept as he held the spindly baby boy in his hands. He wrapped the baby in fur and held it close to the fire in the hopes that the warmth would do something to keep him breathing and alive. But the little boy soon stilled, and when Casper turned with tear-filled eyes to his wife, he realized he had lost her too.

When Dakota came down from the loft, groggy and hungry, he found his father sitting on the floor by a fading fire, holding a leather string with a copper pendant. It was a necklace Kimani always wore, and it would be the only thing Dakota had of his mother. His memories were few and those he did have had vanished in time to where she became nothing but a few stories from his father and the manifestation of his dark skin.

As he grew older, his kind thoughts of her soured as his realization of what being her son brought to his life. When he was alone in the wagon or waiting for his father outside one of the stores, he heard the people of the town call him half-breed and brown-skin and parents shuffled children off if they showed any interest in being his friend. The Shoshone and Bannocks who came to town, were no different. They looked away when he stared at their dark, weathered faces and long braided hair. Dakota wondered if they looked like his mother and what it felt like to be accepted. The older he grew, the quieter and more introverted he became. He started life with the vigor and brightness of his father, and now along with her native features, he also assumed her stoic and muted nature.

Casper loved his son and tried to brush aside the pain both he and Dakota felt from the treatment of others. When they were together alone in the house or the wilderness, they were untroubled and nothing could weaken their bond of father and son.

Like any parent, Casper wanted to give his son everything he could to ensure his happiness and give him a bright future. The guilt he felt trying to raise him on his own weighed heavily, so he tried to make up for the loss however he could. As Dakota grew, Casper realized he could no longer teach him anything regarding school because he had never learned how to read or do anything more than simple math. He was a successful trader, but so much of that came from his ability to beguile, rather than intellect. He wanted more for his son, so he took Dakota and met with the teacher at the one room school house to get him enrolled. The travel to and from school would be challenging, but Casper knew it was the right thing for his son, so he bought a mule that Dakota rode until the winter made the trip too treacherous.

"What if they laugh at me?" asked Dakota, as he watched his father pack a lunch into a knapsack.

"Be kind. They will soon see who you are," Casper answered. In his heart he worried about the treatment of his son, but the school teacher had been encouraging, which lifted Casper's hopes. He helped Dakota onto the mule and made sure he had the supplies the teacher had requested. "Thank her when you leave for the day. She's giving you something that no one can ever take away."

This didn't make sense to Dakota, but he smiled and agreed to do what his father asked. When he returned that evening, he was animated as he described his day. The teacher gave him a slate and chalk and by the end of the day she had moved him into the section of children that were about his age. "She called me a quick study," he announced proudly.

Casper's heart swelled seeing his son so full of joy. Each morning as he sent him off on the mule, Dakota turned back with a big smile and a wave, which kept Casper alight throughout the day. When a week had passed, as the two sat at the table discussing the hunt they planned to take, the sound of a horse and wagon made them both stand and go to the door. It was rare that anyone made the journey to the small cabin, and they never came after dark.

Casper opened the door and found Sheriff Goodwin and the young school teacher. Both the sheriff and the woman looked sad and apprehensive. When Dakota saw his teacher, he greeted her heartily and tried to welcome her into their home, but both the teacher and the sheriff declined. It was then that Casper knew that the visit was not a good one. He directed Dakota to his space in the loft, and with a lantern stepped out into the dark night hoping to keep whatever bad news they brought from his son.

"There are Indian boarding schools for your son," explained the Sheriff.

Casper stood stunned as he listened to why Dakota would no longer be able to attend the school he so dearly loved. "Has he done something wrong?"

"No," said the school teacher emphatically, looking up at him for the first time. "It's nothing he's done. He's a good boy."

Casper shook his head and look pleadingly at the young woman. "Then why?"

She shrugged and looked to the sheriff who sighed deeply. "I'm sorry Casper, but there are people who don't want their children mixed in with the Indians. That's why they have the other schools for the Indian children."

"But my son is half white. His mother died when he was young. He's never lived with the Indians. He doesn't know their language. He's like me, like us," Casper defended.

The young teacher wiped away a tear and pulled her shawl tighter around her shoulders. "Maybe I could work with him separately?" she offered.

"Separately?" asked Casper, shaking his head.

"I'm sorry, Casper. It's the way it has to be. He can't attend this school," said the sheriff. "Think about the Indian school. I'm sure they would treat him well there." He directed the teacher back to the wagon and left Casper standing in the dim light, knowing he would have to go inside and break his child's heart.

The house was cold and still when Casper came back in. He slowly waved the lantern around the room trying to illuminate the empty space. He heard muffled cries coming from the loft. He knew then that Dakota had heard it all. He climbed the ladder and laid next to his sobbing boy. "You are my son and I'm proud," he said, with a hand on Dakota's head. "I will never send you away. It's either this school or no school."

Dakota wiped his eyes on his sleeve and was buoyed by his father's adamant declaration.

Chapter 10

Pocatello, Idaho
August 25, 1896

It had been two full days without food and very little water. Beads of sweat fell into Peri's eyes and the salt stung, but she was too tired to even wipe her brow. When they reached the outskirts of Pocatello, Peri stopped the horse and took a deep breath. She had told Grace to shut up miles ago and to her surprise, she hadn't made a peep since.

"We're almost there. If anyone approaches us and asks questions, just let me talk. Is that clear?" Peri said.

"Yes," Grace said with such defeat that Peri almost felt bad, but she had had it with the questions about Emma's plight, and if Peri planned to go back and retrieve her. She had no intention of doing anything to help Emma, and she also had no intention of talking to Grace about her plans. When she returned to Challis with Marty, she planned to never leave his side.

"There's a hotel next to the rail station. It's called the Pacific Hotel. That's where Marty—,"Peri's heart leapt when she said his name. "That's where he'll meet us."

Grace took a loud and shuddering breath. "What did Marty tell you about me?"

Peri gave it a thought and then shrugged. "He said you were at Cedar Creek and that he was told you were going to marry that old bastard, Deon Dixon. He was worried about you."

Grace was silent.

"Why?" Peri asked.

"Did he tell you why I was at the compound?" Grace asked.

Peri shrugged. "Same reason I was there, I guess."

"You were sold?" asked Grace.

"Sold?" Peri thought for a moment. "I guess in a way we were. Deon paid off our debts."

"I can't believe he's really doing this. I never thought he'd try to get me back," she said softly, almost to herself.

Peri smiled at the anticipated response she hoped she'd get from Marty. She had envisioned it dozens of times and now she was less than an hour away from it being true. She put a strand of hair behind her ear and then realized how unkempt and foul she must be. She could smell the sweat and travel grime wafting off Grace, and *she* had bathed while at the doctor's house. Peri's quick dip in the river did little to help her now. She knew she must look and smell like the dogs that roamed the streets. But it would have to do. They had no options and no time. Peri's only hope was that Marty's appreciation would veil her filthiness.

As they rode into town, people on the streets looked at them with questioning eyes. Peri was used to odd looks when coming into a new town, but this was worse. Her fears of looking soiled and exhausted were confirmed in the disgusted faces of strangers.

When they reached the hotel, Peri tied Chance to the post out front and halfheartedly dusted herself off. She knew it was pointless, but her desire to rid herself of the grime persisted.

Grace walked beside Peri up the short flight of stairs and gave her an anticipatory smile as she pulled open the door. Inside was a large desk made of dark oiled wood and a thin man making notes in a large ledger. He looked up and greeted them with a skeptical look through glasses perched on the end of his nose.

"Yes?" he asked. He wore a stiffly starched white shirt and his hair was combed back in straight lines held in place by grease.

Peri stepped forward. "We're here to meet Marty Busby."

The man straightened. "Are they expecting you?"

Peri nodded. "Yes."

He pursed his mouth as though he still didn't believe Peri. But, after a brief moment, he relented and gave a shrug. "They went out, but should be back shortly. You can wait." He pointed to a wooden bench across the room.

Peri and Grace walked to the bench, then both noticed the large upholstered sofa next to the desk, and made a beeline for it. Peri knew Grace had the same thought—soft, plush cushions under their sore and tired bodies. It wasn't long after Peri took a seat that the exhaustion of their journey made her eyes heavy and she was soon drifting in and out of sleep.

When Grace quietly roused her by nudging her shoulder, Peri opened her eyes and saw Marty standing over her. She startled and wiped her face, feeling the drool start to roll. She stood up and shook her head, hoping she appeared awake and alert. She sniffed and blinked, and then tried to smile naturally.

"Peri," said Marty, taking her by the shoulders and smiling. "My dear, Peri. I knew you could do this. I never doubted you for a minute. You've saved my darling Grace and brought her back to me." He turned to Grace and gave her a quick peck on the forehead. "I'd like to speak to Peri alone. Can you go into the restaurant for a moment? There's someone waiting for you."

Grace grinned at Peri with obvious happiness bubbling up inside her. Peri gave her a big smile back. Grace hesitated, but then she did as she was asked and went through the swinging doors into the restaurant.

Marty took Peri by the arm and led her to the bench, where they sat on the bench. He reached into his pocket and pulled out an envelope. "I know I'll never be able to make this up to you, but I'll never forget what you've done for me. I wanted to give you something to thank you." He handed the envelope to her.

Peri took it and gave him a questioning glance before opening it. Inside was a bundle of cash. Peri's brows furrowed and she looked up at him. "What's this? We never talked about payment."

"It isn't a lot, and you deserve so much more for what you did," he said.

"I don't want money. I never asked for money. I did this for you," she replied, her mind swirling with confusion.

He nodded and squirmed in his seat. "You may need it for the ride back—supplies and stuff."

Peri's shoulders suddenly felt weighted, and the giddiness she felt in seeing him started to fade. "I thought you were planning to have everything ready for us to head back to Challis. I thought we were leaving as soon as Grace was on the train."

Marty looked at the ground. "I'm not going back to Challis."

"What?" Peri shrieked a little too loudly. She covered her mouth and kept her hand over it to prevent herself from saying anything more until he explained.

He paused, looking everywhere except at her. Then he looked at the floor as if gathering his thoughts before he explained. "I took a job in Oregon. Some things came about when I went up there to make the arrangements for Grace."

A well-dressed, *fastidious*, young woman came through the swinging doors of the restaurant, her arm interlocked with Grace's. "Some things came about" rang clear in Peri's head. Her cheeks burned.

Marty stood up and guided the woman forward. "Peri this is Hannah."

Grace looked unsettled. "They're getting married," she said, somberly.

Peri scowled at Marty. "Married?" she asked, his words still not registering, and wondering if it was a dream.

"Yes," Marty said with a hollow smile. "We wanted to wait for Grace to be with us. I've always wanted a family. You know how much we used to talk about it. And now it is happening."

Peri gritted her teeth as she felt her breathing increase and her heart start to pound.

"Hannah's our cousin," said Grace, and then turned to Marty as though pointing out that fact. "I only thought people on the compound married their cousins."

Marty gave her a look and then stepped in front of Grace.

Hannah made a little dip, almost a curtsy, but made no move closer to Peri. "It's such a pleasure to meet you. I feel like I already know so much about you. The way that Marty carries on about Peri this and Peri that." She smiled and raised her thin dark brows.

She was everything that Peri was not. Feminine, sweet, and delicate. When Hannah looked at Marty, Peri saw the adoration in her eyes that Peri felt in her wounded and broken heart. Her stomach heaved and she had to bolt out the main door to keep from throwing up all over her true love's intended.

How could she have possibly thought Marty had feelings for her? Was she really that oblivious to what their relationship was?

Marty was soon on the steps. "Are you all right?" he asked.

She shoved the envelope in his chest. "I need to get on my way." She left him and nearly stumbled down the steps, wanting to run away from the pain. She untied Chance's reins and scrambled onto his back.

Looking back, she saw Grace at the top of the stairs looking lost and forlorn and that made Peri even sicker.

Grace ran down the stairs toward Peri as she turned her horse around. She saw Marty clutching the envelope near his heart, his expression sad as he turned and went back inside the hotel. Her heart sank knowing it would be the last time she saw him.

Grace reached up with both arms to give Peri a hug. Peri leaned down to her. "I'm sorry."

Peri straightened. "For what?"

"I know how you feel about my brother and—"

"You don't know shit," Peri spat back.

"Then why didn't you take the money?" asked Grace.

"That wasn't why I did it. There wasn't ever supposed to be any money," said Peri, her heartbreak slowly turning to anger.

"Then why did you tell me you saved me just for the money?"

Peri huffed. "To get you to shut up."

"Here," said Grace, ignoring her, as she held a small cloth bundle up to Peri.

Peri shook her head. "I told you, I don't want anything."

Grace raising her eyebrows said, "You'll want this."

Irritated, Peri snatched the bundle from Grace and unfolded it. Inside were several pieces of raw silver and more torn out pages of her mother's writings. It was similar to the journal and map that was stolen with her saddlebags, but not the same. She looked down at Grace with both shock and anger. "What's this? Where'd you get this?"

"I took it from Emma," said Grace. "I hid it in my underwear. I guess the witch didn't think to look there."

"Good hell, is there anything you don't steal?" Peri asked, exasperated.

Grace shrugged, unaffected. "I didn't take everything from Emma. Besides, I helped her escape. There is a reason Eliza made her hide in the Spirit Keeper's house. And she told Emma that she wasn't allowed to leave until after she had the baby. That's why they're trying to find us. It isn't just the silver and the map. It's Emma and the baby they want."

"What?" Peri asked. "How do you know that?"

"Emma's baby is the prophet's son. Silas is the only other son. He tried to kill Emma when we were escaping. I think he wants to kill the baby so he's still the only son. Emma told me they wanted the map, so she tore out part of the directions and hid it so they thought they had it and would leave her alone. This is the other half. I tried to tell you, but you never listen to me."

"I don't think it matters," said Peri. "Those people who robbed us have the rest of the map and I don't want to go back to that place, even for treasure."

Grace studied Peri intensely. "But you deserve it. You deserve to have the treasure. Your mother did what she did for you." Grace placed a hand on Peri's thigh. "I'm sorry things didn't turn out the way you'd hoped with my brother."

Peri recoiled in horror that Grace could see her pain. Chance, sensing a change in Peri's tone, sidestepped away from Grace. "What are you talking about? I got you here on time and now I can get on with my life, just like I planned."

Grace nodded knowingly. She looked off to where Marty and Hannah now stood arm-in-arm at the top of the stairs. She turned her back to them and whispered, "If her family didn't have a bunch of money this wouldn't be happening, but I do know that he could never make you happy."

"How do you know what would make me happy?" Peri bent down and hissed at her.

The deafening whistle of the train bellowed from the distance. Marty walked down to Peri and Grace. "It's time for us to go," he said, taking Grace's arm to hurry her along.

Grace blew a kiss to Peri. "Thank you for saving me. Someday I will repay you."

Peri gave a huff. She was glad to be free of her annoying little charge.

"I'll never forget what you did for us," Marty said. He held out the envelope. His eyes pleaded for her to take it. "Please?" he said in a timorous voice.

Peri took a deep breath, snatched the envelope, tipped her hat, stuffed the leather bundle and the envelope into her coat, and started toward the trail to Challis. When she was just outside of town, tears came fast and fierce. She felt betrayed and now lost. She had nothing in Challis to return to, except an empty house and a life full of lies. Her plans and future had all included Marty. Being back there and without him would only remind her of the loss. She was alone with no place to call home. She pulled Chance to a stop and wiped her nose along the sleeve of her shirt.

She put her hand over the bulge in her coat. What was her mother trying to tell her from the grave? A treasure map seemed odd for a religious fanatic who was losing her mind. And yet, maybe this was the only way she could give back. There was no other plan and Peri certainly had nothing to lose. She was going back to claim what was hers. It would be the first time she listened to her mother and she hoped it wasn't the beginning of a long string of bad decisions.

Chapter 11

Pocatello, heading southeast
August 25, 1896

With a new saddle, saddle bags, and supplies, Peri made her way close to the river, but as far off the main trail as possible. The men of Cedar Creek were looking for her, and going back in that direction was risky enough without being out in the open. She figured she could make the trip in less time now that she only had herself and Chance to fend for. Without the other part of her mother's journal, it would be impossible to pinpoint the exact location of the silver, but Peri wasn't sure that is what it all meant anyway. She questioned her decision to travel back toward the trouble almost every minute of the trip, but when it came down to it, she had nowhere else to go.

At a narrow bend in the river, she stopped and washed up quickly, and then redressed in her brother's clothes, shaking off as much of the dirt and sweat as she could. She needed the shock of the cold water on her skin to keep herself awake, as much as to remove the grime that had built up from the long days of travel. Peri never looked down or closed her eyes, even when washing her face. She was never going to be caught naked and unarmed again.

As she rounded the large black lava beds of the Portneuf Gap, she saw the shredded tarp of a wagon flapping violently in the wind, like a call for help. As she got closer, she saw that the wagon was on its side, the belly of the large vessel exposed and its contents strewn about. It wasn't a good idea to go toward the mayhem, but she cautiously guided Chance over the hill. As she looked down to the banks of the river, she saw the remains of James and Tildie's sheep camp.

James' body slumped over the edge of the wagon and Tildie lay dead on the ground. Stunned and sickened by the sight, Peri quickly surveyed the hills and valley in fear that the culprits were still a threat. With no one in sight, she nudged Chance closer to the grotesque and inconceivable scene. Flies swarmed over the bodies. The stench of death filled the air. Peri pulled her handkerchief over her nose in an effort to block the putrid odor.

She wondered about Cooper, the odd young man who was with them. There was no sign of him. Could he have done this? She shook her head and thought, "Why would he? He could never survive on his own."

She pondered the reasons someone would want to kill these people. Peri herself had the desire after they robbed and left her on the trail, but now seeing them like this, she didn't have any feeling of relief or revenge, but instead a sense of dread. Deep in her gut she knew this was part of the evil that followed her. She dismounted and walked to the back of the wagon. There were no signs of her saddlebags or the gun. She didn't expect to find anything salvageable, but she couldn't help wonder if the map had brought the same bad luck to Jim and Tildie as it had for everyone else who possessed it. This violent and vicious act wasn't just a robbery, but a message. The sight of the wreckage had drawn her in and now she wondered if they were simply waiting to pounce.

Peri heard a light crackle of steps on rock and sand coming over the small hill that sloped down to the river. She bent behind the broken remains of the wagon and cursed herself for leaving the rifle in the saddle scabbard.

The shuffle of dirt came again and then suddenly, the white faced mule came up from the banks. Peri felt her body heave a huge sigh of relief, but when she stood up and turned to her horse, she found herself standing with the barrel of a gun leveled at her.

Her heart leapt and she quickly put up her hands in surrender. Peri focused in on her captor and with a mixture of surprise and dismay, realized it was the same man who had caught her bathing naked in the river. She wasn't sure if she should be relieved or embarrassed. She put her head down hoping he wouldn't recognize her.

With his gun fixed, Sam dismounted and walked to her. "Keep your hands up and turn around," he ordered.

She did as he asked and stood quietly as he patted down her sides and legs. She worried he might pat down her chest, but he didn't.

"Where's your gun?" he asked.

Peri motioned to where Chance stood grazing on the lush grass of the river banks, her new saddlebags and the gun she had bought with the money rested in clear view. It made Peri feel even more foolish.

"What's your name?" he asked.

She hesitated. Lowered her voice and lied, "John Johnson."

"Turn around," said Sam. When she did, he tilted his head and took a closer look at Peri's face.

She kept her eyes down.

"Did you know these people?" he asked, looking around with disgust.

"Not really. They let us camp with them a couple nights back, but that's all," Peri said. "I'm heading back from Pocatello. I found them like this."

"Have you seen anyone else on your travels?" he asked.

"No," she answered.

He nodded. "I'm looking for two women. I think they came through this way."

Peri felt her stomach roll. She shook her head.

"They're wanted for murder," Sam said.

Peri's face became hot and she took a deep breath. She was facing the very person who could ruin her plans and quite possibly take her back to face the gallows. "What are their names?" Peri asked. She regretted her question, as it sounded too interested.

"Peri Dixon and Grace Busby," he answered.

Peri swallowed hard, and tried to act disinterested. "Haven't seen anyone on this trail."

An odd and quivering voice came from behind them. "She didn't kill them."

Sam froze, his eyes wide. He looked around and then to Peri to see if this might be part of a trap.

Peri had her hands up, but recognized the voice as Cooper's.

Sam raised his hands.

Cooper emerged from behind a large lava rock next to the river. He looked disheveled and unarmed.

"The men with white shirts and long beards killed them," Cooper yelled. "They took the silver map. That is what they did."

Peri looked at Sam. "I know him. He won't hurt you. He is . . ." She put her hand to her forehead, "not normal. He's odd. Kind of like a child."

Sam cleared his throat and called over his shoulder to Cooper. "I'm going to turn around. Don't shoot. I'm putting my gun down."

"I don't have a gun to shoot," said Cooper.

Sam looked at Peri, who shrugged. "He doesn't. I told you, he won't hurt you."

Sam turned.

Cooper looked scared.

"Put your hands up," Sam ordered.

Cooper looked to Peri for guidance and she nodded.

Sam started to walk toward Cooper, but Cooper backed away with wide eyes. Sam stopped. "What happened here?" he asked, motioning toward the chaos of the wagon.

Cooper wiped his eyes. "The men in white shirts and long beards were looking for Peri and Grace."

Sam's brow lowered. "Peri and Grace? They were here?"

Peri's eyes shot open.

Cooper looked at Peri and then gave Sam an odd look. He stayed quiet as though he didn't understand the question.

"Have you seen Peri Dixon and Grace Busby?" Sam asked again.

Cooper looked again to Peri. "Yes," he answered, cautiously.

"Where did they go?" Sam pushed.

Cooper looked past Sam. "Peri, do you know where Grace went?"

Sam shot a look to Peri and then pointed his gun at her. "I knew it. You're a girl. You're Peri Dixon."

Peri rolled her eyes and sighed.

Sam stepped back and sized her up. He started to ask a question, but then stood with resolve and announced, "You are under arrest for the murder of Deon Heff and Launa Walker."

Peri rolled her eyes again. "That's bullshit. I didn't kill them. Launa killed herself and Deon . . . well I wish I'd of killed that son-of-a- bitch. But I didn't!"

Sam pointed at James and Tildie's bodies. "I suppose you didn't kill these two either?"

"No," Peri said insistently. "I told you, I had just come from Pocatello."

Sam stepped in closer to her. He looked her in the eye. "I just realized who you are." He stepped back and huffed. "I should have arrested you then."

Peri felt her face flush as though she had no clothes on again.

He pointed his gun at Cooper. "Can you ride that mule?" he asked.

"Yes," Cooper answered.

"Get on and come with us. You'll need to answer to these murders," he said, motioning to the bodies.

Cooper again looked at Peri for direction.

"Do what he says," she told him.

Sam took Peri by the arm and led her to her horse. "You will lead us back to Montpelier. Don't try anything stupid. I don't want to have to shoot you, but I will. The warrant was for dead or alive."

"Peri didn't do this," said Cooper, his voice beginning to crumble. "It was the men in the white shirts and long beards. They came looking for Peri and Grace. When Jim and Tildie told them what they knew, the men in the white shirts and long beards shot Jim and Tildie and took Peri's silver map."

"Why didn't they shoot you?" asked Sam.

"I took my mule to the river. I saw a deer. A whitetail deer. That is what they call them. I followed it. When I was coming back I heard their voices so I hid." Cooper kept his focus on the ground. His voice was steady and methodical. "The men in white shirts and long beards wanted Peri and Grace. Tildie said they didn't know Peri and Grace, but when the men in white shirts and long beards saw Peri's saddlebags they shoved Jim and Tildie down and called them liars. They made them tell what they knew. Then they found the map and the gun." Cooper paused. He looked at Peri. "It was the silver map."

Sam looked at Peri, who avoided his gaze.

"Where is Grace?" Cooper asked again, oblivious to the danger they were in.

"Yes," Sam said. "Where is Grace?"

Peri raised her shoulders and shook her head. "I don't know."

Cooper flapped his hand near his ear, as he continued. "The men in white shirts and long beards shot James and Tildie. They took things from the camp and wrecked the camp." Cooper took a deep breath as he finished.

"Are you coming with us or not?" Sam asked, annoyed. He searched Peri's saddlebags and removed the gun. He went to his own saddle and strapped the gun to the side.

Cooper remained in place, flapping his ear.

"Fine, stay here," Sam said, waving him off in disgust.

Peri shook her head in disbelief at the horrifying scene and Cooper's tragic situation.

Sam took another look around the decimated camp, then turned back to Peri. "Let's go."

Peri mounted Chance and looked back at Cooper who now mumbled while petting the mule.

"What about him?" she asked Sam.

"What about him? If he doesn't come with us, I don't care. He's obviously trouble," answered Sam.

"Are you just going to leave him out here?"

"That's where I found him." He mounted his horse and guided Peri toward the trail. "I don't have time for a fool."

Peri looked back as Cooper stood still petting the mule and mumbling into the crisp air. "You have two dead bodies and the only witness out here. You can't leave him. I don't think he'll survive on his own."

Sam scoffed. "Why do you care? You're arrested for murder. Why are you worrying about some useless fool?"

Peri looked back at Cooper and wondered why she did care about what happened to him. She was arrested and facing the gallows, and yet her worry at the moment was for the simple minded man with the white-faced mule.

Chapter 12

Emma

October 8, 1896

When the day of my sealing came last February, I was nervous and curious about what would take place. I spent the morning in the large bedroom that had been prepared for me and my new life as the prophet's seventh wife. I missed Mother and wondered if her sealing to Uncle Deon was similar. I felt her watching me from above, knowing this would keep us together forever.

My soon-to-be sister wives, scurried around me, some helping me dress in the blessed garments of eternal brides, some braiding my hair. It was an important day for them as well. My marriage to Uncle Deon wasn't just between the two of us, but an eternal bond with the entire family. Our marriage ceremony was to include all the wives, as I would be taking my vows with them as well—all married to each other. My children would be sealed to all of them, and theirs to me.

The purpose of plural marriage was to build righteous families who were destined to spend time and all eternity together in the celestial kingdom. It was vital in attaining that highest level of heaven. As members of the Kingdom of Glory church we had been given the calling from God to continue his endowment of plural marriage. It was something the Mormon Church had fallen away from and that is why the Lord called Uncle Deon as the one true prophet. His children were the chosen ones—special spirits sent to earth to continue the plan and then return home to our eternal family and our Father in heaven.

The elders of the church were also promised this if they remained true to Uncle Deon and carried out his teachings. They also had plural wives that the prophet, through revelation from God, chose for them. The children were raised together as siblings. Uncle Deon loved the children and it was common to see him at the playground or with them on his lap reading and teaching them the hymns of our church. When the girls turned twelve they entered the young women's quarters where they began their lives in service and preparation for their calling as spirit wives. The married women on the compound were their teachers, and Eliza, Uncle Deon's first wife, oversaw them all. It was she who called me aside and told me of Uncle Deon's revelation that I be his wife.

"It is meant to be. Your children will be my children," she said, holding my hand with both of hers. "You will help us add to our eternal family and bring us closer to our Lord and Savior. This is God's plan for us."

I was introduced individually to those who would soon be my sister wives. I knew them from living on the compound, but had never really spoken to any of them. I learned that most were sisters or related to each other, and to Uncle Deon. Meek and quiet, and though they smiled, they seemed oddly distant. When Eliza was there, they all brightened up and sat a bit straighter. It was obvious she held the position of first wife and made sure the others didn't forget.

As the newest of the wives as well as the youngest, I was worried about how they would accept me into the family, but as they prepared me that day, I felt loved and comforted by their actions. Eliza spent the day overseeing everything. She rarely spoke to me, but gave me an affirming smile as I stood at the full-length mirror in my white dress, ready to take my vows.

The women surrounded me and escorted me to the chapel. Though I was nervous, their presence comforted me. Inside, stood Uncle Deon. He was dressed in white and his hair was combed back with pomade that smelled of musk and formed slick lines that exposed his freckled scalp. He smiled brightly as I came into view. I tried to smile back but my stomach churned, and I had to watch the ground to keep my focus straight and my resolve strong as I walked forward alone.

Eliza took my hand and placed it in his. Dark spots covered his papery skin. His nails were uneven and yellow, and when I looked into his red and watery eyes, I wondered how a man who spoke directly to our Lord could seem so feeble.

The other women formed a circle around us and bowed their heads as Uncle Deon closed his eyes and spoke to God about the plan of eternal life and the importance of building families to bring us joy in the Celestial Kingdom.

"Sister Emma?" I heard my name and looked up, surprised that I had let my mind drift so far from what was going on around me. Uncle Deon faced me as we knelt across from one another at the large alter. He held my hand in an odd and purposeful grip. I swallowed hard and nodded, hoping no one saw my distraction.

He gave a small smile. "Emma darling, this is called the Patriarchal Grip or Sure Sign of the Nail." He motioned to our hands.

Both of our forefingers centered on the other's wrist. I felt his pulse and it made me quiver.

In a low calm voice he proceeded. "Do you Sister Emma take these vows to be my wife for time and all eternity, with a covenant and promise that you will observe and keep all the laws, rites, and ordinances pertaining to this Holy Order of Matrimony in the New and Everlasting Covenant, and this you do in the presence of God, angels, and these sisters, of your own free will and choice?"

I looked around at the women. Their faces were as white as the dresses they all wore. They looked back at me with absent, anemic expressions. Then I saw Eliza. Her hair was scooped up in a swirl, high on her head. She gave me a directed nod, with scolding eyebrows and I blurted out, "Yes."

Uncle Deon sighed as though he had worried I would say no.

"By virtue of the Holy Priesthood and the authority vested in me, I pronounce that we are husband and wife for time and all eternity, and I seal upon us the blessings of the holy resurrection with power to come forth in the morning of the first resurrection clothed in glory, immortality and eternal lives, and I seal upon us all the blessings of kingdoms, thrones, principalities, powers, dominions and exaltations, with all the blessings of Abraham, Isaac, and Jacob and I say unto you dear Emma, be fruitful and multiply and with my seed, replenish the earth that we may have joy and rejoicing in the day of our Lord Jesus Christ. All these blessings, together with all the blessings appertaining unto the New and Everlasting Covenant, I seal upon our family by virtue of the Holy Priesthood, through our faithfulness, in the name of the Father, and of the Son, and of the Holy Ghost, Amen."

He leaned over the altar and pulled me toward him. He kissed me on the mouth and I smelled a mixture of sweat and old food. My body shivered as my new sister wives came toward me with whispered congratulations and light, disingenuous hugs.

It was done. I was now the wife of the prophet and had secured my place on the compound and in heaven. I would be with my mother again and secure that my children would be cared for, even if I wasn't around. These women would accept them as their own and I would never have to be alone, hungry, or without a place to call home. My marriage to Uncle Deon made everything in my world secure and stable. It was right and it was good. That is what I kept repeating in my head like a mantra.

The humble, gracious demeanor Uncle Deon had always shown changed with our vows. I felt his eyes ogle me every time I looked in the direction of my new husband. I didn't know how to respond, so I looked away and tried to push the vision of his lewd stare from my mind. I was his now and I knew what that meant, but I hadn't processed the reality until that moment.

As the rest of the members of the Kingdom of Glory filed into the chapel to share in our joy, I tried to smile and accept their kind words and blessings, but I knew as the time grew closer to the hour we would leave the gathering and I would have to face him alone and naked in so many ways. I was aware of my role to bear children and grow our family, but along with my fears of what that meant in our bedroom, I also feared that my secret would be exposed and he would come to realize that I was already with child.

Chapter 13

Emma

October 8, 1896

In January, Silas found me alone for the first time. I blamed myself for what happened. I was not in class and knew I was being disobedient. I enjoyed my little secret place in the loft of the horse barn and went there when I felt I wouldn't be missed, so I could think and just be alone.

He grabbed my arm so firmly, I had bruises for over a week, but when he forced me down on the floor and put his hand up my dress, I knew I was being punished for leaving my lessons with the other girls. I screamed out and he clasped his hand on my mouth and then slapped me.

"You make one more sound and I'll strangle you and screw your dead body," he hissed.

He undid his pants and as I tried to pretend it was all just a terrible dream, he took my virginity and my dignity. The pain was tearing and sharp, but I didn't make a sound. He was brusque and his heated breath against my neck made my stomach turn. When he finished, he slid off me and lay on the hay covered floor, eyes closed and panting. I didn't know if I should move, so I lay still until he rose, and told me to get dressed. I knew I was bleeding and I had nothing to clean myself with, so I had to put my torn undergarments back on and hope the others didn't notice.

"If you ever speak a word of this, I will slit your throat like a pig," he told me as I sat looking at the floor.

I nodded and kept my head down.

"Look at me," he ordered.

I didn't want to, but when he yelled it again, I forced myself to lift my head and face him. His face was odd shaped, with a bulging forehead and small chin.

"You're mine now," he said. "Do you understand?"

I nodded slightly, not wanting to comprehend what horror that brought me.

"No one else will ever want you and I'll make sure of that." He left me cowering and huddled on the floor of the only place I had found solace since being brought to Cedar Creek.

From that point on, I made sure that I was never alone. When I saw him in the center park of the compound, I avoided his gaze and went in another direction. He tried to split me away from the others, but I was diligent in staying within the group. And when it was announced that I was to become the prophet's seventh wife, my eyes welled up with joy. Not because I was marrying Uncle Deon, but that I would be secluded away and safe from the man who had tortured me.

My happiness at the thought of being in the prophet's home turned sour when the reality of what my sealing truly meant. My first experience with sex was terrible, and the thought of having to do that with Uncle Deon made me sick inside. I pushed the thoughts from my mind, knowing that the alternative was worse.

I would be easy prey for Silas if I wasn't part of the prophet's wives. This way I had a fortress of both brick and mortar, as well as the constant presence of the only thing Silas seemed to fear, and that was Eliza.

My first night with Uncle Deon was not what I expected. He sat in a chair and read, while I sat on the edge of the bed in my nightgown waiting for a sign from him. He sipped on a glass of water and smiled at me.

"Take off your gown and let me look at my beautiful new bride," he said.

I was disgusted by the thought of standing naked and exposed to him, and he must have sensed my hesitation.

"To obey your husband is your duty in the eyes of our Lord." He walked to me and pulled my gown off my shoulder. He tipped my chin up to him and kissed me with dry lips. "Do as I say," he whispered.

I hesitantly lifted the other side of my gown and let it fall to the floor. I stood straight and pulled in my stomach muscles, hoping he wouldn't notice the small bulge that was starting to form. He stood back and looked me up and down and then cupped my breast. I closed my eyes. He guided me to lay on the bed. I did as he said, hoping this would soon be over. When I opened my eyes, I saw a frail and sagging body. His small penis was limp and as he pulled the covers over us with one hand, I felt him trying to make himself erect with the other. I laid there forcing my mind onto other things. Trying to separate my soul from my body. And that is when I heard the gurgle and heave of his snoring. I looked over to find him, eyes closed and mouth agape. He was fast asleep.

Being his seventh wife would have meant that Uncle Deon came to my bedroom every seventh night, but with Mother gone, it was every sixth. However, because I was new, he spent the first three nights in my bed. Each morning he woke, quickly dressed and left. When night came, I found him already in my room, sitting in the same chair, reading, and sipping his water, and every night he crawled under the covers, showing intentions of consummating our marriage, but soon asleep.

This arrangement didn't disappoint me a bit, except I was pregnant and needed to have him and everyone else believe it was the prophet's child. I calculated I had not bled for at least two months and it wouldn't be long before I was unable to hide the baby growing inside me. Uncle Deon was the only one who knew that we hadn't consummated our marriage, and I wondered just how this would play out when it was obvious I was pregnant. Would he know that the baby wasn't his, or wonder if we had performed the act before he fell asleep? I had to make him think it was his, so one night I used a needle from my sewing box, pricked my finger, and let the blood drip onto the sheet. I then woke him slightly, and spoke to him as though we had completed the act. In the morning, he seemed awkward and drowsy, and left quickly.

Years ago, when my mother was found dead and Peri left in the night, the focus on me intensified. Was I stable? Was I loyal to The Kingdom of Glory and to Uncle Deon? I did my best to assure them that I was. Each night I sat in my room and read the journal my mother had left. Most of it was ramblings about the religion and her desperate attempts to qualify why we were at Cedar Creek, but there was also talk of treasure. When I finished the pages with her longhand ramblings, I found a specifically detailed description using numbers and words that I didn't understand. There was also a roughed out map.

"What are you reading?" Deon asked as he appeared unexpectedly at my door. "I saw your room was still bright, so I thought I'd say good night."

"It's nothing," I answered, wanting to hide it. "Simply notes from my mother."

Deon smiled sadly. "We all miss her. I'd like to read it."

He saw the resistance on my face. "Leave it on my side table when you're finished," he said with a nod.

I heard Eliza's voice behind him and he acknowledged her, then turned back to me. "Good night, my dear. I will see you soon."

"Good night, Husband," I answered. I saw Eliza's quizzical face, just before he closed the door to my room.

I didn't want him to read my mother's odd ideas and beliefs, and I especially didn't want to give away whatever clues she had given me to what she called "the precious treasures." Was the hunk of silver I had stashed in my drawer just a glimpse of what she had hidden? I held the journal close to me. It was the only thing I had left of my mother. I tore the front section out of the journal carefully. It was my mother's last words and even though they were rambling and peculiar, there were names and events that I didn't want him reading. The last part of the journal was meaningless diagrams and letters that looked like she had traced her own chart to heaven—enough to satisfy him and still keep my mother's madness a secret.

I took the pages I had removed and placed the pages with the silver chunk in a pillowcase. I tied the end in a knot to close it and then hid it back in the drawer. I put the rest of the journal on the side table next to his chair. I tied the leather case with the string and hoped he wouldn't notice the missing pieces to her strange and confusing manifesto.

And I especially didn't want Eliza to be aware of the journal. It was she who was mentioned time and again and not in a flattering light. She wrote of the poison Eliza spawned and even wrote of the fear she felt toward her sister wife. I knew if Eliza was aware of what mother had written, she would wonder about me and my loyalty to the family. I was relieved when Uncle Deon retrieved the journal and placed it in the pocket of his vest.

"It's our little secret," he promised.

I remember him saying that when I first arrived at Cedar Creek and he would ask me to sit with him in his office. He called me there while the other girls were at class. He told me to close the door and lock it because he didn't want anyone interrupting our special time together. He always had a treat or gift for me and stroked my arm as he rocked me in the large leather chair.

"Your mother and Eliza would be upset if they knew you were here. You're my prettiest girl and they worry that I will love them less. We don't want to make them sad, do we?" he asked.

Even at a young age, it felt wrong, but the attention was something I craved, so I nodded when he made me promise to never say a word to anyone. When Silas began to stalk me on the compound, I retreated to the company of Uncle Deon where I knew I was protected. Unfortunately, it only took one attack to put me in the state I was in now.

It was Eliza who confronted me about my expanding waistline. I acted demure and unaware that I was showing. The news brought the other sister wives clamoring around me like a swarm of bees, touching my stomach and praising God for this great miracle. Eliza watched skeptically, and when I caught her glimpse as she spoke to Silas in the courtyard, I knew my secret was in jeopardy.

If Silas knew that he was the father of my child, he would most likely kill me to rid himself of the evidence of his betrayal of his father, his prophet, and of his own conscience. I wasn't sure he had one. It would be an easy fix to eliminate me and the baby I was carrying, rather than having to face what he did.

For months, I watched my back and stayed in my room as much as possible. On my nights with Uncle Deon, I used my pregnancy as an excuse as to why I didn't feel well, and even on the nights that he didn't accept that, he fell asleep before the act occurred.

When it was announced that Grace was to become the prophet's new bride, the attention on me faded and he didn't seem to find much interest in his husbandly benefits. The routine continued on the nights he was scheduled with me, but he rarely touched me.

Oddly, this made Eliza warm up to me. She smiled at me as she walked the floors of the main house, overseeing each wife's area and room. During our worship services, she invited me to sit with her. And before I became too large to comfortably walk, we strolled arm in arm in the courtyard.

One evening, when I wasn't feeling well, I returned to my room early and found her standing by the chair and stirring the water that was placed at the side table. She startled and told me she was looking for me. When I asked what about, she stammered a bit and then asked me if I had thought of any names for the baby. I shrugged and admitted I hadn't. She suggested I consider Kathryn for a girl to honor my mother, and Joseph to pay homage to our original prophet. I thanked her and she left quickly. It wasn't completely odd to find Eliza in my area, but she seemed uncomfortable and rushed, which made me suspicious.

I went to the side table and picked up the glass of water. I held it to the light to see if there was anything noticeably different. It was clear. I smelled it and found nothing peculiar. I heard the door creak and quickly put the glass down. I turned to find Uncle Deon watching me.

His eyebrows furrowed. "What are you doing, my dear?" he asked.

"Nothing," I answered, and gave him an innocent smile.

He took a deep breath and bit his lip as he thought. "Do you want me in your bed tonight?" he asked.

I didn't, but I knew that if I said no, it would cause concern. "Of course, Husband," I answered.

He walked to the chair and sat down. "Should I drink this first?"

I felt my face flush. "If you'd like."

He held up the glass. "What would you like?" His voice got louder and turned angry.

"I—um," I stammered, not knowing what he was thinking.

He took the glass and hurled it against the wall behind the bed. It shattered, and I ducked and screamed.

"So tell me again about what happens in our bed. Every night I'm with you we do this thing that husbands and wives do? Is that correct?" He was sarcastic and riotous in his questioning. "Tell me now, which night do you believe was the night we produced this child you carry?"

I wanted to run out of the room. His demeanor and voice grew wild. I could tell he knew something was amiss, that we had never had sex, and that my baby was conceived with someone else. He rose and came toward me. With each step he stripped off a piece of his clothes. I backed up and cowered, knowing my fate. He grabbed my face hard and brought it to his.

"You'll do your wifely duties with vigor tonight," he whispered. He shoved me to my knees. "You can start there," he said, pulling down his pants and exposing a feebly erect penis. His rage was being revealed in a crazed and violent outburst.

I felt an enormous sense of dread and was overwhelmed with relief when a knock came at the door.

"Not now!" he bellowed. He then shoved my face into his crotch.

"Deon, I need to speak to you." It was Eliza.

I wasn't sure if this would be a good thing or make my situation even worse. I fell back away from him and in his frustration, he pulled up his pants and stomped to the door. He flung it open and Eliza pushed past him. She saw me on the floor, with the glass shards and water surrounding me.

"What is it?" he insisted.

She looked up at him. "It's Launa," said Eliza. "She's been found."

Uncle Deon demeanor changed instantly. He stopped raging, and gave an irritated huff. He looked over at me and I looked at the floor. He sneered at Eliza, pulled her out of the room and closed the door behind them. I heard heated mumbles and then the door opened again.

"You clean this up," Uncle Deon ordered me. "I will be back tonight."

"I'll get you another water," said Eliza, coming back into the room.

He took her by the arm and turned her toward him. "I'll get my own damn water from now on," he grumbled.

Eliza was both surprised and disappointed. When she looked at me, I knew that the horror of this day wasn't over.

Chapter 14

Emma

October 8, 1896

It was early morning but still dark, when I heard the door to my room open. I was groggy, but roused quickly when I realized Uncle Deon had returned. I lay still, pretending to be asleep and hoping to be left alone.

"Emma, wake up." The soft voice was Eliza's.

I sat straight up. "I am awake."

She hushed me, and came to the bed. She fumbled in the dark for my arm and pulled me from the covers. "Come on. We need to have you in the Spirit Keeper's house for the rest of your pregnancy," she said.

"Now? Why?" I asked, as she moved me toward the door.

"It will be better for you there until the time comes," she explained.

Fear rose up from my stomach and into the muscles of my neck. "I'm scared," I admitted.

Eliza ignored me as she fumbled and tried to help me put on my shoes in the darkness.

The creak and thud of footsteps on the stairs made us both gasp and freeze.

"Take off your shoes. Pretend you're asleep," she said, shoving me back toward the bed.

I did as she said, and as I pulled the covers around my shoulders, I heard her scuffle and slide underneath the bed on the wood floor. I couldn't breathe, and I lay in the dark, my heart pounding in my ears, as the door opened. The slam was intentional.

"I know you're awake," Uncle Deon said.

I heard the rustle of clothes being shed and then his lumbering steps toward me. The covers ripped from my hands. The rush of air made me shiver, and then he was in the bed and rolling on top of me. He felt my nightgown and leaned up enough to rip it from my body. The fabric burned my neck as it was torn from me and I whined.

"Shut up," he growled.

Just as I felt him about to enter me, he jerked up and turned.

"Who is that?" he demanded.

I heard a small step and then a solid thud. Uncle Deon heaved off me and onto the floor. I heard him thrashing and moaning in the dark. I sat up in bed and scrambled away from him, grasping the covers around me. "Eliza? Where are you?" I asked into the blackness. But there was no answer.

The gasping and writhing faded and soon stopped. Tears poured from my eyes, but I stayed where I was. Soon I heard shuffling and then the metal clank of a tinder box and the crack and strike of a match. The fire shattered the darkness and when I gained my bearings, I realized that Uncle Deon lay naked in a heap on the floor. Eliza stood over him, holding a large tube with a needle.

"Is he dead?" I asked.

Eliza wiped tears from her face. She was shaking him violently. "I was just trying to put him to sleep. I think I may have injected him in the heart."

I moved off the bed but kept as far from the body as I could. I went to my dresser and pulled on clothes. "What is that?" I asked motioning to the large syringe.

She kept shaking him and pounding on his chest. She put her ear to his mouth, then sat back and sighed. "He's breathing."

I nodded as I slid my shoes onto my feet. "What do we do now?"

"Help me put him in the bed," she ordered.

I took his hands, she took his feet and we tried to lift Uncle Deon's body onto the bed. We only got his head and shoulders up far enough onto the mattress, so I had to move down and help Eliza push the rest of his limp frame onto the bed.

"Leave," she said.

I nodded. "Should I wait in the hallway?"

She looked over to me with tired eyes. "No. Leave Cedar Creek."

I stood stunned. "What? Why?"

"He knows," she said, intently. "He knows about you and Silas. He won't stand for it. You need to leave this place."

"Where would I go?" I asked, feeling my tears well up again.

Eliza took a deep breath and ran her hand over her forehead. "Stay quiet and don't ask questions. Go and stay in the Spirit Keeper's house until we can get you out of the compound. You can't let anyone see you there."

I felt a chill as I thought about going into that house. I remembered seeing my mother dead and wondering what had brought her to that point. I knew it was a place that only a few were allowed to enter. It was sacred because that is where the new spirits came into this world and where the ones who had served their time returned to our Lord. It was only the sisters who were called upon by the prophet to be Spirit Keepers who had access. Those there to give life or coming to their end had limited entry. No one spoke about what they saw because it was only between them and God. It was the most important place on the compound.

I looked down at Uncle Deon's sluggish form. "What will happen with him?"

"I'll take care of this. When he wakes up, he won't remember much, but he'll be looking for you. Put together some clothes and follow me."

I went to the chest of drawers and stuffed some clothes and garments in to a bag. I tied the pillow case with my stash to the waistband of my nightgown and let it dangle by my side. I went to Eliza who was waiting. She slowly and quietly peeked around the door. The light spilled out and she pulled the door so only a crack was visible. The house was still. She took a deep breath, then led me into the hallway. She locked my door behind us with her master key, and we softly padded our way out of the house and to the courtyard. In the darkness, we ran to the house where I had found my mother dead. Eliza used her key to unlock it and when we were inside, she pulled all the shades in the room and lit a candle.

"Don't open the window shades, and don't answer the door," she ordered.

A small knock from one of the rooms inside startled us both.

The door opened, and there stood Grace, wide eyed. "Eliza, is it time?"

Eliza put her hand up to hush her. "No, not yet. Emma is going to stay here with you. I don't want either of you leaving this house. I'm the only one with a key, so don't answer this door for anyone." With slumped shoulders from exhaustion and the weight of what she had to do, she left us alone to wonder what would happen next.

"Who are you hiding from?" Grace asked me.

"Uncle Deon," I answered. I went to one of the doors and opened it to find a small room with a bed covered in clean white sheets.

Her eyes lit up. "The prophet?" She turned skeptical. "But he's your husband."

I raised my eyebrows in response. I had nothing to say. He was my husband and he was our prophet. I went to the next door and opened it. I found a similar room.

"That's why I'm hiding too," she said. "I'm supposed to be sealed to him on Sunday, but my brother's coming to get me."

"How?" I asked, knowing that no one ever left the compound, and if they tried, it always turned out badly.

"I don't know, but Eliza said he was coming. He's taking me back with him to Challis where he works in the mines," she explained.

"Challis?" I asked, surprised. I walked back and sat next to her on the bed. "That's where I came from. Is your family in Challis?"

Her eyes lit up again. "You're from Challis? Well, I'll be," she mused. "I was only there a short time. My momma married a man who took her to Utah, and when I was old enough I was sent here to Cedar Creek. My brother had to stay in Challis. My momma's new husband didn't have room for him."

I looked at her in the small amount of candlelight. She was small and fair skinned and seemed so young. "How old are you?" I asked.

"I turned fourteen last Sunday," she said.

She didn't just look young, she was young, too young. I shook my head. "And he wants to marry you?" I asked. As I look back now, I see how silly my thoughts were. I was barely twenty and had been married to him for months. He was almost seventy. Wasn't I also too young?

She nodded. "When the sister wives told me what he was planning to do to me in our bed, I didn't believe them. Then they told me it was what the wives had to do. I wanted to run away right then and there." She looked at my protruding belly. "Oh my. Did you have to . . .?" her question faded off.

We both sat silent for a moment and then she turned to me and grabbed my wrists. "Come with us," she said. "Come with us to Challis. You can go back to your family."

The initial excitement of going home was tempered by the harsh reality of having no family left. The only family I had was a sister, and even if I knew where Peri was, she had made it clear the night she left, that she no longer considered me her family. "I don't have family there any longer. That's why I'm here. I don't have anywhere to go."

Grace tipped her head. "But you do. You can come with us. Please, Emma. Don't stay here."

It was early morning when Eliza came back and unlocked the door to the house. She led Launa inside. Launa looked tired and dazed. She was dressed in white and clenched a small blanket to her chest. We had heard that Launa tried to leave, but that is all we knew. I didn't know her well, but saw her in the courtyard always looking tired and depressed. She was married to an Elder named Joseph, but when she first came to Cedar Creek, I had heard she was already married to another man. It wasn't long before he left the compound. The Elders said he wasn't worthy to remain, and Launa soon became the fifth wife of a man she had never met.

Eliza opened another door that led to the room where years before I had found my mother dead in Peri's arms. I felt my neck hairs tingle as we walked in. She placed Launa on one of the beds in the large sterile room and tucked a blanket around her. She was gentle with her, as though she would crack and fall apart.

"I'll bring you all breakfast in about an hour. Stay here. And again, don't open the shades or let anyone know you are here." Eliza slipped out and left us staring at each other.

Grace went to Launa and sat on the edge of the bed. "What happened?" she asked. "Where'd you go?"

Launa's face became pained and her lip quivered. "I know my baby isn't dead," she whispered. "I heard it cry. Right in this room I heard it cry and then they took it away."

Grace looked over to me for help.

I went to Launa and sat next to Grace. "What did they tell you? Didn't you get to see the baby?"

"No," she said and started to weep. "They just took it away into the back room. I don't even know if it's a boy or a girl. They came back and told me it had died. When I asked to see it, they refused. I know it was alive. I heard it. I heard my baby cry."

Grace wrapped her arms around Launa as she cried. I sat stunned and put my hand to my belly. When Eliza came back with the food, she saw from our faces that we had been talking.

"The Lord blesses us when we obey and he punishes us when we don't. Remember that," she said, looking at Launa.

"I'm faithful," cried Launa. "I brought a child into our family."

"The Kingdom of Glory needs precious and perfect souls. We can't build our eternal families with those who are already damaged," she explained. "The Lord knows this and removes those quickly from this earth. They return to him where they'll have perfect bodies for the resurrection. You should find comfort in that."

Launa stayed quiet, but I felt her trying to hold back sobs.

"If you stay true to the Lord, you'll be given the chance again," continued Eliza. "Uncle Deon is speaking with your husband and is asking him to forgive you and take you back. If you're faithful, you'll be given another chance at a child." Then she repeated her warning about staying hidden and slipped out the door.

"What did you do?" asked Grace.

Launa shook her head. "Nothing. Joseph says the reason the baby died was because I sinned. He said that God took the baby because I wasn't worthy." She started to cry. "He told me I'd be better off dead. I left because I knew he was going to kill me."

Grace and I kept trading horrified stares. I brushed Launa's hair from her face. "Grace is leaving. Her brother is coming to take her away. You should go with them," I urged.

Grace nodded. "Yes. You should."

Launa pulled away from us and put her hand to her mouth. "I can't. I tried. But I saw it."

Grace and I looked at each other knowing, but not wanting to ask. We didn't have to.

"I saw the demon in the willows. It was awful," Launa said in frantic whispers. "It chased me back. I felt it as I ran." She broke down.

We all had been told about the demon. The ghastly phantom that hovers in the trees and swoops down to claw at the faces of anyone who tries to pass through on the trail leading away from Cedar Creek. I had heard the warnings during our Sunday services and, like the other women of the compound, knew that if I was found wandering alone, that whatever happened was my own fault. It was unacceptable in the eyes of the Lord to not have the protection of another faithful member. Going in twos was the teaching and it was for our own good. And even though I had heard tales of the demon and the warnings of what it did, I had never heard about it from someone who actually saw it.

Our desire to pepper Launa with questions about the demon was stifled by her frantic tears every time she started thinking about it, so we let her rest. Grace and I went to the other room and talked in circles until we found ourselves questioning our beliefs. Grace was committed to the teachings of the Kingdom of Glory, but now found herself in conflict and unsure where her loyalties lay.

After hearing Launa's heartbreak over the loss of her baby and the veiled discussions with my mother, I wondered what was really happening to the children of Cedar Creek. The few babies that survived were all girls. There were no boys on the compound, with the exception of a few that were part of families being brought into the church. And even then, none over the age of fourteen. Boys who hit that magic age were given jobs in other towns and never seen again. The girls were primped and primed for a life of being a spirit wife.

Why no boys? The reason was becoming frighteningly clear. Boys had no value in a world meant to benefit men. They became competition. It was then I wondered if Launa's baby was a boy. And if it was, did he die or was he killed? I put my hand to my belly and knew that I had to leave quickly. I expected my baby to be born within a couple weeks, and if it was a boy I feared they would destroy it. But even if my baby was a girl and was free of the risk of extermination, her life if we stayed in The Kingdom of Glory compound was, to me, even more horrifying.

"I want to come with you," I told Grace.

She smiled and nodded.

When Eliza came with our lunch, I told her I planned to go with Grace.

"No, not yet," she explained. "Not until after the baby."

I looked at her shocked. "You want me to stay here hiding until after I have the baby? Why? You said I needed to leave."

"Yes, but," she set the food on the table as she spoke. "When the baby comes, I'll make arrangements for you to leave."

"But I don't want to wait. I believe it's best for me and the baby that we leave soon. Isn't that what you said?" I was pleading.

She turned at me with a face of stone and shook her head. "I'll decide what is best for the baby. When you were sealed into our family, you were told that all the children born into it were sealed to all of us. This baby isn't just yours. If this child is a boy, he is our future prophet." She picked up the tray and left. I heard the key turn and knew that I wasn't being protected but held prisoner.

I went to Grace, feeling like I'd been punched in the stomach. I cried in both fear and anger.

"Don't worry, Emma. We'll get you out," Grace said, stroking my head. "Marty will be here tonight. We'll act like we're leaving, but then we'll sneak back to get you. We'll meet at the stables. There's an old wagon there. Hide in the back."

"But how will I get there? She's locked us in." I felt helpless.

Grace pulled me into the larger room, where Launa still lay in a ball on her bed. She hadn't eaten or even moved since she told us about the demon. Grace pointed to the back where a storage area had racks and shelves with bottles and medical looking devices. A large window was blocked with empty wooden boxes. There was another door and I went to open it, but found it locked.

"We'll break that window in the back and have you crawl out," said Grace.

I shook my head. "When she sees I'm gone, they'll come looking."

"You won't leave until after she takes me away. She'll see you here. When we leave, crawl out the window and get to the stable. It'll be dark and no one will be out. I'll keep talking to her to give you time to get to the corral. I promise we'll come back for you. I won't leave without you." She squeezed my hand.

I walked to the window. The shelves had gardening tools and when I peered outside, I saw the large lush bed of dark purple flowers that Eliza was so passionate about tending. It was as if her yearning for children of her own was transferred to the love and care of her garden.

"My mother brought them with her from England. They remind me of her," Eliza told me as we went for our stroll before things changed. "I miss her terribly. I wish that Silas could have known her."

The mention of his name made me cringe.

"Someday Silas will lead our church, and then someday his son will follow as well. That is how it works. When Father died—" she stopped and caught herself. "When a prophet dies, only his blood can carry on the revelations of our Lord. Deon received a vision from our Lord that he must lead us as the new prophet. That calling can only be for the next son in line. We follow the only true prophet. We practice God's commandment of the principle of plural marriage. The others we were with before have fallen away and no longer practice it. They follow a false prophet who follows the law of man, not of God."

I nodded my agreement and wondered why she was telling me all this. Did she know that the baby I carried was Silas's? If my child was thought to be Uncle Deon's and was a boy he would challenge the fate of Silas as the prophet. I looked at Eliza and she gazed back at me with smiling eyes. We were sealed together as part of an eternal family, but I began to wonder if she didn't have other intentions for me in this life. The more I thought about my situation and role, the more her eyes shifted from smiling to sinister.

Chapter 15

Emma

October 8, 1896

With the wooden handle of a small hand shovel, Grace broke a window in the back room. We hid the shards of glass that fell onto the floor or were still stuck in the jambs, and then rolled and placed a sheet around the frame and on the sill to guard against any sharp edges. We restacked the boxes to hide the opening, then we sat and waited.

"What should we do about Launa?" Grace asked in a whisper. "We can't just leave her here."

I bit my lip in contemplation. I stood and walked to the room where Launa lay. I nudged her and she turned to me, still groggy. I sat on the bed next to her and stroked her shoulder as I spoke. "I want you to be strong. Come with me and leave this place. We can find a new life outside."

Launa took a deep breath as she took in what I said.

"I know it's hard, but there is nothing for you here now. Get up and get dressed and we will escape together." I tried to sound confident but I could tell my voice exposed my fears.

"What about my baby? I can't leave without my baby," she said in a surprisingly clear and aware tone.

I tried to be comforting, but time was short and I'm sure my words did little to soothe her. "Your baby is in heaven and is safe there. There is nothing left for you here and nothing you can do for your baby. You must save yourself now."

She cried, but it wasn't so much in pain as acceptance of her loss. "But the demon," she murmured.

"We'll have help. We'll be safe," I tried to assure her, and yet I found myself feeling the same misgivings. "Will you leave with us?"

She wiped her eyes and nodded. I hugged her and then left to tell Grace the news.

"That's good," Grace whispered. "It shouldn't be long now. The sun is going down."

We sat huddled on the birthing bed silently waiting. I felt the rolls and kicks of my baby as if it knew I was terrified. I placed my hand on my belly, hoping it would sense the comforting touch. I would either escape to a life that was completely unknown to me, or be caught and severely punished for trying to flee. They would take my baby and label me an unworthy mother for my sin. And what about the demon? There was something in those woods that Launa saw. All my sensibilities told me this was a tale, but it added to my worries none the less.

The rattle of the key in the lock startled us both. We had drifted off to sleep, leaning against each other. We both jumped to attention as Eliza, dressed in dark clothes, entered the house.

"It's time. Let's go," she ordered Grace.

Grace grabbed her knapsack of clothes, hugged me hard, and then followed Eliza. She looked back at me for reassurance and I nodded. But before the door closed, Eliza turned back with a glare. The look sent a chill so cold and stinging throughout my body that it left me paralyzed with fear. When the door was closed and locked, I stood with my heart racing, trying to bring myself back and prepare for what I had to do.

I went to the window and pulled back the shades slightly to see the two shadowy forms scurry across the courtyard. It was time. I took a deep breath and steadied myself. This wasn't just to save me, but my child. Being pensive would only put us at risk. For the first time in my life I had to be more than strong.

I went to the room to get Launa. I walked to the side of her bed and bent down to call her name and wake her from her stupor. A large pool of blood spread across the sheets. A triangular shard of glass stuck out, embedded in her wrist. I gasped loudly and had to hold back a wail.

"No!" I pleaded, as I gathered up Launa's limp body, shaking her as if she was only asleep. She had agreed to leave with us, but this was her exodus. She was free of pain and in the presence of her baby is what I had to tell myself as I left her, and with blurry eyes made my way to the broken window that had given Launa the tool she needed to escape.

I moved the boxes and climbed up the rack and through the window, using the sheet to shield me from the remaining sharp edges of glass. As I fell to the cold dirt outside, I realized there was no retreat. I had to make it to the corrals.

I ran to the edge of the house and peered around to see if I was alone. My white nightgown billowed in the breeze and would be easily visible even in the dark. I knelt on the ground and quickly smeared dirt on my clothes to camouflage myself and then sprinted to the back of each house, stopping every time to scout the area before I made the dash to the next one. My chest ached and my belly grew heavier with each sprint, but I made it to the meeting point and found the wagon Grace had described. As I heaved my pregnant body up into the bed of the wagon, someone grabbed me from behind and pulled me down. I didn't scream out because I didn't know who it was until I heard his voice.

"You're not going anywhere." It was Silas.

I struggled against him and found myself on the ground being dragged across the corral. He kicked at me to make me move and his boot slammed against my head and shoulder. Then he stopped and grabbed my hair and started to pull, which made me cry out in pain. He slapped my face hard.

"Shut up!" he hissed, as he hit me again. "Stand up and walk or I swear I'll kill you."

I couldn't catch my breath and stumbled as I got to my feet. He grabbed my arm hard and thrust me forward toward the barn. It was the place he had violated me and I had no idea what his plans were now. I knew he would kill me if he got me inside that barn, so I struggled against his grip and freed myself briefly, I quickly took hold of the dangling weighted pillow case that was tied to my waist. I didn't know where he was or what I was aiming at, but in the dark I stepped back and swung the heavy chunk of silver my mother had given me with all the force I could muster. I heard a solid thud, a distinctive moan, and the sound of a body hitting the ground. My first instinct was to continue swinging my weapon, but in the dark, I didn't know where he was or if he would still be coming after me. I scrambled to my feet and ran back to the wagon.

"Emma?" I heard Grace calling softly into the night.

"Yes!" I answered. My voice was weak and I was terrified that Silas was on my heels. When I reached her at the wagon, I saw the figure of a young man on a horse. "He's coming!" I cried.

"Who?" Grace asked.

"Silas!"

"Hurry," she shouted, helping me into the back of the wagon. I fell to the bed onto a large woolen blanket. Within seconds the wagon bolted forward. I was thrown and jostled violently as we raced from the compound. It wasn't until we were miles away that I felt myself take a breath.

When the wagon came to a stop. I heard Grace ask our rescuer. "What is it?"

"Be quiet!" I recognized the voice. It was Peri. I couldn't believe she was there. She had returned to save us and yet she didn't know she would be saving me too. I tried to sit up and called out to her. "Peri!"

"I said be quiet!" she ordered.

I laid back down and wrapped myself in the blanket. The silence was horrible. I heard every branch in the breeze and each leaf flutter. They all sounded like footsteps rustling toward me. I wondered when Eliza would make it back to find Launa alone and dead. The waiting overwhelmed me with dread. My back began to ache and when I rolled to ease the pain, I felt a gush between my legs. Had I just wet myself because of the fear? It was then I heard a large bell ring out into the blackness. It was the sentry bell that alerted the entire compound of danger.

I tried to sit up, but the pain in my back was now under my belly and all I called out in a desperate moan, "It's the sentry bell. They're coming!"

The pain subsided and when I tried to peer out the back of the wagon, I was told harshly to stay down.

They were looking for me. I had escaped, I had taken the heir of the church with me, and there was a dead woman left behind. The pain in my belly returned gradually and soon became grueling. I tried to keep from crying out, but the agony was too much.

"Keep her quiet!" I heard Peri hiss back at Grace.

"What's wrong, Emma?" Grace asked me from the seat of the wagon.

I couldn't answer. The pain was too great. I tried to steady myself in the bed of the wagon, but my body was thrown, and rolled as we resumed our escape. Frantically, we rode away from Cedar Creek and into the dark void of the wilderness. My head began to buzz and then my world went black.

It was the pain that woke me. I felt it again, slowly coming on. It intensified to the point I knew I couldn't take it any longer, and then it started to wane. When it was gone, I realized the sun was up and the rock of the wagon was now steady and the jostling had subsided. I lay listening to Peri and Grace speak, still stunned that my sister had returned and was with me. It wasn't long before I realized she too was surprised that I was there, and I felt my heart fall when I realized she wished she had left me behind.

Chapter 16

The story of Dakota
Montpelier, Idaho
1885

The night the schoolhouse caught on fire, was the first day of winter and the wind was already strong and cold. It whipped the flames high above the cottonwood trees and embers flew into the brush starting other smaller fires. The townspeople scurried around frantically half-dressed and some barefoot as some formed bucket lines and others used large blankets to smother the flames. But it was hopeless. It had been burning at least an hour before someone became aware of the fire, and by that time, it had brought down the beams and most of the brick walls that supported the structure. It was the noise of the collapse that aroused the people living close by.

Sheriff Goodwin had been shocked out of bed by Deputy Clyde's fists banging on his door. When he opened it, he saw the glow and smoke plume in the night, went to his room and threw on his clothes and holster. The two ran through the dark town toward the fire and flurry of people. When they got close,

Sheriff Goodwin felt the intense heat from the building. The flames had died down and yet the schoolhouse seemed to heave as the heat radiated out.

When Ben arrived, he dove off his horse before bringing it to a halt and ran to the charred and burning remains, screaming out in horror at the sight. Two other men held him back as he tried to grab at the ash and burnt wood, scorching his hands and leaving him covered in soot, sweat, and tears. It was then that they recognized the charred and lifeless body lying where the door to the schoolhouse once stood.

"Oh God, Jessica," Ben sobbed, as he fell to his knees.

Sheriff Goodwin ran to his deputy's side and bent down to comfort him. "How do you know it's her?" he asked. The sheriff was confused at Ben's sorrow but also at how he knew that unrecognizable body was hers. Like everyone in Montpelier, he was aware that Ben and Jessica knew each other, but it was a small town and as a deputy, it was Ben's job to know everyone. Sheriff Goodwin was puzzled at Ben's emotional reaction. He looked at the other two men but they only gave him sad, unknowing shrugs.

Sheriff Goodwin held Ben under his arms as he walked him to an isolated area still aglow in the surrounding darkness. "How do you know it's her?" he asked again. "And why was she here so late at night?"

Ben wiped his eyes and, still in shock, explained their secret meetings and the rule that kept them from being a normal married couple. "I should have never left her alone," he sobbed.

Sheriff Goodwin stood with a mixture of shock and grief, as he processed what Ben was explaining and how truly tragic this all was. "Was it the stove?" the sheriff asked, trying to find answers.

"No. She never lit it in the summer," Ben answered. Ben poured out his soul as he grasped the reality that their secret didn't matter any longer. So much planning and effort to keep their love from being exposed. The casual hellos they exchanged as they crossed in the mercantile, the separate homes they rented, and their plotted meetings at the schoolhouse in the cover of dark to hold each other and envision their life together. The effort it took to not be seen together and for what? Jessica suffered a horrible death and he hadn't been there to save her. He should have never left her alone. Ben thought his life was starting over and now he was again left forlorn and heartbroken.

"Someone did this. And I'm going to find them." His voice was low and guttural.

Goodwin put a hand on Ben's shoulder. The act of blame was what Ben wanted to help ease his pain, but the sheriff believed it was nothing more than a horrible misfortune.

The sheriff walked back to the burning building and told one of the men to fetch the undertaker. He surveyed the crumbling walls and metal outlines of the children's desks. The front of the building was destroyed, but the back of the room, where the stove sat, remained practically untouched. Sheriff Goodwin scanned the room several times as the inconsistency soaked in. As he continued to contemplate, he stepped closer to where the disfigured body of the young schoolteacher lay. He paused and surveyed the area. Small smoke spirals floated up between the splintered and burned wood like ghosts. At the front of the school, an eerie orange flickering glow lit the surrounding area, casting everyone in a ghoulish tableau. Sheriff Goodwin lifted his chin to the night sky, and there it was, the smell of kerosene. Ben was right. This was not an accident. He pulled aside the nearest person, Doc Baker, and pointed out the odor.

"Why would anyone want to burn down a school?" the doctor asked.

Sheriff Goodwin felt the hair on his neck tingle. It was then that the memory of the hurt and angry eyes of a father burned into his mind. The realization made him gasp. He went to deputy Clyde and told him to come with him. Sheriff Goodwin kept the information to himself as they walked in the dark to his office. He didn't want to go alone knowing what he was facing. At sunrise he would be making another visit to the small cabin in the woods.

When the pink glow of morning spread across the valley, Goodwin wished the day wasn't as still and pretty as it was. This visit was one of the hardest things he had to do as Sheriff and he dreaded each step of the horse as it climbed the narrow canyon toward the clearing and the cabin.

"Can you tell me why we're headed out here?" Deputy Clyde asked. "Do you think Casper had something to do with the murder?"

The sheriff took a long and deep breath as he rode. "That fire wasn't murder. It was revenge. Casper didn't know that Miss Jessica was in there. But that doesn't make him innocent."

"Why did he do it?" Clyde asked.

"He was angry about his boy being taken out of the school because he's Indian," the sheriff answered. "Miss Jessica and I came here a couple nights ago to tell him the news. I knew he was mad, but I had no idea he would do this."

Deputy Clyde nodded sadly. "What's gonna happen to Dakota? Will he go to the tribe?"

The thought of the young boy stabbed at Sheriff Goodwin's heart. "I don't know. We need to bring justice to Miss Jessica and then things will be figured out for the boy."

He heard the words that came from his mouth, but in his mind he was scared of the future that lay ahead for the child. The white families wouldn't want him and, just as Casper had argued, the boy had never been with the Indians and had always been around the people of the town. He knew nothing different.

When they reached the cabin, it was silent and still. A small waft of smoke came from the chimney, so Goodwin was confident Casper and Dakota were there and awake. He told Deputy Clyde to stay back as he walked to the door and knocked twice.

They waited and soon the door cracked open and the weary and rumpled face of Casper peeked through.

"We need to talk, Casper," said Goodwin, quietly.

Casper nodded knowingly and opened the door to expose both his hands wrapped in long strips of cotton cloth. He lowered his head and wept. "I didn't know. I tried to save her. I'm so sorry."

When Dakota came down from the loft, he looked surprised and concerned.

Casper looked at Sheriff Goodwin with pleading eyes. "Please take care of my son. He has nowhere else to go."

Hearing this, Dakota ran to his father and clutched his leg. "I don't want you to go!" he yelled. "Don't leave me!"

Sheriff Goodwin felt his insides break at the sound of the child's desperate cries. He called to Deputy Clyde and asked him to stay with the child until Dorothea could come up and get him. She was the only woman he knew who would watch him until they figured out an alternative. He ignored putting handcuffs on Casper and simply helped him up and onto the Deputy's horse.

Casper moaned every time his hands touched anything. When they both mounted, Casper looked back at the house where Deputy Clyde struggled to hold back the frantic, screaming boy.

"When his mother died, I promised I would never leave him," Casper whispered, his voice breaking through tears.

As they rode toward town, the cries of Dakota faded, however the muffled sobs of Casper stayed fixed in the mind of the sheriff for years.

Chapter 17

The story of Dakota
Montpelier, Idaho
1885

They arrested Casper for the fire, and for the destruction it caused. Dakota sat each day just outside the window of his father's cell. They spoke, but most of the time, Dakota drew pictures in the dirt with a stick and avoided the mournful and demoralizing looks from the people of the town.

"What will become of him?" he heard them whisper. They all knew that Casper had been sentenced to hang and they all agreed it was the right punishment for the crime. The trial made it clear that he didn't mean for the fire to destroy life, but he purposefully set it, and that had him sentenced as a killer.

Dakota stayed at Dorothea's but every morning he was out the door and at the sheriff's office, with his back against the wall of the jail.

"He can't stay there," Sheriff Goodwin told Ben. "I won't let him witness this."

Ben shrugged. He agreed that the sins of the father shouldn't be carried on to the little boy, but his anger and hurt at what Casper had done still boiled under his skin. As much as Ben tried to live his creed as an officer and knew that his job was to enforce the law, not decide it, he couldn't bring himself to stop wanting to avenge this crime himself.

At night when he was alone with his thoughts, he plotted and planned. No one would care if the punishment was carried out quickly with a bullet rather than a public hanging, and who would blame him for doing it? It wasn't murder when the sentence was already death.

One night when sleep eluded him again, he dressed and walked from his small house on the far side of town, down the dark road to the jail. As he approached the building, he drew his gun, but then he paused. He heard the soft sobs of Dakota, still at his post on the side of the building, and Casper's voice from the window trying to calm him. Ben stopped and in the veil of moonlight listened to the desperate and sad conversation.

"I will be with Mommy and your little brother. You must live a good life so you can be with us too," Casper said with confidence.

"I want to go with you now," Dakota cried. "Please take me with you."

There was a long pause and Ben wondered if Casper was trying to gain his composure. How could he not be distraught hearing his son's pleas?

"I want you to be with the men in this office. Stay here and learn from them," Casper said.

Ben stood frozen, stunned at what he heard. Why did he want the people who were about to hang him be in his son's life?

"Don't let anyone take you from here. This is your home. I will watch over you from the hills and we will never be apart," Casper continued.

Only sniffles and cries came from Dakota.

"It's okay to cry. But I don't want you to stay sad or mad. You need to be happy and live your life. My father went to heaven when I was younger than you. I learned to be happy and that's how I got you. If you let the anger take over your heart, there won't be room for me."

Dakota piped up, "But you said you'll watch me from the hills."

"I will," said Casper. "And if you are full of anger and sadness, you won't be able to hear me and I'll be sad. I want you to be happy so I can be happy. If you need me, you can come into the hills and we can talk. I'll always be listening. You'll hear me when you stand still and close your eyes. I'll speak to you from the wind in the trees."

Ben felt his eyes sting with tears. He decided to go back home, but when he turned to leave, he tripped over a small stone in the dark and the sound echoed through the street. He turned to find Dakota, red eyed and swollen faced, staring at him from the corner of the wall.

"Go on home," Ben said, trying to recover.

Dakota disappeared around the corner.

Ben waited and heard Casper's voice. It was hushed, but firm. "I'll always be there, but for you to find me there must be room in your heart. If you're filled with anger, there will be no place for me."

After several minutes, Dakota appeared again. He walked to Ben and stopped in front of him. With large dark eyes in the moonlight, Dakota peered up at him. "Can I stay with you?" he asked.

Ben felt his chest clench and his throat tighten. "Why do you want to stay with me?"

Dakota shrugged. He looked back at the building and took Ben's hand.

Ben's first reaction was to flinch. He'd never been around children and the small hand in his felt awkward and strange, but the boy leaned into him with such trust and ease, that Ben's hesitation vanished.

"My dad is going to wait for me in the hills," Dakota explained.

"Yes, he is," Ben agreed, knowing what awaited Casper, but now wanting so badly to give the boy hope.

"Let's go," Ben said.

They walked hand in hand, across the dark and empty streets of the town to Ben's home. When they arrived, Dakota stood on the porch and looked toward the mountains.

"When do you think he will be there?" Dakota asked.

"Soon," answered Ben.

"How will I know he's there?"

Ben took a deep breath wanting to comfort the boy, but also exhausted and losing his ability to craft an appropriate tale. "You'll know," he said. "He will be wherever you are and you'll know."

"Do I have to go back to Dorothea's?" Dakota asked.

"Not tonight. You can stay here," said Ben.

Dakota looked disappointed. "Why can't I stay here all the time?"

Ben had no good answer, except that it wasn't what he had planned. He looked at the boy, his face dirty and smeared with tears and sweat. "Why do you want to stay here?"

"My dad says you and I are both alone now. So, I want to stay with you," Dakota said.

Ben felt his heart throb. He wasn't sure if he should feel pain or incredible relief from the young boy's words. "Come inside," he said, directing Dakota into the house and to a small room off the kitchen. "You can sleep here tonight." Ben pointed to a pile of flour sacks. He found a blanket and gave it to him. "We'll talk about things tomorrow, okay?"

Ben was tired and now he wasn't sure what to do in the morning. At seven Casper was set to be hanged. He knew he couldn't have the boy witness his father's death, and since the sheriff had already directed Ben to distance himself from the situation, he figured he had a good excuse to be absent.

"Will you take me to the hills tomorrow? Then we can both talk about it with my dad," Dakota said simply.

Ben wondered how much Dakota was aware of. Did he know his father would be led to the gallows? He had to have asked him during their jail wall talks what the men were building in the empty dirt field next to the jail. "Yes. But only if you go to sleep now."

Dakota lit up and gave a satisfied sigh.

Ben watched as the boy curled into bed. So young and so innocent of the horrors planned the next day. It's so unfair, he thought. And without realizing it, he took upon himself the role of raising a boy whose father had taken the most precious thing in Ben's life.

Chapter 18

Sixty miles northeast of Montpelier, Idaho
August 25, 1896

"Is he still there?" Sam asked, annoyed.

Peri gave a quick glance back. There was Cooper, riding the white-faced mule about a quarter mile behind them. She smiled to herself, knowing the irritation was because her captor had given in and allowed the odd young man to come along. "Yes," she replied.

Sam gave a loud irritated sigh.

They rode in silence for another hour, then stopped where the trail sloped down and into trees where Peri had some privacy to relieve herself. It seemed rather ironic considering Sam had seen her completely unclothed and now diligently searched for a place to keep her hidden. When she returned and mounted her horse, she raised her eyebrows. "What about you?" she asked.

"I went while you were down there," he said, pointing at the small bunch of trees where she had squatted.

"It must be nice being a man," she said, and then huffed.

Sam looked over to her. "You must think so."

She shot him a glare.

Sam shrugged. "Well, why do you dress like that?"

"Why do you care how I dress?"

Sam nudged his horse toward the trail. "I don't. I'm just curious. So, why do you?"

Peri had no desire to open up about her life and her reasons for disguise. "Do you always carry on like this with your prisoners?"

"No," said Sam as he slowed his horse and waited for Peri to come alongside him. "It's a long ride back. I thought we could pass the time."

"You arrested me for something I had nothing to do with, and you want me to carry on a conversation with you so you won't get bored on the ride back to the jail?" she groused and shook her head in frustration.

Sam smiled. "I'm just doing my job. I don't think you did it, but that is for a judge to decide. My job is to find you and take you back."

Peri slowed Chance and studied Sam. What reason was there to believe she was innocent? And she wondered why it mattered to her what he thought. She noticed him watching her and she snapped to and blurted out, "How'd you get that job?"

Sam smiled widely. He took a deep breath and paused a moment. "I guess I've always kind of had this job. I like to hunt and when I got old enough, I started tracking down people. I grew up around the office, so I learned stuff there too. I never really thought about it until now."

"What do you mean you grew up around the office?"

Sam smiled again. "When my dad died, I didn't want to be alone at home, so I hung around Ben and the other deputies at the sheriff's office."

Peri nodded. She thought about the turn her life took when her own dad passed away. "How old were you when he died?"

Sam sighed. "I'm not sure because we aren't really sure just how old I am. We lived in the hills and my parents didn't care about days and years. I think I'm about twenty-two. So, I think I was ten when he died."

"That's really young to live on your own," she said.

"I wasn't alone. I had Ben and the other men. They all took care of me."

Peri took a deep breath. "I was twelve when my dad died."

Sam's smile faded. "How'd he die?"

Peri stared ahead at the trail. "Cholera."

Sam nodded knowingly. "It took many lives in the towns of the area and those who traveled along the trail."

"What about your dad?" Peri asked. "How'd he die?"

Sam set his shoulders back with resolve. "He did something bad and he was hung to pay for it." He looked over to Peri who was silent.

She thought a moment, contemplating if she should pry. "What did he do?"

"He killed someone," Sam answered. "It happened right in town. Sometimes I wonder why I stay, but it was a long time ago and I can't change what he did." He kept his eyes diverted.

With brows knitted and eyes large, Peri opened her mouth to speak, but the words escaped her. She had started to warm to him. She knew too well that he felt a sense of nakedness when peeling back the scab that covered his past.

Sam said, "I shouldn't have told you all that. I'm sorry."

"No, I'm glad you told me. It's just . . ." Peri searched for words to convey her thoughts. "You were raised by the people who hung your dad?"

Sam nodded.

Again, she struggled for the right thing to say.

"It sounds strange, and I guess it is, but that is what happened," Sam said. "Ben's been good to me. But I still miss my dad."

Peri smiled sadly. "So do I."

Sam grinned at her. "So, I answered your question. Now you answer mine."

Peri shot him a quizzical look.

"Why do you dress like a boy?" he reminded her.

She shook her head and kicked Chance to pick up the pace.

Sam followed. "That's not fair," he complained. "I just opened up to you, and you won't tell me why you dress like that?"

Peri pulled the horse to a stop and whipped around to face him.

Sam stopped. He looked into her fierce and troubled eyes, as if wondering if she was going to bolt or simply break down and cry.

Peri's face turned sullen and then she looked at the ground. "I dress like this so I'll never forget."

Sam walked his horse closer to her. "Forget what?"

Peri looked up with a stone-faced stare. "The worst day of my life."

Chapter 19

Cedar Creek, Idaho
1892

Peri knew from the first week she was at the compound, that it wasn't a place she wanted to stay. She tried to convince her mother to leave, but that only upset Kathryn and made her avoid confrontation or even conversation. This infuriated and confused Peri, making her even more adamant in her anger toward the compound and intensified her desire to leave.

When they first arrived in Cedar Creek, Peri was allowed to stay in the main house along with her mother and Emma. They had two rooms, but Peri and Emma's room was on the opposite side of the large house. The other wives were meek and kept to themselves in their own rooms in the sprawling house. Only Eliza, Heff's first wife, was in the same area with Kathryn.

It wasn't long before they saw less and less of their mother, even living in the same home, they passed through the halls with only glimpses of each other, and when Peri called out to her, Kathryn only glanced back with empty eyes and would soon be out of sight.

It was later that summer that it was announced that Peri had been chosen as a spirit wife. Uncle Deon claimed that God himself had appeared to him and professed that Rolly Wilson, Uncle Deon's nephew, was the intended.

Peri bristled at the announcement and openly refused. What followed made Peri realize the mother she adored and loved was gone, replaced by an impassive woman who tried to convince her to marry into a life of servitude and isolation. Peri wanted to get her mother out of the compound, to bring her back to life, but she worried it was already too late.

Her indignant words and posture eventually got Peri moved from the main house and to the young women's quarters. Peri hated this even more. These girls weren't like her. They had no interest in horses, games, or being outdoors. They only spoke of sewing, cooking, and marriage, and she felt isolated and alone. Peri spent her time staring out the wavy glass panes of the windows, plotting her escape. She waited to see her mother go from the main house to the Spirit Keeper's house, then she tried to catch her before she went in and locked the door behind her.

Emma tried to reason with Peri that the life on the compound would bring them joy and eternal life, but Peri only scoffed at her gullibility. At night in her bed she cried out of anger. She kept her sobs quiet, not wanting the others to know her weaknesses.

One of the girls who had been married soon after Peri was assigned to the house, came back one night, weak and shivering. Some of the other girls huddled and whispered, but none spoke or comforted her. She was stone-faced and unresponsive for days, and when Peri refused to go to the day's lessons, she found herself alone in the dorm with the girl. She was still curled on her bed, eyes open, but seemingly in a daze.

"What happened to you?" Peri asked, sitting on the bed across from the girl.

The girl blinked, but that was her only response.

"If you don't eat, you'll die," Peri said. She really didn't care what happened to the girl, but her curiosity made Peri continue to pry. "Did your husband do this to you?"

The girl's eyes widened and looked at Peri.

The reaction encouraged Peri to continue. "You married that old man, Gordy, didn't you?"

The girl took a deep breath.

"What happened? Why are you back here?" Peri pressed.

The girl swallowed without speaking, but seemed to come back to life.

"What's your name?" Peri asked.

"Clarissa," the girl whispered.

Peri sat on the bed with the girl. "Tell me what happened to you."

The girl closed her eyes and shook her head.

"Why? Are you afraid?" asked Peri.

The girl nodded.

"Why are you back here? Why aren't you living in your husband's home?"

The girl looked up at Peri. "I've been banished until I can be faithful again."

Peri squinted, trying to understand. "What does that mean?"

"He says I sinned and I'm being punished. He threw me out after my baby died." The girl's lip began to quiver and she put her hand to her mouth.

Peri bent closer to her, almost unsure of what she heard. "Your baby died? How?"

The girl thought for a moment as tears welled in her eyes. She shook her head and answered, "I don't know. After it was born they took it and then they told me it was dead."

"Who told you?" Peri asked.

The girl stammered as she told her story. "The Spirit Keepers," she said, as though Peri should already know. "I heard the cry and that was all. They took it away." She paused a moment and wiped her eyes and nose. "They told me it died because I was unfaithful."

Peri shook her head and gave her a puzzled stare. "They blamed it on you?"

The girl peered up at her through large wet eyes. "But if I'm faithful, I can return," she paused. "If I'm faithful." She rolled to her side and sighed. "I must be faithful," she mumbled to herself.

Peri watched her for a moment. She tried to reason how someone could be so obedient and so credulous when their own child had been taken from them forever. Is this what had happened to her mother and Emma? Had they chosen their faith over everything else in life, including her?

Peri went to the window and looked out over the courtyard. She watched some of the other young women walking back from their lessons. They all looked alike with their long braided hair and long dresses. They chatted with shoulders close as they clutched their books to their chests. Peri had heard their conversations. They spoke about their dreams of motherhood and who they hoped the prophet might choose to be their husbands. They giggled at the thought of being sister wives and how much they wished for it to be. Peri spoke to no one and no one spoke to her. They knew of her obstinacy and wanted nothing to do with anyone who wasn't on the same path to salvation.

Peri gave a relieved sigh. Just the day before, she had been given word that Paul had help and was on his way to rescue them. He was to meet them with horses to take them to freedom. She was eager to leave, but she worried that Emma was too imbued with the faith to break her vows and escape. This made getting her mother out even more difficult. Kathryn was no longer speaking or even acknowledging those closest to her. She spent all day in the Spirit Keeper's house and away from everyone else. She was a shell of the woman who brought them to the compound. That woman had been confident in her choice to become a member of the Kingdom of Glory Church and was honored to be chosen as the prophet's sixth wife. Peri didn't understand her devotion to the principle of plural marriage, but figured she was trying to do her best for the family by grasping to the idea of an eternal life together in heaven.

Unexpectedly, it was Eliza who slipped Peri a note with cryptic instructions for escaping the compound. Peri wasn't sure if it was to help them leave or to rid her home of the one person who seemed to get the prophet's attention. That person was Emma. At only 16 years of age, she was regularly summoned to his office and out to walk the paths into the woods that surrounded the settlement. He was smitten with her graceful, classic beauty and especially her innocence. This wasn't lost on the others of the group, especially Uncle Deon's other wives, and Eliza in particular.

When Eliza gave Peri the dog-eared note hidden in a hymnal, Peri worried that it may be a trap to expose their plan. She wondered how Eliza had helped to arrange the escape and why she was helping them, knowing how it would upset the prophet.

~*~

Eliza was Uncle Deon's closest confidant. She married him at age twenty when she was without parents or others who knew her past. She had run away from home and married a man when she was fourteen. Her father disowned her, and when her husband died just a few months later from influenza, she found herself alone and surviving anyway she knew how. It was six years later, after her father died, that Eliza was able to come home to Deon, the only family she had left. He offered to support her and give her a place to live, but that's not all he offered.

Eliza knew their union wasn't right, but he charmed her and made her feel safe and adored. He convinced her of the righteousness of their union and that God himself would approve because of their divine lineage. She became his partner and supporter for over twenty years. She believed in him and was unquestioning in her loyalty. They had seven children together; five boys and two girls, but only their oldest son, and the two daughters survived. That son was Silas Heff. He had been born small and sickly and remained that way his entire life. He was coddled and indulged, and at age twenty-five was named the president of the quorum of elders that managed the church and the colony of Cedar Creek.

It was the untimely deaths of their other sons and Eliza's inability to get pregnant again, that Uncle Deon was able to convince her of the necessity of the principle of plural marriage and the role it would play in the building of their eternal family. Their daughters were given as wives to one of Leroy's closest advisors as a gift for his loyalty. Eliza had been raised in a family where her mother was one of three wives, and had never contemplated a life that didn't include the principle. And yet, the idea of other women giving Deon children when she couldn't, was a pain that only dulled slightly over time.

The commandment of plural marriage wasn't just for the sake of expanding their family but that of the other faithful men of the Kingdom of Glory Church. They needed new blood to keep their family growing and that meant women being brought into their fold.

Even though she was raised in a polygamous household, the decision wasn't an easy one for Eliza, but Deon treated Eliza like his comrade and partner in the work of the Lord. Even when other wives came into the family, he made it clear that she was first, not only in order in the family, but in status. It wasn't until Kathryn brought her daughters to live at the colony that Eliza felt her position was in jeopardy. They were the first outsiders, and while Eliza knew that is what their family needed, she knew that if Emma stayed, she would soon become the prophet's seventh wife, and most likely his new favorite. Her children would be healthy and carry on the prophet's lineage. It was a threat Eliza wasn't willing to risk.

Chapter 20

Thirty miles north of Cedar Creek
1894

"I have to go back," Peri said.

Dutch scowled and huffed. He had been hired to help in the escape and had no ties to Peri or Paul. He needed the money and wasn't about to risk his life to do anything more than what he had agreed to. He loaded the packs onto the mule's back and tied the halter rope to the back of his horse's saddle.

The escape had been successful, at least in Peri's mind, but Paul didn't accept that Emma was unwilling to leave. When Peri told him what had happened to their mother, Paul became even more adamant about going back to find Emma.

"I can't bring my mother home. I have to try and get my sister or she'll end up dead too," Paul had argued with Dutch the day before.

With the light of the rising sun, they discovered that Paul had left in the night. He had argued the entire trip from the compound to where they had camped, that he needed to go back for his sister, and when Dutch and Peri woke up the next morning, he was gone.

"He doesn't know the area and won't know where to find her," Peri argued.

Dutch shook his head. "I don't get paid for trying to rescue people who don't want to be rescued. And I certainly don't get paid if I am shot and killed while doing this. That is why we follow the plan."

Peri gave a big sigh. She didn't want to go back any more than Dutch did, but she knew that Paul was in trouble and she would never forgive herself for leaving him behind. "Can you wait here for just a day? If I'm not back then you can go on without me. Give me one day to try."

"And have you lead them straight to me? No thanks," Dutch said, as he climbed into the saddle. He looked back to Peri. "If you go back, you're on your own and those people are not the kind to be forgiving those who take their property, and that is exactly how they feel about the women there. You will be heading back to men who won't think twice before killing you for what you tried to do. And they will be on alert."

Peri mounted her horse and had to rein him hard to get him to face the opposite direction. It was as if Chance was giving his own opinion on the situation.

Dutch rolled his eyes. "I can't save your brother. If he accomplishes what he's planning, then they'll be on his tail back here. We need to leave and get to where it's safe. Wait a year and then we can talk about coming back."

"A year?" Peri asked, distressed.

Dutch shrugged. "Even then it's a risk." He paused, watching Peri think.

She looked up at him with anguished eyes.

"I'm not waiting . . . for you or anyone else," he said. "I'm going back to Challis and if you aren't coming with me, I want to know now."

The trail ahead stretched over the hills and then dipped down into a valley of sage, junipers, and willows. Peri turned back to the path they had just traveled and spotted the large gray clouds that made her decision seem even more ominous. She heard Dutch exhale as his horse began to move. When she turned to him, he was heavy in the saddle with no intentions of joining her. She was on her own and felt like she was in retreat.

Tears of anger stung her eyes and her stomach knotted. She hated her sister for what she had done. Her betrayal could cost Peri everything she cared about. She wiped her nose on the sleeve of her dress and turned her horse toward the trail. She had only a short window of time to find her brother, and yet she saw no need to spur her horse into a gallop. In more ways than she ever imagined, she was riding into the middle of a storm.

The day was slowly fading and the clouds were low and rumbling. A spit of rain seemed to needle at her circumstances. Peri pulled the collar of her coat up around her neck. She was wearing a flimsy gingham dress, the clothing mandated by the colony for women, but had managed to fish a pair of denim pants from her satchel to put under it. It was a layered mess that made sitting in the saddle a chore. And now with the rain, it was even more uncomfortable.

It had taken over four hours to reach the camp that first night after the rescue. She wondered how far Paul had made it before she and Dutch woke up to find him gone. There was no telling how long she had to ride to catch up or if she even could before he made it back to Cedar Creek. Peri had no idea what to expect and with almost no supplies, she was even more vulnerable. The trod of the horse's hooves went from a solid clomp on the packed dirt, to an uneven crunch and crackle as she made her way through dead fallen limbs of a large grove of cottonwoods and willows. She pulled the horse to a stop when she thought she heard voices. Trying to calm the thudding in her chest, she took a deep breath and let it out slowly. She was about to continue on after hearing nothing but a rainy breeze in the leaves, but then she heard the voices again.

Peri quietly dismounted the horse and tied Chance to one of the trees. She cursed her noisy footsteps on the dead leaves as she sneaked through the trees and closer to the voices. She couldn't make out whether or not it was Paul, but her concern was that it sounded like more than one voice. As she got closer, her shoulders sank, as she recognized Paul's voice. He was pleading with someone, which meant he was in trouble.

Peri pulled her gun from the holster around her waist and bent low to the ground as she made her way up a slope, tucking the hem of the dress into waistband of the pants as she moved close to the sound of the voices. At the top she dropped back when she saw three men at the bottom of the hill. Laying on the ground she scooted back to the top and peeked over.

Paul knelt on the ground. Dirt and blood covered his swollen face. Two men stood next to him. She didn't recognize them as being part of Cedar Creek, but she was certain they were ordered by the prophet and his quorum to go after her and her small band of fugitives. Now they had captured Paul and he obviously wasn't giving them the answers they wanted. It wasn't like the people of Cedar Creek to use violence. They professed to be Christ-like and kind, but she also knew they didn't take lightly to members leaving the church. In hiring these men, they could remain without the stain of violence on their conscience and still maintain the order of the members.

Peri looked to see if they had guns. It seemed unlikely that bounty hunters would be unarmed. She knew she could shoot one of them from her vantage point, but if she did, she wasn't sure what the other would do to Paul. She lay still and strained to hear their words.

Paul's voice was hoarse and mumbling and Peri couldn't make out what he was saying.

One of the men kicked him in the back making him fall forward into the mud. Paul was obviously not giving the answers he wanted.

"I'm going to ask you one more time," the man yelled, standing over Paul. "You tell us where the rest of them are going or I'll shoot you right now."

Peri's eyes widened. So they did have guns.

Paul looked up, his head bobbing unsteadily.

Peri wanted to jump up and run toward them, shots ringing out to save her brother, her twin, but instead she stayed lying on the ground as though frozen to the dirt and sod. Was she more concerned about her own fate that she would allow this to continue? It was she these men had come after, and now Paul was paying the price. Had Peri stayed behind with her mother and sister, these men would have no reason to come after Dutch and Paul, except as a warning. But because Peri, a promised spirit bride of the colony, had made it out, they had orders from whom they were told was God himself to do whatever was needed to bring her back.

She swallowed and went for her gun and then hesitated. That is when the shot rang out. It cracked through the entire valley and Peri's face hit the ground as she flinched from it. When the silence returned, she looked up to see her brother lying still on the ground and the two men arguing over him. She felt her breath being sucked out of her as she stifled sobs and the words that rose in her throat. No, no, no! How could she let this happen? No-o-o-o. She wanted to scream out. She could have saved him.

She buried her face in her coat to choke back her horror and grief, as tears spilled onto her face and from her nose.

"What did you do that for?" the taller man yelled, panicked and annoyed.

"He wasn't giving us anything and he was already half dead," said the other man using his boot to nudge Paul's body. "He was no use. We only get paid for the women we bring back."

Hearing that, Peri looked up and over the slope. She wiped her eyes. These men were bounty hunters working for Uncle Deon. They weren't believers, but outlaws living amongst them as though they were.

The taller man huffed nervously and took a sweeping look around. "You murdered him. Deon said, no killing. Nothing to bring attention."

Peri remained watching, but kept low to the ground, silent.

The shorter man stood tall. "What does that matter? No one is going to come looking for him and the coyotes will take care of the body." He walked to his horse and untied it. "We only have a couple hours of daylight left. Let's go."

Peri closed her eyes, hoping they wouldn't ride straight to her. She held her gun close, wanting to kill both of them, but knowing it wouldn't change a thing and possibly bring another search party looking for her.

As the taller man mounted his horse and followed the other, Peri saw him look back at her brother's lifeless body and give a regretful shrug. They rode parallel to her but far enough to the east that she was able to go undetected.

When they were gone and she could no longer hear their voices or the sounds of their horses, Peri's horror exploded. She scrambled to her feet and ran frantically to her brother. Her legs felt heavy as she stumbled through the brush and mud to reach him. She fell to her knees at his side, but when she went to touch him, she was unable to move. Her hands wanted to feel him, to shake him, and erase the last few moments when she should have done something to save him. A low and guttural groan escaped her.

"Paul," she cried and touched his back. "Oh, Paul."

He was still slightly warm as she rolled him over. The sight of his mangled and lifeless face made her immediately regret it and she threw her hands to her mouth and then flung herself to the side and vomited until she was rid of everything that was inside her. She continued to purge until her head started to spin and she was at the verge of passing out. The pain and emotions overwhelmed her. Her sister had betrayed her, her mother was dead, and now her twin brother had been murdered right in front of her. Her body shivered from the cold and the realization of what her life had become.

All of this pain and loss was because of Uncle Deon. He isolated her mother, married her sister, and tried to pawn Peri off on a man she hardly knew. He had taken all their money when he married Kathryn and kept them indentured there, feeling like they owed him for saving them. And now her only brother was dead. It was Paul who had kept her going. The thought of him living free and coming to save them is what Peri dreamt about.

When she heard he was really coming for them, she felt light and happy for the first time in years. She had hoped that they could escape and be a family again, and now as she sat sprawled in the wet and soupy floor of the valley, regret and revenge simmered in her mind. Not only did she blame Uncle Deon but also her sister Emma. It was she who believed that Uncle Deon was a prophet and called of God. She was a simple-minded fool for being duped into his church and his bed. When Peri arrived at the meeting place without Emma, she tried to explain to Paul how Emma was now. Paul was sure he could convince Emma to leave. He had always been headstrong.

Peri took a deep breath and smoothed Paul's blond hair. She had been sitting there for several hours trying to make sense of what had happened. She had cried until she had exhausted every ounce of fluid in her, and now she just sat in a lump, staring out at nothing.

What did she have to live for now? Her family was gone leaving her in a world that only held betrayal and pain. She looked down at Paul's damp hair and knew she had to do right by him. She wasn't sure why or what good it would do, but deep in her chest she felt it. She had no home to take him to be buried. There was no place that she felt he should be. Their father had been cremated and scattered amongst the pines and spruce that he loved so much, but that was miles from where they were now and she knew that to try and take his body there would be impossible. Peri pulled herself to standing. Her legs shuddered with exhaustion. Mud and Paul's blood covered the front of her dress, and it made her cry again.

The walk back to Chance seemed long, and she was relieved to see the horse where she had left it. When Chance heard the rustling of Peri's footsteps, his ears perked up at alert, but he eased when he saw who it was. Peri untied him and walked him to the clearing. The horse shied when they entered the clearing where Paul's body lay. Peri hushed him and led him to a tree out of view of the body. She pulled a tin plate and a bowie knife from her saddlebag and started the arduous and wretched task of digging her twin brother's grave.

~*~

Dusk was quickly sliding over the valley as Peri rode through the trees and back toward the trail. She decided to go back to the house in Challis, even though she had no idea what she would find there. It was home, but what did that mean anyway? At least she knew she had a place to stay and could plan what to do from there.

She was thinking back to when she and Paul were children living in the house near the mines, running through the back yard surrounded by a large iron fence and ivy that had grown through to hide the outside world. Their life was so easy and simple then.

Emma was just two years older and even then she was a beauty, with long dark hair and large brown eyes framed with dewy lashes. She was a lighthearted and happy girl, but when their father became ill, Emma seemed lost like her world had turned upside down. Her posture and poise were noticeably dark, and she rarely smiled. On the night their father died, Peri saw for the first time a streak of gray hair along the side of Emma's face. Peri wasn't sure why their father's death seemed to rock Emma more than the others, but she was never the same sister Peri remembered before. It may be why she wasn't completely surprised when Emma turned against her and stayed at Cedar Creek.

It was this musing that allowed her to ride through a clearing and right into the path of the two men who she had watched kill her brother earlier that day. When she realized what she had done, all she could do was stop and wait for what would happen next. Even Chance stood stunned as though he too was caught off guard.

Peri sat up straight, accepting of her situation due to her own carelessness. When she raised her head and looked them in the eye, she saw something she didn't expect—terror. Both had stopped and their faces showed the look of men who were facing a monster. Eyes wide, mouths agape, and even from fifty yards Peri saw them breathing heavy and frantic. Peri wondered if there wasn't something or someone behind her, but before she could turn to see, the men had reared their horses, turned them, and bolted. One yelled back, "Lord, forgive us!" as they sped away.

She watched, bewildered at their actions. They ran their horses until she lost sight of them and even their dust trail. Then she looked down and realized why they looked at her with terror. They had seen a ghost. When she buried Paul, she took his clothes and hat. She had first taken his boots to remember him by, but then as she prepared him for the ground, she decided to wrap herself in whatever was left of him. She also needed to rid herself of the dirty, bloodied dress, so she used it to wrap his body before placing him in the cold shallow grave.

She felt good in his clothes. They fit her, as she knew they would, and not only comforted her, but made her feel stronger. In doing this, she not only looked like a man, she was the spitting image of her twin brother. And now she was the unsettled ghost of a murdered young man, seeking revenge against his killers. These vagrants weren't members of The Kingdom of Glory, but their fear of God was no less. The sight of their frantic skedaddle made it obvious they wouldn't be following after her, and would most likely be telling their story of the boy who came back from the dead and now haunts the willows to anyone who would listen.

Peri gave a small grunt of a laugh. The realization of what happened lightened her mood, knowing Paul would have also found the humor in it. She pulled Paul's hat down snug on her head and gave Chance a nudge to continue on the path of what was sure to be an uncertain future.

Chapter 21

Northeast of Montpelier, Idaho
August 25, 1896

The night was closing in and Sam knew it was time to stop and make camp. He felt his stomach rumble with hunger and looked forward to a meal and the bottle of whiskey in his pack. He found a place that was surrounded by trees and began to tie off his horse as he waited for Peri to join him. Sam had allowed Peri to hang back and ride with Cooper for a bit, when they heard him whimpering in the distance. When they came upon the camp, Peri looked sad and Cooper's eyes were red and swollen.

Sam made a fire and laid out two bedrolls. He put out an old blanket for Cooper, but was still not happy about having to bring him along. Peri gave him an appreciative smile, which helped.

"He's having nightmares about what happened even when he's awake," Peri whispered to Sam. "I think Jim and Tildie were the only parents he knew and now he's alone."

Sam looked over at the peculiar young man. "A lot of people don't have parents," he said and looked at Peri for emphasis.

"Yes," she answered, understanding his point. "But he's so strange and simple. It's like he's still a child."

"A child that is a lot of work," Sam said, annoyed.

Peri watched and smiled to herself as Sam took Cooper a bowl of dried venison and a piece of bread. He then went to his packs and found another blanket that he offered Cooper.

Cooper went and sat by his mule, away from the others, as he ate.

When they finished eating, Sam pulled out his whiskey and offered the bottle to Peri.

"This got me into trouble last time I drank," she laughed. "I think I'll pass."

Sam pushed it toward her again. "How much more trouble could you be in?"

She laughed louder and took the bottle, uncorked it and took a swig. She made a sour face and shivered.

This made Sam laugh too.

"How long have you been a deputy?" she asked.

Sam scoffed. "I'm not a deputy."

Peri looked at him puzzled. "But I thought you worked with the sheriff."

Sam raised his eyebrows and sighed. "I do, but I can't be sworn in because I'm half Indian, so I do this instead."

Peri shook her head. "Do what?"

"Track down people like you."

Peri sat up surprised. "You're a bounty hunter?"

Sam smiled. "Yep."

"So this is about money?" she asked. "Not about the law?"

"That's right," he answered. "You're not wanted in our town. You're bounty is out of Cedar Creek."

Peri groaned. "You're not taking me to Montpelier?"

Sam shook his head.

Peri sulked for a moment, then sat up. "How much am I worth?"

Sam smiled. "Not near enough for all the hassle," he chided.

She glared at him and then lifted an eyebrow. "So, how much?"

"Five hundred," he said. "In silver."

This made Cooper perk up. "They stole the silver map. The men with the white shirts and the long beards."

Sam looked back at Cooper and then to Peri. "Why does he keep talking about that?"

Peri brushed his question aside. "What if I paid you a thousand to let me go?"

Sam threw his head back and laughed. "If you had that kind of money, you wouldn't be in this mess."

Peri straightened her shoulders. "I do have that kind of money and it's one of the reasons those men from Cedar Creek are after me."

"You stole their silver?" he asked.

"No. I didn't. But I think my mother may have. The men Cooper talks about with the white shirts and long beards are the elders from The Kingdom of Glory church. They're after me because I helped some girls escape and because they think I know where treasure is hidden."

This got Sam's attention, but he was still dubious. "What kind of treasure?"

"It's a silver mine," Cooper yelled to them as he squatted under the mule and sorted small pebbles into piles. "They stole Peri's silver map. It had AG. That is silver. AG is silver."

Peri smiled and sighed. "I don't think it's a mine. I think my mother took a bunch of Deon's silver and buried it near the compound. She kept a journal with notes and a bunch of letters and numbers that made no sense, until Cooper saw it and said it was silver."

"It's an aliquot plot," said Cooper, still sorting. He didn't look up, and continued talking to himself. "Like a placer claim. It's a silver mine."

"How does he know this stuff?" asked Sam.

Peri shrugged. "I don't know, but he's the only one that's been able to make sense of it."

"And I'm supposed to trust what he says?" asked Sam. "That's asking a lot."

Peri took a deep breath. "I know you're in this for the money, but I didn't kill anyone. I went down there to bring a girl back to her family. Their prophet was going to rape a fourteen year old girl and I helped her escape. I didn't kill him, but I would have. They aren't men of God, they're monsters who prey on girls. That's what they do there. They lied to my mother to get us to Cedar Creek and then held us at that compound. If I hadn't escaped all those years ago, I would've had to marry a man that was over thirty years older than me. My sister married their false prophet and he's in his sixties. Emma was seventeen and he already had six other wives. If you take me back there they will kill me. And not because they think I murdered Deon, but because I know what they do."

"Did you get paid to bring that girl back?" Sam asked.

She nodded.

"So you did do it just for the money?"

Peri's chest tightened as her mind was brought back to the real reason she sacrificed so much to save Grace and how her world had been upended with the truth at the end of the journey. "Yes," she lied.

"Then I guess you're a bounty hunter too," mused Sam.

Peri shot him a look.

"What guarantees do I have that you'll pay me what you say?" he asked.

"Take me to Montpelier. I can get the money there," she answered. "If not, you can take me to Cedar Creek."

Sam gave her a lifted eyebrow. "Where do you have money in Montpelier?"

"It's with my sister Emma," Peri answered.

Sam sat back and looked at her with apprehension.

"What?" Peri asked, seeing his obvious reaction.

"Your sister's gone. The marshal came looking for all of you and when we went to Dorothea's to ask her some questions, your sister was gone. I half expected to find her with you," Sam said.

Peri's breathing stopped and her shoulders sank. "The baby?"

"Gone too." Sam went to his bedroll and brushed off the dirt. "We can still stop in Montpelier to see if she's returned, but with a bounty on her head, I doubt it."

"Why is there a bounty for her? She didn't do anything but escape that nasty place." Peri pulled her bedroll to the farthest place from Sam.

He pulled it back. "You're still my prisoner and you will stay close." He put rusted metal hobbles on her ankles. "They say she kidnapped that baby," Sam said as he crawled into his bedroll. "That it isn't hers. They say she killed a woman and that she stole it."

Peri blurted out a laugh. "Stole it? I was with her when she had it! Those people are vile. They want to take Emma's baby, make Grace marry an old man, and hang me for a murder I had nothing to do with." Peri took a deep breath. "They're offering all that money because they have three women that know what really happens down there and they want to shut us up for good." She looked at Sam with purpose in her eyes. "I guess none of this matters to you though. As long as you get that money."

Sam was tucked in his bag. He laid back and closed his eyes. "If it mattered so much to you, why'd you take off and leave your sister behind?"

~*~

Peri started to spit words back at him, but realized she had nothing to say. She laid down and turned away from him. She laid there wondering where Emma had gone and how she had traveled alone with a baby. Did she decide to go back and surrender to a life of abuse and imprisonment? When Peri left, Emma probably lost hope. Peri's guts churned with the guilt of what she caused. Her disdain and anger for what happened in the past was overshadowed by her new found compassion of what her sister had endured. Peri's need to escape the bounty was now even more urgent. She didn't just have her own life to save, but that of her sister and nephew as well.

Chapter 22

Challis, Idaho
1892

Seeing her brother murdered would haunt Peri for the rest of her life, but as she rode, wearing his clothes, back to the home she once knew, she felt him with her, watching over her. She knew it was probably the exhaustion setting in, but she took some comfort in feeling he was there.

She arrived in Challis with a new identity. She wondered how long it would take before she was exposed and what would happen. At that moment, she was so hungry that being revealed only worried her as long as it was after she had dinner.

She rode Chance through town and to her family's small home on the hill. When Deon convinced Kathryn to marry him and move to Cedar Creek, he agreed to pay off the house and the back taxes. It was the perfect plan to rid himself of Paul. He was able to keep him away from the compound and back in Challis. Now Peri was utilizing Deon's scheme to her benefit. She had a home. However, she had no money or job and her plan to impersonate Paul would be dicey when she tried to do his work in the mine. With no other options, she cut her hair short, dressed in his clothes, took his miner's shovel and tools, and tried to remember when she watched Paul and the other men headed for work.

Her insides squirmed as she reached the mine and saw the men in line for the cage to take them in. She paused, trying to build her courage.

"Hey, Paul," she heard over her shoulder. She looked to see a young man walking toward the large mine shaft. She nodded at him as he kept pace with some others. She put Chance into the corral and started for the cage. When she got there, no one paid her much attention, so she kept her head low and followed their lead.

At the end of the day, she surfaced to find the sun had gone down and the only daylight she would see was what she basked in each morning on her way to work. Her muscles ached and quivered. Dirt covered every inch of her, even inside her nose and ears. She tried to shake what she could off her clothes before going into the house. She was starved and yet she had no energy to cook. She grabbed for jerky and bread and before she ate half of it, she was asleep.

Weeks went by without issue. She was even surprised that her lack of strength and production wasn't noticed. As long as she stayed busy and didn't draw attention, she felt she could pull her transformation off without a hitch. But what then? she thought one night as she sat alone in the candlelit kitchen, her hands bruised and cracked, and her demeanor crushed. Was this what she expected for the rest of her life? It was better than the future she faced at the compound, but it wasn't a life she enjoyed. Facing years of hard labor with no family, and as a man, wasn't something to look forward to.

The next day as she sat against the rock wall eating the small lunch she had packed, she heard a familiar voice.

"So you made it back?"

She looked up. It was Dutch. Peri's stomach clenched and she wanted to beg him not to reveal who she really was.

"Did your sister find you?" he asked.

He didn't know. Maybe it was the darkness of the mine or the dirt that covered her face, but either way, he thought she was Paul. Still unsure, Peri cowered back trying to hide from him. Without thinking, she blurted out a low and throaty, "Uh, yes."

Dutch gave a satisfied grunt. "I didn't expect that. I thought you were both goners."

Peri gave a nod, took another bite of her lunch, and tried to act uninterested.

Dutch started to leave and then called back to her. "You still owe me that last forty. I expect to see it."

Peri nodded. "You will," she said in her man's voice.

He looked at her oddly with squinted eyes. After a moment, he shrugged and walked off. When Dutch was out of view, Peri let her breath out and felt her shoulders sag in relief. She had pulled it off for now, but dreaded a life of continual hiding. It was getting to her and she could tell the other men wondered about her odd behavior. The ones she spent most of her time with didn't talk much and that was a relief, but when she was moved to a different area, she found herself surrounded by young men her age who weren't going to let her just hang back and hide.

They were loud and raucous. They swore often, made lewd comments about each other, and seemed to shove or punch even when they agreed on things. They tried to bring Peri into the mix, but she held back and tried to brush off their boisterous play by acting annoyed and ornery. It all made Peri even more anxious about her situation. She wasn't sure how, but she needed to get away from them.

When she was leaving the mine, she saw one of the supervisors standing by the stamp mill. Without giving herself time to change her mind, she went to him and asked about positions in the mill or the smelter. When he turned to her, she was taken aback at how young he was and the incredible blue of his eyes. He smiled and she blushed. Then she remembered herself and cleared her throat.

"Mr. Busby, I . . ." she stammered.

"Call me Marty," he said. "And what should I call you?"

"I'm Paul Dixon," she said in her best low voice. "I'd like to move out of the shaft and up top here."

Marty put a hand to his smooth, square chin. "It doesn't pay as much."

"That's okay," Peri said.

"It takes a week of training and I only pay half for that week. You sure you still want to switch?"

Peri nodded emphatically. "Yes."

When the other young men on her crew learned she was leaving, they chided her, even calling her a girl. It may have struck her funny, if she didn't actually worry. She was so relieved, when her last shift underground was over she found herself smiling as she made her way up the shaft and outside.

It was late summer and the sky was still bright when she surfaced. It felt like a new beginning and she was happy she had left Chance at home instead of riding him to the mine that morning. The sun, the warmth, and a new life outside of the hole, had her almost skipping toward home.

In the distance she heard a mixture of laughter, whooping, and screaming. She diverted her path home, wondering what she'd find.

As Peri came to the top of the hill, the hollering that caught her curiosity turned to horror as she looked down on the scene.

Three of the young men she knew from the mines were tormenting an Indian girl they had surrounded. She was down on her knees, her dress was ripped, and one of them had her by the hair. She looked at the ground stoically.

Before Peri ducked out of sight, they saw her and called loudly, "Hey, Paul! We caught you a live one. Time to be a man." They all laughed. It was a common taunt due to Peri's girlish features and skinny frame. She had to wear her clothes loose to hide her curves and this made her look even scrawnier. One of them groped the girl's breast and she swatted their hand away. This angered the young man and he slapped her hard.

Peri gasped and started to turn, but before she ran, one of the boys had her by the arm and was flinging her toward the group. She tried to keep her composure and her secret intact, but they were bigger, and her thin frame was easily tossed toward the girl.

Peri tried to keep from falling, but she ended up on her hands and knees next to the girl. She saw them shove the girl to the ground on her back and within seconds Peri was heaved up and slung on top of the girl. She heard them calling out what she should do to the girl, but Peri looked up and into dark vacant eyes. There were dried tear streaks on the girl's dusty brown skin but her face showed no emotion. She was defeated physically, but she wouldn't let them crack her soul. For a moment Peri thought she saw the spark of a fire in those eyes, but before she processed through the chaos, someone rammed their boot on her butt, pushed her into a rocking motion on the girl and yelled, "Got a boner yet?"

Peri tried to squirm away from under the boot and off the girl, and then she heard a stern voice behind them all. The boot released and Peri rolled off the girl to see Marty on horseback and a bluster of dust surrounding him.

"Are you all crazy?" he yelled. "Do you want the tribe down here fighting with us?"

"We didn't do nothing," said one of the young men. "We were only playing with her."

Marty looked down at Peri.

Peri shook her head. "I didn't . . ." is all she could muster from her place on the ground.

Marty scoffed. "There are plenty of whores in town for this. Don't be stupid. Now go on," he ordered.

The young men shuffled off in haughty swaggers, but Peri stayed on the ground. Marty dismounted and went to the girl. He helped her up and apologized.

"They grabbed me and pushed me on her," insisted Peri. "I have no interest in doing stuff like this. I swear."

Marty tipped his head and studied her. He then looked at the girl for confirmation.

The girl nodded her confirmation of what Peri said.

"Go on home then," Marty said to Peri.

Peri got to her feet and walked off feeling ashamed and annoyed. Not only was Marty her boss, but having him think badly of her was worse. She pondered this and how bizarre it was that she cared what he thought, even when she was doing everything she could to keep him from knowing the truth. She hoped when she showed up at her new job tomorrow, he didn't decide to send her away.

Chapter 23

Challis, Idaho
1895

An older man with heavy side burns and a prominent scar across his cheek and nose met Peri at the mill. Thomas was gruff but seemed willing to spend whatever time she needed to learn her new position as a picker along the conveyor belt coming out of the crusher.

"How old are you?" he asked, as they took a short break for lunch.

"Seventeen," she said, in her best strong voice.

"You need to eat more. You're skinny as a rail. And look at your hands," Thomas said, motioning to Peri's long thin fingers. "They look like piano playing hands, not picking hands."

Peri was concerned that he might tell Marty she wasn't fit for the job. "I work real hard. I know I'm small, but I can do the work."

Thomas grunted and walked off.

Each day, Peri did her job with focus. She came early and left late, always making sure Thomas saw her progress. He rarely gave her compliments, but a quick survey of her work and a head nod was what she needed to begin feeling secure.

She kept to herself and rarely spoke to the other men in the mill. Some days she caught a glimpse of Marty going from one level to the other. She found him watching her and Peri quickly turned away in hopes he didn't think she was just standing around day-dreaming. Marty always had a ready smile, which had her wishing he spent more time in her area.

When her training was finished, she felt satisfied that Thomas would give her a good recommendation to have the job permanently. It was nearing the end of her shift, so Peri decided to ask him what he thought and what would happen now.

"You keep doing what you're doing," he said with a sigh. "If you want the job, it's yours."

She almost hugged him with excitement, but instead she smiled wide and thanked him for his help.

Thomas grunted, told her to wait until he returned, and left her with her job. He didn't return for another two hours, and when he did, Marty was with him.

Peri felt her heart jump when she saw his face.

He smiled. "Thomas says you're picking it up well enough and that you're the man for the job."

Thomas gave another grunt and walked off to another part of the building.

"He also says you're too scrawny," Marty said with a laugh.

Peri tried to smile, but worried whether that affected her status with the job.

"How about you come to my place for supper tonight?" Marty asked.

Peri looked up at him in shock. She felt a mixture of excitement and terror.

"I guess we need to try and fatten you up," he said.

She swallowed hard. "All right," she answered.

"Good," Marty said as he clapped her on the shoulder. "I'm just around the corner from the feed lot. The small house with the large spruce." He walked off.

She watched, still in a daze at what had just happened. When Marty turned back and saw her still staring, he smiled and waved.

She waved back wondering if he was this kind to all the men who worked for him. Then she became frantic that he might already have figured out her secret.

As Peri cleaned up and prepared for the evening at Marty's house, she found herself worrying about things that most women care about. How did she smell? What should she wear? What would he think about her? She knew it was silly. After all, in Marty's mind they were two men having a meal, not a man courting a woman.

When Peri arrived at his house, she was surprised at how clean and orderly it was. Her own home wasn't this tidy.

"Sit," he said motioning to a chair at the table. "Drink?" he offered, holding a bottle of whiskey.

She accepted and tried to shoot it like she had seen the other men do. It burned her throat and she gave a throaty moan.

Marty laughed. "Another?"

She shook her head and put a hand up.

He brought over plates and trays full of meat, potatoes, and carrots. "Eat up! This should make Thomas happy," he teased.

The food was delicious and Peri found herself relaxing back in her chair and enjoying his company. She wanted to tell him the truth, but even after a second drink, she knew it was not the right thing to do.

When they finished, they both sat back and Marty lit a cigar. He offered one to Peri but she declined. She watched his mouth as he took in the smoke and then let it slowly billow out as he leaned his head back.

He looked over to her. "I think I know something about you."

Even with the haze of the whiskey, Peri sat up straight with worry.

Marty put his hands up in defense. "It's not a bad thing. I'm glad. Very glad."

She studied him wondering just how much she should divulge. "What do you mean?"

Marty gave her a drunk smile. "If I kissed you would that be a bad thing?"

This made Peri's eyes shoot open.

Marty laughed. "So I'm right, aren't I?"

Peri sat back in her chair. "Please don't fire me. I need this job."

"Fire you?" he said loudly. "I'm so happy to have you around. I'm tired of working with a bunch of disgusting pigs. I knew you were different."

Peri took a deep breath feeling a bit lighter. "So, you won't tell anyone I'm a girl?"

Marty cocked his head and looked at her. For several seconds he sat and stared.

"Please," begged Peri.

He swallowed. "Why would I tell anyone that?"

"I don't know, but I want to keep it a secret. When my brother Paul was killed, I took his clothes and it is the only way I was able to work."

Marty's eyes narrowed and he seemed to sober up. "Uh, of course. I would never give your secret away." He stood up and started taking plates to the wash basin. He turned back to her. "A woman? I mean…" he stammered, then caught himself. "Why are you pretending to be a man?"

She shook her head. "I didn't know what else to do. When Paul and Dutch helped me escape from Cedar Creek, I thought I'd come back here and live with Paul. But now I'm alone. I didn't have anywhere else to go. I couldn't find a job here unless I was a man."

"You're from Cedar Creek?" he asked, surprised.

"Yes," she answered. "But Challis was my home before I was taken there."

Marty thought to himself for a moment with brows furrowed. "Does Dutch know about you? Being a girl and all?"

"No," she answered and then explained how Paul had tried to go back and save the others and what had happened in the grove. "He thinks I'm Paul."

"Paul went to rescue you," Marty pondered to himself. "He was killed and you took his place."

"Yes," said Peri.

"Did you know all the other women at Cedar Creek?" he asked.

She shrugged, wondering why it mattered. "Not all. Most of the girls who were unmarried lived in the young women's house, but I got kicked out of there. The other women who were married lived in the houses with their husband's and sister wives." She studied him. "Why?"

"My sister went there about two years ago. It was a terrible situation. Do you know Grace Busby?" he asked.

Peri shook her head. "I don't. I'm sorry." She apologized mainly for the fact that his sister was still captive at the compound.

"How long do you plan to be a man?" he asked.

Peri raised her shoulders. "I guess until I can find a way to live and just be myself. But I don't know if that will ever happen.

I've got a house. Deon Heff paid all the back taxes when he took us to the compound and then sent Paul back here."

Marty gave a sad and knowing nod. He motioned to his own home. "It sounds like we have a lot in common."

Peri stewed. "Deon's buying girls. It's terrible. He lies to these women who are widowed and poor and brings them to that place and then . . ." she looked up to see Marty's horrified face. "I'm sorry, but that is what he's doing. You don't see many boys on the compound. Just women and young girls. He sends all the boys away."

"He probably would pay quite a bit to get you back?" Marty asked.

Peri shrugged. "I'll die before I allow that to happen. If I hadn't escaped, I would've had to marry Rolly Wilson. He's over fifty years old."

"Do you think that's what is going to happen to my sister?" Marty asked.

Peri dreaded the question. All she could do was look up at him with apologetic eyes.

"He told me he was a man of God," Marty mused. "When my father died, he said he'd take care of my sister and me. He wanted to marry my mother, but she ran off."

Peri huffed. "He married my mother, but it was only to get to my sister and me. He sent Paul back here."

Marty started to pace with the realization of his own situation.

"Deon is their prophet. Everyone calls him Uncle Deon. He has everyone down there thinking he really is a prophet and that if they don't do what he says they're going to hell. He's got a lot of money and he uses it to make them think God himself is blessing him." Peri became angrier the more she thought about what Deon had done and was still doing. "Even if they don't believe in it, the women are stuck there."

"Do you think they'll come looking for you?" asked Marty.

"They already did, but I don't think they will any longer." She felt her heart sink as she relived the day she watched them torture and kill her brother. Her eyes began to sting as she thought about him buried in a shallow grave next to the large cottonwood tree. The anger grew.

Soon there was nothing but silence as they sat, deep in thought about what they had both come to realize that night. When Peri was ready to leave, Marty squared her shoulders and then lifted her chin. "Thank you for telling me your secret. I'll keep it and make sure you're taken care of." He gave her a weary smile and sent her home.

That night Peri lay awake replaying the evening and all the things they said. She wondered how Marty would be with her at work and if her secret would bring him closer or keep him at arm's length. Even with the weighty conversation, she came away with the desire to be with him. She had escaped an arranged, loveless marriage, and now she was living a lie and unable to be with the man she wanted. The unfairness of it all, paired with the loss she had already endured, made her stomach ache and her breathing labored. However, when she woke the next morning, her body and mind felt light with just the thought of being at work and the possibility of seeing Marty.

Chapter 24

Challis, Idaho
1895

Peri's wish of simply seeing Marty at work was granted tenfold. He made every effort to speak to her, have lunch with her, and spend time after work hours hunting, fishing, and riding their horses in the hills. For weeks, they spent almost every day together, and yet their conversation about the compound at Cedar Creek and Peri's secret of being a girl was never mentioned. Peri found this odd, but didn't push the subject mainly because she didn't want to cause any ripple in their relationship. She was buoyant and felt her life might possibility have the happiness she never envisioned before.

On a warm night, as they sat on the porch, drinking whiskey and talking about the day, Marty reached over squeezed her shoulder and told her he loved her.

"I love you too," she answered.

Marty took a deep breath. "You're the best friend I've ever had. I hope we'll always be together."

Peri smiled. "Me too."

"You ever think about having kids?" he asked.

Peri never wanted children because she saw nothing but sadness when it came to her own experiences as a child, however with Marty those feelings were starting to change. "Sometimes," she answered.

"I do," said Marty. "I would love to have children, but I never thought about marriage and stuff."

Peri laughed. "You can't have children unless you're married."

Marty nodded in thought. "What about you? Do you want to get married?"

Peri's heart leapt as though his comment was a veiled proposal. "Sure. Some day."

"You'll have to start dressing like a girl then," he chided her.

"Unless I find a man who likes wearing dresses," she countered.

Marty choked on his whiskey and they both laughed loudly.

Peri realized it was late and started to leave, but Marty held her back.

"I need to ask you something," he said. His face was serious and pained.

Peri nodded for him to continue.

"I want to go and rescue my sister. Some of my family are in Oregon and I think she could live there with them," he explained.

Peri smiled. "That would be good."

He looked at her and took a deep breath. "Will you help me? Will you go with me to get her?"

Peri sat up straight, surprised at what he was asking.

"I don't know that area or even how to get there. I know it's a lot to ask, but I wouldn't want to do it without you. You're my only hope that this will work."

"What about Dutch?" Peri asked. "He knows the way."

Marty lifted his eyebrows and raised his shoulders. "Yes, but I really wanted this to be you and me."

Peri was flattered and enjoyed his obvious need of her, but the thought of going back there made her stomach turn. "I don't know—"

"Think about it," he interrupted her. "Don't give me an answer now. We'll talk about it later." Marty walked Peri to the edge of the street and kissed her cheek.

She didn't remember the walk home. She lay awake all night weighing the benefits of helping him, with the pain of going back. When she saw him at work the next day, he didn't mention it and after several days, she wondered if he had changed his mind. They spoke often, but even at dinner or a long horse ride, the conversation centered on their day to day life and nothing else.

It was during a summer thunder storm that she came to his home to find him rumpled and upset.

"What is it?" she asked, concerned.

He shook his head. "Nothing. I can't do dinner tonight. You'll have to leave."

She was thrown back by his withdrawn and cold disposition. "What's wrong? Did something happen, Marty?"

Finally, he slumped into a chair and told her that he had been in contact with someone at Cedar Creek and they informed him that his sister Grace would soon become the prophet's new bride.

"Oh no," Peri moaned as she took a seat next to him.

"She's fourteen!" Marty yelled. "What am I going to do?"

Peri wanted to hug him, hold him, and make it all go away.

"I'm going. I have to save her," he said with resolve.

Knowing it was a sure death sentence if he went unguided and on his own, she took his hand and agreed to come along.

The next day they planned out the trip. He promised to arrange things at the mine so that they could return to the jobs they had before. Peri had no idea how he pulled that off, but didn't question him. The only thing she made sure of was that Grace was aware and ready for them. Marty was in contact with someone who assured him she would be at the meeting place each night for three consecutive nights to give them some leeway in their travels. She would have a horse and proper clothing for travel.

On the day they planned to start their journey, Peri arrived at Marty's house, packed and ready. She found it odd that his horse was still in the corral, unsaddled. She went to the house and knocked. A weak voice called to her to come in.

Inside, she found Marty in bed, looking pale and exhausted. He slowly lifted his head as she approached the side of his bed. "I'm sorry, Peri. I can't go."

"What happened? What's wrong?"

"I have the fever. The doctor was here already and said I can't go anywhere. He thinks its influenza." He let his head fall back against the pillow.

Peri straightened and backed away from him, stunned at this turn of events. She figured they would wait until Marty was well and then start again. She was saddened and surprised when he asked her to go without him.

"We don't have time. She's going to be waiting for us. And if you don't show up to rescue her," he paused and gave a shiver. "I don't want to think about that."

"But . . ." Peri started. Her voice began to falter as she realized her situation.

Marty reached for her hand. "I'll never be able to repay you for this. You mean the world to me. I'll meet you in Pocatello on the date we planned, and after I get Grace on the train to Oregon, we can ride back home to Challis together." He squeezed her hand. "I'd kiss you," he said with a weary smile, "but I don't want you to get sick too."

She squeezed his hand back and tried to smile. When she closed the door of the house and walked toward Chance, tears spilled onto her cheeks and down to her shirt. She was about to set out on an almost three hundred mile trek across the rugged and wild Idaho countryside to a place that only brought her sadness and pain, and now she would be doing it without the one person that brought her happiness and hope.

Chapter 25

Montpelier, Idaho
August 26, 1896

The relief Peri felt when she realized Sam was actually taking her back to Montpelier was crushed when they arrived and found the Bear Lake Marshal Larry Hobbs there as well. He congratulated Sam on his find and offered to take her off his hands. It surprised both Peri and the marshal when Ben stepped forward and asked that she be kept in his jail until the trial.

"What's the point of that?" asked the marshal.

"I'd like to discuss the whereabouts of my stolen gun with her. Besides, you said yourself your own jail was full. I'll have Sam bring her down next week. You can wait to pay him then. That'll guarantee she'll get there." Ben slapped the marshal on the shoulder with a smile.

The marshal looked confused and flustered, but gave a halfhearted smile back and agreed to Ben's terms. When Peri was locked tight in a cell, the marshal gave a satisfied nod and began his journey back to Bear Lake County.

When Sam left for the office outhouse, Peri walked to the bars of the cell and grasped the cold steel. "I didn't take your gun. That was Grace," she offered.

Ben leaned back in his chair. "I know. I also know that she's the one who shot Deon Heff. They found his body you know."

Peri cringed. Why hadn't she done a better job of hiding it? she thought, beating herself up for being so careless. "She was trying to save me. He was going to shoot me and she shot him before he could."

Ben nodded. "I know that as well. However, they have your gun with your initials on it."

Peri cringed.

"I also know that you stabbed one of their men and he almost died." He stood up and walked to her.

"How do you know all this?" Peri asked.

Ben ignored her question. "Why didn't you just tell me all this before?"

Peri shrugged. "Why would you believe me?"

"Why not?" asked Ben, annoyed. "Now it's blown up to where I don't know if I can help you. Without Grace or Emma as witnesses, you don't stand much of a chance."

"Why do you want to help me?" asked Peri.

Ben shook his head as though wondering that for himself.

"And how do you know all this? Did Emma tell you? Where is she?" Peri asked.

Sam walked back into the office and both Peri and Ben looked at him awkwardly.

"What?" he asked. "What are you two talking about?"

"I asked him about my sister," Peri said.

"What about her?" Sam asked. "I told you she disappeared in the night. No one knows where she went." He looked at Ben, who looked at the floor.

Sam furrowed his brows. "Is there something you're not telling me?"

Peri went and sat on the cot in her cell.

"So what should I do with that kid who followed us?" he asked Ben. "There were two people murdered in the Portneuf Gap area and he saw it happen."

"Bring him in," said Ben. "I'll talk to him. I'll send word up to Bannock County to get the bodies. It will be their investigation."

Sam scoffed. "That could be a mess. He's nuts. He talks in circles and does this flapping thing," he said, as he demonstrated Cooper's tick.

"He has some problems," Peri tried to explain. "But he's actually very smart. Those people who were killed were like parents to him. He has nowhere else to go."

"Take him to Dorothea," Ben said with an exhausted huff, and see if she can take him for a couple days." He turned to Peri. "I can see if they'll take him at the insane asylum by Pocatello."

"He's not insane," insisted Peri. "He's just odd."

"Right now you can't look after him and neither can I. What else do you suggest?" asked Ben.

Peri shook her head. "Is there a way to get word to Grace about my trial? What if she comes back and tells them what really happened?"

"That's hard to do when we don't know where she is," Ben said.

"I know where she is. I took her to the train station to meet her brother." The thought of Marty and his betrayal stabbed at her, but Peri continued. "He was sending her to live somewhere in Oregon."

"Oregon is a pretty big state," Sam said. "What city?"

Peri racked her brain trying to remember the name.

"Why do you think she would risk her own life to save yours?" Ben asked.

Peri thought for a moment. "I don't know. But without her or Emma, what am I supposed to do?"

Ben took a deep breath. "Sam, take the kid over to Dorothea's. I'll meet you back at the house for supper and then you can bring some to . . ." he looked down at the wanted poster. "Periwinkle?"

Peri felt her heart stop. "It's Peri," she said sternly.

Sam snickered and Peri shot him a glare. He walked out to go get Cooper.

Ben stood at the cell door. "I have to do some arranging, but I don't think you'll have to spend the entire week here."

She looked up at him quizzically.

"We'll talk in the morning," said Ben, as he left her.

It was perplexing. All of it. She had been arrested for murder and yet the sheriff seemed more conflicted about her situation than she was. He knew more than he was letting on, and her core throbbed with the knowledge that he held the keys both literally and figuratively to her fate.

When the door closed, Peri's demeanor fell. She sat back against the cold stucco wall and let her fears and exhaustion come to the surface. She cried so hard, she fell asleep. She dreamed of Marty and her past life in Challis. She saw her father in his last days, weak and feverish and unable to look her in the eye. Her sleep was long and deep and when the clank of the lock stirred her, she rolled up and through blurry eyes saw Emma standing at the cell door.

"Emma?" Peri asked, still wondering if she was in a dream.

Dressed in a dark hooded wrap, Emma nodded.

"Where've you been?" Peri stood and walked to her. She looked her up and down. "Where's the baby?"

"I've been hiding. The baby is safe. They came here looking for us and they say I killed someone and stole her baby. They want to take my son."

"They're evil dogs," Peri grumbled. "I'm in here because they say I shot that bastard prophet."

"Yes, I know," said Emma. "Did Grace make it back to her brother?"

Peri's stomach rolled. "Yes," she answered.

Emma sighed. "She may be our only hope in this mess."

Peri pondered what she said. "What's going to happen? Are you going to tell them what you know?"

Emma licked her lips and took a step back. "I don't know what to do."

"But Emma, if you don't tell them I didn't do it, I'll hang," insisted Peri.

Emma's eyes began to tear. "Peri, if it was just me, I'd turn myself in and do whatever it takes to free you, but it's my baby that I have to save. They want Paul and they'll do anything to get him."

"Paul?" Peri's heart leapt. "You named the baby Paul?"

Emma smiled.

Peri felt her eyes fill. "Thank you," she whispered.

"I loved him, too. And I miss him, just like I've missed you," Emma said.

Peri let the tears roll down her face. She wiped her nose. "How did we end up like this?"

Emma wiped her eyes and shrugged. "I don't know, Peri. I wish I did. I wish I knew how to make things right."

"If it's both of us saying what happened, they'll have to listen." Peri spun and put her hands through her hair. "I can't believe this is even happening. They are monsters and we are the ones on trial."

The front door of the sheriff's office opened and Ben peeked through. One hand was on the door, the other held the baby cradled in the crook of his arm. "It's been long enough. We need to get you back," he said to Emma.

Peri cocked her head and studied him, he looked away as though her gaze made him uncomfortable and he closed the door. She looked back at Emma. "Is he the one helping you hide?" she asked.

Emma nodded. "Yes. Please don't tell anyone. No one knows. Not even Sam or Dorothea. I told him what happened and he believes me."

"Then why doesn't he say something? Why doesn't he make them leave you alone?" demanded Peri.

"He's the sheriff, not the judge, and unless I can prove that Paul is mine and I didn't murder Launa, there isn't much he can do." She took a deep breath, "Except keep me safe from them . . . for now." She took a quick glance at the door and then back to Peri. "I have to go. I'll come back and we can talk more. Please think about how we can get Grace to help us. I don't know what other options we have." She went to the cell door and reached through to Peri.

Peri went to her and they hugged through the steel bars.

"Pray for us," Emma said. She turned and pulled the cloak close around her face and left Peri alone in her cell.

Peri walked to the small barred window and watched the wagon lumber away, lit only by the moon. She continued to watch until they were out of sight. The sound of the horse and wagon were soon gone, leaving Peri alone in the silence. It was then that Peri noticed a plate covered in cloth sitting on the table next to her cot. She removed the cloth to find bread, shredded chicken, cheese, and two boiled potatoes. She wondered if Sam had left it while she was sleeping or if Emma had brought it in.

Her stomach grumbled and she dove into the food. It was bland, but she was so hungry that everything tasted divine. She couldn't remember the last good meal she had eaten. When she cleared off every last crumb, she folded the cloth and placed it on the plate. It was then she remembered the cloth bundle Grace had given her at the train station. She pulled it out from the front of her pants and began to leaf through the pages.

It was her mother's handwriting, graceful and swooping. Peri recognized the ragged pages as the missing part of the journal she had been carrying. But this section was filled with more than plot lines, dates, and diagrams, it was filled with her mother's words. She tugged the thin blanket from the cot and wrapped it around her shoulders. Cross legged, she sat back in the fading light and began to read what messages her dead mother had left behind.

The cryptic and odd words, described ceremonies and beliefs on the compound. Kathryn wrote of Deon and his promises to her if she was faithful. She described being placed into the position of a Spirit Keeper and her heartbreaking realization of what that meant. The need to save the treasure and create a plan to give her daughters an escape. Dispersed throughout the writings were lists of landmarks that Peri remembered in the area. Kathryn gave these points numbers and sorted them into directions. In the few last words she had with her mother, Peri now realized that as odd and disturbing as they were, Kathryn was giving her the clues she needed to find the only thing her mother had left to give, stolen treasure and the truth of what she had done.

The next morning it was Sam who woke Peri. He carried another plate with a cloth, and she realized it was he who had left her dinner the evening before. He opened the cell door and placed it on the table.

"Can you leave me alone for a minute," she asked, still groggy.

Sam looked surprised and almost hurt.

She sighed. "I have to pee," she explained.

"Oh," said Sam. "Sure." He walked out the door and left her to do her business.

When she finished, she washed her hands in the wash basin and tried to straighten her clothes and hair. Then she yelled to him.

He walked back in with a smile. "Boiled eggs and salt pork," he announced. "I made it myself."

She raised her eyebrows as she pulled the cloth from the plate. "And bread," she said, taking a bite of the large crusty hunk.

"Dorothea made the bread," Sam admitted.

At the mention of Dorothea, Peri wondered how Cooper was getting along. She was still puzzled at her sense of responsibility for him.

"It looks like you and your gang are famous," Sam declared, pulling a folded newspaper from the back of his pants. The wanted poster with rough sketches of all three of them covered an entire page. A large banner stretched across Peri's face that read Captured.

Peri groaned, not so much about being labeled a wanted killer, but having her real name out for everyone to see.

Sam stood and read the story next to the poster. He looked over at Peri with a smile. "Looks like I'm famous too," said Sam. He read aloud. "Accused murderess and kidnapper, Periwinkle Dixon, was recently captured by Indian bounty hunter Dakota Samuels, the son of Casper Samuels the man who . . ." His words drifted off. He kept reading for a moment in silence. He crumpled the paper.

Peri looked at him oddly. "Who's Dakota?"

Ben walked into the office and closed the door. He noticed the balled up newspaper in Sam's hand and gave him a solid pat on the back. "I read it. What happened in the past doesn't matter now. Let it go."

"How'd they know? It's been years," Sam complained. "My real name. They knew my real name."

Peri stood back quietly wondering what it was that had Sam so upset.

Ben nodded. "I agree, but it makes for good gossip and that sells newspapers. Just like stories about murderers and kidnappers." He looked over to Peri. "You two have a lot in common. Both caught up in a mess caused by somebody else."

She gave him a questioning look, but he didn't respond.

Sam walked to Ben. "You don't think she did it?" he asked.

Ben shook his head. "When the men came through here last week, I asked them what evidence they had, and they showed me a gun with Peri's initials on it. They told me the woman you're accused of murdering was shot. Before I told you anything, you told me that girl cut herself. It doesn't add up."

Peri nodded, still unsure how much she should trust him.

"The problem we have now, is that they know you're here. They'll be expecting you down in Bear Lake County to stand trial," he said, pacing the wood floors of the room. "I'm not sure how we'll do this, but I won't have you going down there to face them alone."

"Let me go and say I escaped," Peri pleaded.

Ben took a deep breath and nodded. "I've already got them wondering about me after I let you all escape the first time, but that was before I saw the warrant. We'll stall until next week and then I'll escort you down there myself."

"Can't you talk to the judge and tell him what you know?" she asked.

"I can and I will," said Ben. "But I want more than my word against the men of Cedar Creek. They have money and power in that county and I'm betting they pay the marshal and judge pretty well."

"That's bullshit," growled Peri.

Sam choked on a laugh.

"It is!" she continued. "And you were ready to take their filthy money too," she spit at Sam.

Sam stood straight. "I brought you here didn't I? I could've drug you right back to Cedar Creek, but I didn't."

"Only because I told you I'd pay you more than they would," Peri countered.

"Whoa," interrupted Ben. "You two can fight it out later. Right now, we need to keep you from swinging."

Both Sam and Peri stopped and watched Ben gather his gun and vest. "I'm going to Dorothea's to talk to that boy about the other murders. I have other business after that. Stay close," he ordered Sam.

Sam nodded and looked at Peri, who slumped down on her cot.

For the next week, Peri saw little of Ben. It worried her and when she asked Sam if he knew anything new about her fate, he simply shook his head.

Sam brought Peri her meals, and often found tasks around the office to allow him to stay and talk with her.

"Tell me more about this silver you claim to have," Sam asked as they sat playing cards through the bars of the cell.

"AG. That is silver," Cooper's voice called from outside the window of Peri's cell.

Both Peri and Sam's eyes went wide with surprise.

Peri pushed her chair back and went to her window and looked out. "Cooper?" she called.

His face popped up and filled the window. This startled Peri, making her stumble back.

Sam laughed.

"What are you doing out there?" she asked.

"Sitting," Cooper answered.

"Come inside," she told him. She looked at Sam and they both waited until the door creaked open and Cooper stepped inside.

"It's getting cold out there," Peri said. "You can sit in here."

Sam started to object, but realized there wasn't much of a reason.

Cooper took a seat in the corner and stared at the floor. He took a rock from his pocket and used it to draw on the old wood slats of the floor.

Sam looked over at Cooper. "I think it's odd that you care about him."

"Why?" she asked.

Sam cocked his head. "It seems like you don't like or care about much of anything. It doesn't fit that you have feelings for anyone else."

"That's not true," countered Peri. "Why do you think that?"

"You left your sister behind and told me you had no use for her. You talk about Grace like she's a pest. You hate everyone on the compound, but I guess that's understandable. I don't know. I'm sorry I said anything."

Peri went to her cot and faced away from him.

"I said I was sorry," Sam appealed.

"I guess I deserve to hang. Is that what you're saying?" she asked, still with her back to him.

"No!" said Sam. "I didn't mean it like that at all."

Peri turned to him. "Then what did you mean?"

Sam paused and looked at her.

"What?" she asked, uneasy with his gaze.

"Every time I look at you, your eyes . . ."

Peri recoiled, "What about my eyes?"

"They look like they're on fire."

Peri winced. "What do you mean?"

"They're fierce with anger or hate . . . or something."

Peri looked down.

"Why?" asked Sam. "Why are you so angry with everything? If I took you and rode up through the canyon, we don't know what we'd find there, but I'm pretty sure you already hate it. You need to forget whatever happened to you that made you this way or you'll be alone and sad."

"I'm sitting in a cell accused of murder," she announced. "I've lost my father, mother and . . . " her lips started to quiver. "My brother. I'm angry because the rotten people who caused most of this are now going to hang me for something I didn't do. Yes, I'm angry."

Sam nodded as he said. "I lost my mother and father too. But after a while you have to keep living, or the anger will take over."

Peri scoffed. "Why do you care?"

Sam sighed. "I don't know why. I guess because there are some moments when I can see your eyes without the flames and you look like a completely different person. I wish that is how you always looked. But then I'd want to look at you all the time." He smiled and looked down.

Peri was confused but felt her stomach clinch. Did she really hear what he said? She tried to clear her mind. She was angry, hurt, and baffled. She lowered her shoulders in a sulky pout, and then felt childish, which made her even more upset.

"I'm sorry. I'll leave," said Sam, as he pulled the chair back.

Peri knew that if he left, she'd stew for hours and then be left alone with her thoughts and Cooper's rock carving noises. "No. I was winning," she said pointing at the cards.

Sam hesitated a moment and then Peri gave him an impatient head tilt and pointed at the chair.

Sam shrugged and took a seat. After they had played several hands, he went back to his original question. "So what's the story with the silver?"

Peri sat back. "I'm not sure, but I think my mother stole a bunch of silver from Deon and hid it. I have a bunch of her writings that talk about the church and the people on the compound, but there's another part that was taken. James and Tildie took that part from me and from what Cooper told us, the men from the compound took it from them when they killed them."

"It was the men with the long beards and white shirts," mumbled Cooper.

"That's how they all dress on the compound," Peri explained. "There's no one else who knew about the map or whatever it is. I think they want to find us because of Grace, Emma, and the baby, but I think they're also after the silver." She took the cards and leaned back in her chair. "I'm pretty sure they know they only have half of what they need to find it."

"Why did your mom steal it?" asked Sam.

"I'm not sure. I know there was something strange going on when she died. She was definitely up to something. She must have taken a lot of their treasure. She talks about it in the journal." Peri paused. "When I had the other pieces of the journal, it looked like a diagram or chart, but I'm not sure. It was Cooper who looked at it and said it was a silver map."

"AG. That is silver," Cooper said, still carving at the floor.

"If they have the map, why do you think they're still after you?" Sam asked.

"Without this other part," Peri said, holding up the bunch of papers, "They only have the final piece. What I have is all the directions leading up to the place she buried it, and without the part they have, we can only get so far. I have no idea the exact location because they have the diagrams."

Sam took a deep thoughtful breath. "So, no one can get to it without the other?"

Peri nodded.

"What if we offered them the part of the journal you have in exchange for letting you off?" asked Sam.

Peri's head jerked up and she shot Sam a stunned look.

"If the silver is that important to them, they might take it."

"That would leave you with nothing," she reminded him. "If they don't have me, you don't get your bounty."

Sam gave her a small smile. "I told you before that you are more trouble than you're worth."

Peri sat back against the wall, but kept her gaze on him. "You would do that?"

"I have to feed horses and make lunch," he said, seeming awkward with her question and under her stare. He walked out of the office and left Peri dumbfounded.

When he came back with lunch, he made an excuse to leave and it wasn't until dinner that he seemed to settle and feel he could stay and talk.

"Even if they refuse that offer, I'll let you go and we can ride to Montana. They won't find us up there," he said.

Again, she looked up at him bewildered. She started to speak, but then felt his hand on hers and looked down. "I know you didn't do this. And I won't let them take you."

"Okay," she whispered.

He smiled at her and nodded. "We can talk to Ben about it tomorrow."

"Do you think he'll agree to that?" she asked.

"The offer will have to come from him. They won't trust me. They won't even let me bring you down there to turn you in. They told Ben only white men are allowed into Cedar Creek."

Peri gave him an odd look and then a small laugh. "Why does that matter?"

He smiled. "It shouldn't. But it does. I guess they're afraid I might muddy up their perfect pure world just by being there."

"Ha!" scoffed Peri. "That place is nowhere near perfect. They may try to act pure, but that place is nothing but filth. They are making those young girls marry those vile old men. It's sickening."

Sam tilted his head. "I wish we could save them. Those girls."

Peri felt her stomach sink. It was something she had never considered, and now she felt selfish and inconsiderate for not even pondering the fate or even existence of all those girls she once lived amongst. She was more worried about her own fate or about treasure, rather than the lives of others. The thought overwhelmed her. There were so many and even if they were able to free those young women and girls, what would they do? Life in the compound was all they knew. It meant renouncing their prophet, their religion, and in their minds, their salvation. Even if they could set them free, Peri wasn't sure they would view it as liberation, but rather upheaval. "I'm not sure they would see it as being saved."

"You did," Sam pointed out.

Peri nodded. "Yes, I did." She wanted to explain it to him, but life on the compound was so complex and mired in lies, she didn't even know where to start. Could they save the girls of Cedar Creek? At this point Peri wasn't sure her own life was safe.

Chapter 26

Montpelier, Idaho
August 30, 1896

The wind had picked up and clouds covered the sun. The air felt troubled. Peri had an overwhelming sense of dread. She watched the storm roll in from her window and now she sat in her cell, with Cooper in his corner, knowing something was amiss. That is why she wasn't surprised when the door to the office opened wide and, with the wind and rain, Silas and three other men walked in. She gasped and got to her feet.

Silas stood with a satisfied and loathsome grin.

Peri stepped to the back of the cell and wondered if she should scream out the small window for help. Instead her instincts took over and she puffed her chest. "What do you want?" she growled at him with confidence.

"You hanging from a rope," Silas answered with a smug laugh. His hair hung in damp strings over his protruding forehead, and a red and angry gash was still visible above his left eye.

Cooper cowered in the corner and started mumbling, "The men with long beards and white shirts. The men with long beards and white shirts."

Silas looked over at him and raised his gun. His face turned to a sneer. "What is that?" he asked referring to the quivering form. He walked toward Cooper.

"Leave him alone," Peri warned.

Silas bent down and studied Cooper as he continued to repeat his phrase. "What the hell is wrong with him? Is he some kind of a freak?" He took a step back as though Cooper had a disease he might catch. "Get out!" he ordered Cooper. "Get away from me."

Cooper did as he was told and scuffled to the door, cringing and continuing to mumble.

"Someone should've drowned him when he was born," Silas said.

The other men nodded in agreement.

Peri was disgusted. "Because he isn't in the image of God?" she mocked. "Or is that why you cover up your weird ears and have a beard to hide your deformed face?"

Silas went to the cell and pointed his gun. "I ought to kill you right now!" he hissed at her.

Peri flinched back.

The door to the office opened and Ben rushed in. "Drop it!" he shouted. His gun was pulled.

The other men raised their hands slightly and backed away. Silas lowered his gun and turned slowly.

"You have no jurisdiction here," Ben said. "This is my prisoner until a judge orders me to release her."

"This prisoner—our prisoner—should be in the Bear Lake jail, not here," Silas huffed. "We're taking her back with us."

Ben shook his head. "No, you're not."

Sam stepped into the office and gave Peri a look of concern.

Silas sighed. "She's wanted for the murder of one of our women. She's hiding evidence in the murder of our prophet. She was supposed to be taken to our county to stand trial. This trial will go forward and I want no delays."

Sam stepped forward. "Things have changed," he countered. "She may be needed for another murder trial of two people near the Portneuf Gap. We have a witness that says it was a group of men with long beards and white shirts." He took a moment to look the men up and down.

Silas scoffed. "You're nothing but an Indian half breed. You don't know anything." The other men shuffled a bit, but their faces stayed stoic. "That brainless freak can say whatever he wants. No one is going to believe a mutant."

"They believe you," Peri hissed.

Silas turned back to her with a scowl.

"You need to leave before this goes bad," Ben said to Silas. "We will listen to a judge and bring her when we are told. Until then, she's staying right here."

Silas stood defiantly.

Sam stepped forward. "Do you want to discuss the murders of those two people now or later?" he asked.

"I'm not discussing anything with a filthy Indian," Silas grumbled.

Ben stepped forward. "The sheriff of Bannock County will be the one looking into this and I'd be happy to notify him if you all want to stick around. Otherwise, I think you need to head on back and wait for a judge."

Silas relented, his stringy hair swinging as he turned abruptly. The other men trailed after him without hesitation. Both Ben and Sam followed them out and onto the street.

Peri tried to look from her cell through the open door of the office, but could only hear the sounds of horses' hooves on the hard dirt as they rode away.

Chapter 27

Montpelier Idaho
September 3, 1896

The day before Peri was to be taken to Bear Lake County for
the start of her trial Ben came into the office. He was smiling.
Peri was a bit disturbed that he seemed so happy, considering
her dire situation.

"You won't be leaving today. Or any day for a while," he
said. "We got word this morning of the death of Judge Morris.
The poor man was kicked by a horse. They'll have to find a new
judge and that could take weeks."

Peri felt her shoulders ease. Death had yet again affected the
course of her life, but this time it was to her advantage.

Sam came in quickly and before he realized Ben was there,
he blurted out with joy, "You don't have to leave!" When he saw
Ben, he gasped and then tried to turn his smile into a more
somber expression.

Ben looked at him and then to Peri.

"They have to find a new judge because the old one died,"
Sam tried to explain in choppy awkward words.

Ben shook his head. "I have to go check on some things. We'll talk more about what to do later." He gave them a knowing look and left the office.

Sam went to the cell. "It's great news. It will give us more time to figure out how to get things worked out." He put his hands on the bars. "I wish we could have you stay somewhere else. Somewhere without bars."

Peri agreed, but gave a defeated shrug.

Sam paced the office and walked to where Cooper sat trying to balance two rocks. They kept falling each time, but he stayed at it over and over again. "Cooper," Sam said, annoyed. "You've got to stop scraping up the floors. I told you. It ruins it."

Cooper ignored him.

Sam looked at the drawing. He studied it a minute. "Didn't you say that Cooper called Silver, AG?" he asked Peri.

"Silver is AG. That is what they call it," said Cooper to himself.

"Yes," answered Peri. "Why?"

Sam crouched down next to the drawing. "What is this, Cooper?" he asked.

"AG is silver," Cooper repeated.

Sam went to Peri and unlocked the cell. He led her to the drawing and they both stood staring at it.

"It's the map," Peri said, stunned.

"It's a silver map," said Cooper.

"How do you know it's the actual map?" Sam asked. "He's probably just scribbling stuff."

Peri shook her head. "No, this is the map. I remember a lot about it and when I first met Cooper, it was James who said Cooper is able to remember things even when he's seen them just once." She bent down to Cooper. "Is this the map you saw?"

"It's the silver map. It's your silver map," he repeated.

Peri looked up to Sam and smiled. "We have the map. We have the entire map." She looked around, feeling like an animal realizing the cage door was open.

Sam went to her. "We have more time to plan getting the treasure. I'll find a way to copy this and then we should cover up the carving." He looked at her apologetically. "I should probably get you back inside there in case Ben comes back."

She nodded and returned to the cell.

Later that evening, Sam brought a piece of parchment and a smooth stone. He placed it over the intricate carving on the floor and rubbed it with the stone until the entire piece had been covered. He then lifted it carefully and turned the drawing toward Peri.

She looked it over carefully. "It transferred well, but there's a problem."

Sam turned it back and looked it over. "What?" he asked. "What problem?"

"It's all backwards," she answered.

Sam studied it. "It is," he realized, disappointed. "I guess I can try to draw it myself by looking at what he's done."

"Or you could have Cooper do it?" she said with a smile.

"Do you think he would?" asked Sam.

Peri thought for a moment. Cooper did things on his own terms. She wasn't sure how he'd take to an assignment, but she told Sam she would speak with him when he arrived as he did each day at the office.

"Can I have the one you made?" she asked Sam, reaching through the bars for the sketch. "I'd like to keep it."

"But it's wrong," he said, handing it to her.

"I know, but I still want to keep it." She folded it, and tucked it into the waistband of her pants and under her shirt. She patted it softly and smiled.

The next morning when Cooper arrived at the office, Peri asked him if he would redraw the map on paper. Sam handed him some parchment, but he didn't take it. He looked at Peri oddly and then crouched down to his carving and studied it.

"This is the map. This is your silver map," he tried to explain.

Peri made every effort to assure Cooper that she knew that and was pleased, but needed it to be on paper so she could carry it with her when she left to find the treasure.

Hearing this, Cooper stood and looked upset. He began to pace and flap at his ear.

"Cooper, what's wrong?" Peri asked from her cell. She turned to Sam, "Let me out, so I can talk to him."

Sam quickly unlocked the cell and Peri went to Cooper. She didn't touch him but bent her head close to his, the way she had witnessed James speaking to him when he was caught with her map. "Cooper, it's okay. You don't have to draw it."

"James and Tildie are gone. Grace is gone," he mumbled. "They're gone."

She looked up at Sam, realizing the reason for Cooper's angst. She put up her hands to try and stop his pacing. "I'm not going to leave you, Cooper. You won't be alone."

"They're gone," he mumbled again.

"I'm not gone. I'm here," she persisted.

He suddenly stopped pacing and turned to her. For the first time Peri could remember, he looked her in the eye. For several seconds they both stood silently, as if validating what she said through the trust he found in her eyes. He blinked several times and swallowed. He took a seat in his corner, and picked up his rocks as if nothing had happened.

Sam went to her and guided her to a place in the office where they could talk without Cooper overhearing. "You're not always going to be here. What then?" he asked.

Peri took a deep and labored breath. "I don't know. I guess I figured Dorothea will take care of him, but I had no idea he felt attached to me."

"He does come here and sit with you every day," Sam pointed out. "If we leave, we can't take him with us. It will be too much if we're on the run."

Peri agreed. "Can you bring Dorothea here so I can talk to her about this?"

Sam nodded. "I'll bring her with me when I bring your dinner." He paused a moment. "How much should we tell her?" he asked.

"I'm in jail for murder," Peri said, incensed. "What else does she need to know?"

Chapter 28

Montpelier, Idaho
September 14, 1896

Sam watched as Ben explained the reasons he had decided to risk his career and possibly his life, to hide Emma and the baby. He understood Ben's reasoning as he spoke, but it was the strength of purpose and determination he saw in Ben's eyes that surprised Sam. There was more than a desire to keep Emma safe that was driving him.

"With the judge dead, and things going on as long as they have, I felt it was time you knew," Ben said, as he stood at the hearth of Dorothea's parlor.

"At my cabin?" Sam asked.

Ben nodded, taking a chair next to Dorothea. "No one goes there, so they're safe."

Cooper stood up and went to a corner, where he crouched down, and looked at the grain of the wood floor. "Emma's at the cabin," he mumbled to himself.

Sam thought for a moment. "That's good," he said. The memories it held were too much for Sam to be there himself, but it made him happy to know that someone was living there. "What about Peri?" he asked.

"She knows," answered Ben.

"No," said Sam. "What I mean is, why can't she stay there too?"

Ben smiled, and Sam could tell from the way his eyes also grinned that Sam's feelings for Peri were obvious, but then Ben's face turned ominous. "No one knows about Emma, and it has to stay that way," he urged. "If Peri goes missing, it won't be good for any of us. I've only told you because I plan to have Emma stay here. Permanently." He took a deep breath, waiting for them to realize what he was saying.

It was Dorothea who understood first. She looked at Ben and then stood up and went to him. She put a hand on his shoulder. "I'll do whatever you need."

Sam watched the exchange. "Can we see her?"

"Eventually," Ben answered. "But it has to be very secret. If this gets out, she'll be in danger."

Sam knew that was true. "Have Peri and Emma been able to see each other?" Part of him was sad to hear that Peri hadn't trusted him enough to tell him.

"Yes, but only once," Ben answered. "I decided it was too risky for them to meet again. Emma needs to stay hidden in that cabin until all of this is resolved or becomes forgotten, and I have no idea when that will happen."

"Emma is at the cabin," Cooper mumbled again.

"What about him?" Sam asked, motioning to Cooper.

Ben gave him a half glance. "Nobody listens to his ramblings. Most of the people in town avoid him completely. He never goes anywhere except here and to the jail. Or out to the corral to talk to his mule, and I don't think the mule will give it away."

Sam agreed, but was still a bit unsettled with the strange young man knowing such weighty information.

When he spoke with Peri that night, she looked pleased that he was in on the secret and this soothed him. He was now sitting in the cell with her in the evenings when the public didn't visit. They still played their card games and talked innocently, but he began to move his chair closer to hers, and when he rose to leave that night, Peri gave him a light kiss on the cheek, which both surprised and elated him. He rode home that night with the moon bigger and brighter than he had ever remembered. It was fitting. His chest seemed ready to burst, and as he traveled the solitary road home, his smile never faded.

~*~

The sun was already up when Peri awoke. The sound of horses and men's voices made her heart race as she wondered if Silas and his men had come back. She stood up and walked to the cell door, awaiting their entrance. Ben walked in, followed by Sam who went to her quickly. He unlocked her cell and then stood back as if to let her pass by.

"What's going on?" Peri asked perplexed.

"You're free," Sam announced with a smile.

"What?" she asked, stunned. Had Sam and Ben already made a deal with the map? How did it happen so quickly? Then she looked up as another man walked into the office. It was Marty. She gasped and took a step back. "Marty?" she asked, not believing her eyes.

He went to her and embraced her, picking her up and twirling her around. He set her down and took her face in his hands. "My dear Peri," he said. "I was so stupid. It was you. It was always you." He kissed her lips.

When he released her, Peri couldn't breathe and was still stunned that he was there. She looked around and caught Sam's eye. His face had fallen and he looked devastated. She wanted to say something, but he turned and quickly left the office. She looked back to Marty. "What's going on? Why are you here?"

Marty took her by the hand and sat with her on the bench. Cooper scooted away from them, but watched carefully.

"When we read the news that you'd been captured, Grace told me what really happened and I knew I had to rescue you. I went to Cedar Creek and talked to them. We made a deal and I got things taken care of. You're free and we can be together again." He put a hand on hers and smiled.

Ben walked forward. "I have the signed record from Cedar Creek saying you're free to go," he said showing her the paper. "They've dropped the charges."

"We can leave today," Marty said.

"Today?" asked Peri. "Where's Grace?"

"She's waiting for us. We need to get going. It's a long way," he said, hurrying her along.

"But what about Oregon and Hannah?" Peri asked, still hurt from her last encounter with him.

He gave her an apologetic look. "I was stupid. I knew that the minute I saw you at the hotel. I'm so sorry, Peri. It's all over. Let's go back to Challis and start over."

Peri sat staring at him and wondering how it was all happening. She was elated and yet conflicted, and this made her even more unsettled. "But what about Emma?" she asked thoughtlessly, looking back at Ben. The moment it left her mouth she cringed inside.

Ben shot her a look.

"Emma's at the cabin," mumbled Cooper in the corner.

Marty looked at him quizzically and then turned to Peri. "Your sister is here?"

"No," said Peri emphatically. She laughed uncomfortably. "He's a bit slow," she tried to explain. "He says things that don't make sense." She continued to try and divert his attention from Cooper. "What if Emma comes back here looking for me?"

Marty sighed. "I did what I could for you, but there's still a warrant out for Emma. The men at Cedar Creek said she went missing about the same time you and Grace left. Is that correct, Sheriff?" he said, turning to Ben.

"Yes," Ben answered. "We didn't know about a warrant for any of these women until after they had left."

"But without me and Grace, there is no one to tell what really happened. She'll need us to be witnesses," Peri explained.

"If they find her, we'll all come back," said Marty.

Peri looked to Ben again. Her eyes searched his for guidance. She had only seen Emma once and now it looked as though she may never see her again. It wasn't that long ago that she would have been fine with that, in fact, she would have been living her dream of being with Marty, but now it all seemed rushed and unresolved.

"It's already late morning," said Ben. "You should stay the night and leave before dawn, that will get you a better start and you'll have a night's rest in a good bed."

"Yes, that's a good idea," Peri said. "We can leave in the morning and make sure we have everything we need."

Marty put his hand on her waist, urging her to stand. "I've already made sure of that," he said with a half-smile. Grace is waiting and I really want to get on our way. It's going to be great, Peri." He looked into her eyes.

Peri stood and looked back into the eyes she had loved and trusted. She took a deep breath and nodded. "Okay."

As Marty escorted her out the door, the brightness of the sun made her squint. She raised her hand to shade her eyes and saw Sam standing against a post across the street. She stopped and stared at him. She lifted her hand to wave, but it seemed inadequate. Marty took her arm and moved her toward the wagon.

"My horse," Peri said. "I can't leave without him."

"We can get him later," said Marty.

"No, I have to have him," she demanded, feeling anxious and unsettled.

Ben motioned to Cooper. "Gather Peri's horse and bring it here."

Cooper shuffled off toward Dorothea's house where Chance was being boarded.

"That's fine," Marty relented. "But we'll have to hurry before they change their minds," he urged.

Peri looked at him oddly, as he rushed her to the seat and slid in next to her.

"Come on, Peri, give me a smile. I'm chiding you," he said, pushing his shoulder into hers.

She gave him a halfhearted smile and sat waiting for Cooper to bring Chance and trying not to look at Sam. Once Cooper arrived, Marty quickly tied his lead to the wagon and placed the saddle bags into the back.

"Thank you, Sheriff!" Marty called to Ben.

Ben looked disturbed and unsure. "Are you sure you don't want to stay over and rest before your journey?"

"The sooner we start, the sooner we'll get there," Marty answered. He turned the wagon west and gave a hearty click of the reins. As the horses moved forward, Peri caught Sam's eye.

Marty noticed. "Who's that?"

"The bounty hunter who found me and brought me here," she answered softly.

"You don't say?" said Marty intrigued. "An Indian working for the Kingdom of Glory?" "I'll bet he's burning mad I took his bounty," he mumbled with a smug smile.

"What'd you say?" asked Peri, surprised.

"Nothing, darling," Marty said as he moved the wagon into the dirt street and toward the route out of town.

Peri's gut was filled with a terrible sense of foreboding when she turned back to see the town fade in the distance. Cooper sat on his white-faced mule in the middle of the street, watching the wagon lumber along into the distance. She had broken her promise.

She finally turned back and when she did Marty put a hand on hers and squeezed it. He nodded toward the bed of the wagon. "Take a nap. I'll need you to take over while I sleep a little later."

Hesitantly she nodded and crawled into the back.

"There's a jug of water there. Have some. We'll eat a little when we switch places," he directed.

She did what he said and then laid down on a bed of straw covered by a large cow hide. Within minutes she was lulled to sleep by the rhythmic rocking of the wagon.

Peri was unaware how long she had slept, but when she awoke, her hair stuck to her face with sweat, and something pounded inside her skull. She lifted her head to see that it was already getting dark. She pulled herself to sitting and looked around. She watched the setting sun and as she became more awake realized the sun wasn't setting, but actually rising, which meant they were heading in the wrong direction. She looked up at Marty troubled. "Why are we going this way?"

He ignored her and kept looking ahead.

She asked again and then sat and studied the area more closely. Peri then realized she must have been out for more than just hours, because instead of heading northwest toward Pocatello, they had traveled at least two days on a trail she knew well—the one headed south toward Cedar Creek. She scrambled up to the wooden seat of the wagon. "Where are we going? What are you doing?" she demanded.

Marty stopped the wagon, but kept his eyes forward and answered. "We are going to find the silver." He then yelled, "Git ya," to the horses to start them again.

"Marty?" Peri was both confused and panicked. How does he know about the treasure? she thought. "What do you mean?" she asked, trying to act oblivious.

Marty turned to her, but his face had become brooding. "Come on now, Peri, we never kept secrets before. Grace told me about the map. The silver will help us have the things we'll need to set up our new place."

"What did Grace tell you?" she asked, alarmed.

"She told me about the map and that there was silver buried somewhere around Cedar Creek and that the men from The Kingdom of Glory are also trying to get it."

Peri felt the impulse to flee. "Where's Grace?"

"I told you that she's waiting for us." He stopped the wagon and turned to her. "You do want to share this with me, don't you? Isn't that what we planned, my love?"

Peri felt her body tense. She didn't want to speak but felt she had to answer. "What about Hannah? *That* isn't what we planned," she countered. "Why are you really here?"

"I made a mistake. Don't tell me you never made a mistake." His voice was flat, toneless. "I'm here now. Stop bringing up the past and let's go find that treasure."

"I don't want to go near that place." She spoke with force as she turned toward Chance. "I want to go back."

"Turn around and sit still." He grabbed her arm, pulling her back onto the seat to keep her from jumping. "We're almost there."

Peri settled back on the seat and pretended to relax. He released her arm. "How long have we been traveling?" She put a hand to her aching head. "What was in that water?"

Marty was silent. He removed his gun from its holster on his belt and pointed it at her.

Her scalp prickled as she thought he would shoot her right there. "What are you doing?" Her voice shook.

"I'm not going to hurt you, just give me the map."

She had to think fast if she wanted to live. "I don't have it. It was stolen by some people on the trail."

He gave an annoyed huff, dropped the reins and dove at her, groping her body, searching her clothes. Peri lunged away from him, but he grabbed her arm and pulled her back. "If you don't have the map, the only thing you're worth is the bounty on your head. I gave them Grace as a guarantee I'd bring you back. If you don't get me that silver, I'll turn you in and get the bounty."

His breath was hot and heavy on her neck as his hands ran down the length of her back and inside her trousers.

"You gave them your sister?" she gasped as she tried to push him away.

Marty leaned away enough to cock his head and smiled.

"But you sent me to rescue her." Peri was frantic. "Why? Why would you do that and then turn around and sell her?"

"It's you they wanted," he said. "We'll just call it like it is. Grace was bait."

Peri stopped struggling and stared at him as recognition of who he really was dawned on her. She'd been such an idiot to trust him. "When you said you had the influenza. You wanted me to go alone so they would catch me? You *sold* your own sister to those monsters."

Marty laughed, an ugly, sardonic laugh. "And how do you think your brother was able to keep your house? I bet you and your sister fetched a pretty penny."

Peri was enraged. "My brother had nothing to do with me being at Cedar Creek."

Marty shrugged. "Someone sold you to Deon." He picked up the reins and clicked at the horses to keep them moving.

"We didn't know what they were about. You knew and you still sold her to them. How do you live with yourself?" she said.

He shrugged. "There was a time you claimed to love me. And I almost thought I loved you."

Tears burned as she remembered the night he wanted to kiss her. "That's when you thought I was a boy."

She couldn't bear to think about him any longer. She folded her arms and scowled at the back ends of the horses as they plodded along the trail.

They rode in silence for a while until the trail leading up to the grove of willows came into view. "You're going the wrong way," she said.

"I was just here. I know the way," he answered.

"If you want the treasure, this is the wrong way."

"Give me the map," he ordered. "I know you have it."

She knew what she had to do if she was to live. "If I give you the map, will you let me go?"

He sneered at her knowingly. "Prove you have it," he ordered.

Peri scooted to the far side of the bench and lifted her shirt to expose the map tucked in the front of her britches. It was the one Sam made of Cooper's carving. "But this is only the last half. The other part is just what I remember reading. I can get you close enough so this map will get you to the treasure, but only if you let me go once we get there," she said.

"I don't have to negotiate with you," he answered quickly. "If I kill you and bring you to them, I'll still get paid." He gave the reins a good flick and the horses picked up the pace.

"I'd rather die than go back there. If you kill me, even with this map, you won't find the silver. You can't get there without me," Peri said sternly. "You have to promise me, if I take you there, you'll let me take my horse and leave."

He thought a moment. "And how do I know you're directing me to the right place to start looking?"

"There's a place that's on the map that will show that we're there. You'll just have to follow the diagrams on the map after that," she said.

He nodded. "Fine."

"You promise you'll let me take my horse and leave?" she asked again.

"Yes," he said smugly. "I promise."

Peri nodded, hoping she was right to trust him. "You have to go around the grove of willows and up the hill behind the compound."

Marty reined the horses and then turned and nudged them in the direction Peri had given.

She took a deep breath.

When they came to the place Peri described, Marty stopped the wagon. "We're here, now give me the map," he demanded.

Peri shifted her weight, prepared to jump from the wagon before he could grab her again.

He pulled his gun.

Furious at him and at herself for trusting him, she put up her hands. "If you shoot me, you'll never find it. Let me get on my horse and then I'll give you the map. You promised you'd let me leave."

He snickered. "Haven't you already learned that I don't usually keep my promises?"

"I have a gun!" a shaky voice called from behind a large bunch of junipers. "It's a real gun!"

Peri recognized Cooper's voice and while she cringed inside, part of her was ecstatic that he was there.

Marty looked around frantically. "What do you want?" he yelled to the hidden voice.

Peri jumped to the ground and headed toward Chance. "I'll give you the map," she said pulling it from under her shirt. "Just let me go."

He looked at the map and then back at where the voice had come. "How close are we?" he asked.

She unfurled the parchment, held it up so he could see it, and pointed to a large arrow. "This shows north," she said. "This big circle with the jagged lines is that hill of lava rock." She pointed to it in the distance. "It shows that if you go north for two miles, you'll see another hill like it. The rest of the map begins right at the edge of that hill. It gives exact feet between each stone where she buried the silver."

"If I let you go, who's to say he won't just shoot me?" he asked.

Peri gave a huff. "I've never betrayed you and I've always kept my promises."

He stared at her coldly. "Tell whoever that is to back down. Give me the map and I'll leave you alone."

Peri nodded. She yelled to Cooper to stay where he was and to not shoot. She folded the map and tossed it onto the seat of the wagon. She untied Chance, grabbed the saddlebags and moved behind the wagon to a spot that was least likely for him to aim at her. She stood behind Chance as a shield and watched as the man she once loved and trusted rode away with a map that would take him nowhere and bring him nothing but frustration and fury.

When Marty was far enough away, Peri called to Cooper.

He stepped from behind the trees, leading the white faced mule behind him. A pistol hung from his hand.

Peri ran to him and without thinking, hugged him. He flinched back awkwardly.

"Why did you follow me?" she asked.

Cooper went to the mule and pulled something from the saddlebags. He walked back to Peri and handed her a folded piece of parchment. "I did your map on paper. It's your silver map. You said to draw it on paper," he explained.

She looked down and unfolded the drawing. "Oh, Cooper," she said, warmly. "You saved me. And you drew the map. You're so brave."

Cooper didn't respond but stood by the mule and looked out at the sky. "It's that way," he said, motioning the opposite direction that Marty had taken.

"Yes, it is," Peri agreed. It was enough of a sign that Peri knew it was time to follow the path to the treasure. "Will you come with me?" she asked Cooper.

He didn't answer, but mounted the mule and waited for her.

She was weak from lack of food and unsure of even how many days or hours had passed, but they had one chance and they needed to do it quickly. It wouldn't take long before Marty figured out that the map was incorrect and backward. Peri knew once he figured it out, he would come looking for her and the real treasure. She figured she had several hours and with Cooper's gun, she at least had a way to defend herself.

She smiled and went to Chance. She mounted him and with the map in hand, turned to the south and started toward the place her mother had hoped she would find.

They traveled the short distance at a quick trot and finally reached the area her mother had described and the map had indicated. It was a plateau of green surrounded by the jutting and jagged rocks of a prehistoric volcanic eruption. Peri felt anxious as she contemplated walking in her mother's footsteps, as she was taking such a risk to hide what she felt was their means of escape. She directed Cooper to go back to the top of the hill and watch for anyone coming their way. She wanted to be alone.

"If you see someone, come and tell me. Don't yell," she directed. They were close enough to the compound that with the right direction of breeze, their voices might be heard.

The plot was laid out in perfectly sectioned squares and unmistakable stone markers. Peri looked at the map again and decided to start from the beginning with stone number one. She knelt and brushed the debris and dirt from the rock. A jagged faint line was scraped into the stone. Peri retrieved her shovel and started to dig. Within minutes she hit something hard and hollow. She dug around the small perimeter and then lifted a large wooden bread box from the shallow hole. She shook it and heard a solid knock and some other light rustling. She smiled at what felt like a good sized chunk of silver.

Peri took the box and sat in the shade by Chance. She pried the lid off and found the shiny brilliant nugget she had anticipated, but underneath was a bundle wrapped in a white cotton cloth. She figured it was padding to keep the nugget of silver safe, but as she lifted the cloth from the box, it unraveled. Peri stumbled back on her haunches as the box and bundle tumbled away from her. Her eyes had flown open and now she clenched them shut, trying to erase what she had seen. It was the tiny remains of a child. Her stomach heaved and she clasped her hand to her mouth to keep a horrified wail from escaping into the breeze.

Chapter 29

Near Cedar Creek
September 14, 1896

When Peri came to, Cooper stood above her. The sky was gray and the wind made the trees bend and whip. The memory of what she discovered flooded back to her and again she heaved. It was only bile. She had thrown up so many times, she was now weak, dehydrated, and delirious.

"We need to go back," she muttered softly. Ben needs to know about this, she thought.

Cooper looked uneasy. "This is the silver mine," he said, but he looked around as though he wasn't sure.

"It is," she said. Letting him know what was also buried with the silver would only make him frantic. "Cooper, you need to help me. I need water."

Cooper had started to pace, but went and brought her back a jug.

She drank then handed it back to him. "Go make room in your saddlebags," she directed.

He began to rock back and forth and mumble.

"Cooper," Peri pleaded. "Please help me."

He steadied himself and did what she said. He stood by the mule and kept his gaze at the horizon.

The task of digging up each small grave and removing the bundles was more than Peri could handle. Several times her stomach overtook her, and the entire time she dug, she wiped tears. She had no idea how they died, but because of her mother's cryptic notes, she knew the evil beliefs of the Kingdom of Glory were to blame.

There were twelve stones. Each stone she found was another lost life. They were so small and barely registered as weight in her hands. She kept the bodies, or what was left of them, wrapped, and tucked them all carefully into the pouches of both hers and Cooper's leather bags. Twelve lives cut short. She placed the accompanying nuggets of silver in another pouch and secured it all with the leather straps.

Peri stood on the plateau and surveyed the mounds of dirt by each of the empty graves. She wanted nothing to be left when Marty or the men on the compound ever discovered it. She shook her head and felt tears of both sadness and rage overtake her. Peri knew she didn't have time for emotion, so she swallowed back her cries and took hold of Chance's lead rope. She directed Cooper to do the same and they both walked from the mesa down to the valley floor. Peri checked their packs and then led them toward the trail to Montpelier.

The longer they rode, the more Peri began to falter. Her vision was blurred and she shivered in the cold breeze. It took all her concentration to stay upright in the saddle. Her head was spinning and she held onto the horn of the saddle, hoping Chance knew the right way back. Hunched over and barely hanging on, her thoughts turned to Grace. Peri had ignored her prattling, and in the process disregarded her warnings. Grace knew what Marty was and saw the path Peri was taking. Peri wondered what would become of Grace now. Being brought back to the compound would make her a literal prisoner, isolated and locked away until she proved her devotion.

Peri's intention to show Ben the crimes committed at the compound included her desire to save her former charge. If Ben and the marshals went to confront the men of The Kingdom of Glory about the deaths of twelve innocent children, they would see that the girls of the compound must be saved too. Her daydreams of rushing in and rescuing Grace and the other girls and having Silas, Rolly, and the others arrested kept Peri from passing out and falling off her horse.

The air had become cold and damp. A storm was upon them and they still had hours on the trail.

Cooper pulled back on the mule. "It's the men," he stated. "It's the men."

Peri tried to look up. Her heart leapt. She was certain it was Marty and the others coming after her. "Where?" she shouted, trying to focus her blurred eyes.

"They're coming," Cooper said, loudly.

She raised her head to see two forms in the distance. Even in the cool dampness of the day, their dust clouds were visible. Peri pulled the pistol from her saddlebags, then she turned Chance and kicked him as hard as she could muster. "Cooper! Hurry!" she yelled, as Chance bolted away.

"It's the men!" he yelled again as he followed her.

Peri held the saddle horn with one hand and the gun and a handful of the mane in the other. She tried to make a plan, but her head still throbbed as she was jolted forward.

Cooper tried to keep up with her, but the mule was no match for Chance. Peri was frantic. She debated stopping and having it out with them rather than running. She knew she couldn't aim to actually hit the men, but she fired the gun back toward them with the hopes of slowing them down.

Chance barreled forward, his ears back and his breathing loud. Again, she shot back into the air. Then the sound she dreaded. The thunder of hooves. They were gaining on her. She saw a thicket of brush and reined Chance toward it, but the turn was too much and she slid from the saddle and landed hard on the cold dirt, the gun flew from her hands. Her instincts were weak, but she crawled chaotically in search of the gun. Within seconds they were upon her. She felt the stomp of hooves and heard the quick thud of their dismount.

"Peri," Sam called as he turned her over. "Peri, it's me."

With fists flailing, she blinked and saw his face. Before she said anything tears came and she wrapped her arms around his neck. She held him for several minutes and then looked through blurred wet eyes to see Dutch. "Dutch?" she said, drained and surprised.

"Yep," Dutch answered.

"He came because he knew what was going to happen. He couldn't stay, knowing what Marty had planned," explained Sam.

Cooper caught up to them. "It's the men," he said, breathless.

Peri sighed. "Yes, it is." She remembered what she was carrying in the saddlebags. Her chest became full and as she explained what she'd found, her voice trembled along with her hands.

"Good hell," said Dutch. "And you have them with you?"

Peri nodded. "I couldn't just leave them there. Those monsters culled them like unwanted animals." She looked up at Chance as she realized the irony. "My mother at least tried to give them a burial. She risked her life to do that and to let us know where they were."

Sam listened, a hand over his mouth, his eyes wide in horror.

They sat for a while in silence as Peri drank water and waited for her strength to return. The wind blew cold under the misty clouds.

"We need to get back and tell Ben," Sam said. "Those men must be brought in. They're killers."

Peri agreed.

"Are you well enough to ride?" Dutch asked.

Although still drained by the extraordinary discovery of dead infants and silver nuggets, she responded with a firm, "Yes."

"Then let's get going," he said.

When she was back on Chance and pointed toward the trail, Peri stopped. "Wait," she said. "I need to do something."

They looked at her quizzically.

"I need to go the other route, through the willows. I need to …" her voice trailed.

Dutch shook his head. "We've been through this before and I think you forgot how bad that turned out. We need to get back."

"I have to do this, Dutch" she pleaded. "This will be the last time I ever want to come here. I have to say good-bye. It's only a few miles off the trail. It won't take long. Please."

Dutch gave a long labored breath and shook his head.

Peri hadn't forgotten, and by doing this one thing, maybe she could finally start.

~*~

Sam spoke up. He saw Peri's determination and without knowing anything more, he understood what she needed. "Dutch, you go with Cooper and wait for us on the hill just below Hawkes Peak. We can do this for Peri and still make it back before it gets too dark."

"This is a bad idea," Dutch repeated. "You know they're going to be looking for her. We'll be risking her life just like her brother risked his."

Sam nodded. "That's why you must watch for them." He turned to Peri. "Let's go, quickly."

Peri nodded and then shot Dutch a look of gratitude and apology.

Sam and Peri galloped the horses through the open field until they reached the border of the grove. Peri pulled her shirt close around her neck, trying to keep out the chill. Clouds had already darkened the sky, and snow had started to come down in steady large flakes. They rode up the hill to where Peri had hidden, and then witnessed her brother tortured and killed.

Sam saw her heartache as he watched her relive the horror of that day. "We don't have to do this," said Sam. "You can say good-bye right here. He'll know."

"No," she answered. "I must do this. I need to be where I should've been. Near him."

As they approached the grove, they both saw a billowing white figure high in the trees. Peri stopped her horse and watched it sway in the wind and snow. It was the demon. It was just as she had been told.

Sam stopped his horse too and when Peri dismounted, he looked at her for direction. "What is it?"

By this time, Peri's eyes were spilling over and she put her hand to her mouth to quiet her cries.

Sam dismounted and ran to her. "Peri, tell me what's wrong," he begged her.

She fell to her knees. "It's him," she sobbed. "It's Paul."

Sam looked up at the billowing figure, and realized it was a person hanging, clothed in a white dress. "How do you know it's him?"

"He's wearing my dress. The one I wrapped him in when I buried him. They dug him up and hung him like that."

"Oh my God," Sam said, as he watched the ghastly image.

"It's a message—a warning. They did it to punish me for leaving. They hung him up there in a dress and then told everyone there was a demon who haunts the forest. They let him hang there and rot." she cried. "I hate them!" She rose and ran to the tree.

Sam ran after her.

When she reached the trunk, she grabbed madly at the rope tied at the bottom in an attempt at freeing it and letting her brother's body be released. She scratched and pulled at the rope, but it had grown into the tree and was partially rotted. She sunk down to the wet dirt and sobbed, defeated.

Sam knelt beside her and put an arm around her. Peri felt his touch and leaned into him, her face in his chest. He wrapped his other arm around her and held her while she cried. He wanted to comfort her, help her, and make it all go away.

"I can take care of this," said Sam. He helped her to her feet. "They won't be able to use him like this any longer. They sent you a warning? I'll send them an even bigger one."

Peri wiped her eyes and shivered.

Sam walked Peri back to her horse. "Ride to Dutch and Cooper at Hawk's Peak and wait for me."

"What are you going to do?" Peri asked.

"Make all this go away."

"How?"

Peri saw the set of his jaw, the determination in his eyes, as he spoke. "The only way I know how."

Peri hesitated. "I don't want to leave you," she said quietly.

Sam put his hand to her face. "Do you really think I'll ever let that happen again?"

She looked at him with a faint smile.

"Wait at the top for me. I won't be long," he said.

Peri nodded. Sam helped her onto the horse and she turned Chance toward the hill.

~*~

Sam watched until she was out of sight. He then got to the task of trying to clear away one of the most painful events of Peri's past. He pulled his bow from his pack. He wrapped a piece of cotton cloth behind the tip of the arrow, and then took sap from a rotted pine tree and coated the rag. He lit the pitch-covered cloth. It flared and he quickly drew back and aimed. Sam winced when the arrow struck Paul's chest, but it was exactly what he had planned. The cotton dress ignited and within seconds the body was engulfed. He stood and watched to make sure it would be complete in turning the remains to ash.

~*~

As Peri reached a tall ridge, something told her to stop and look back. She pulled Chance to a halt and turned back at what was calling her. In the misty haze of light snow, Peri watched the flames take her brother's battered and rotted body and turn it into a plume of silver smoke. Instead of horror and sadness at the sight of the fiery mass, she felt an overwhelming sense of release. As tears filled her eyes, Peri felt she saw her brother's spirit rise softly into the sky.

She watched the glow in the late evening horizon. She wiped her eyes and took a cleansing breath. She turned Chance and continued on to where Dutch and Cooper waited. When she reached them, Dutch looked apologetic and unsure.

"Thank you for waiting," Peri said, her eyes still wet.

Dutch simply nodded and turned toward the grove. They all watched in silence as the orange burn of the fire grew as the sky turned dark.

Peri cried softly, but as she waited for Sam to return, her soul seemed to lighten, knowing Paul was free. The fire spread to the tree, and started to smoke as the steady fall of snow dampened the flames.

"So much for getting out of here unnoticed," Dutch mumbled to himself. "Kind of hard to hide a raging fire."

Peri continued to watch. "I've been hiding most of my life and I've had enough."

Dutch gave her a knowing nod. "So, did you find what you were looking for down there?"

She thought for a moment and then saw Sam riding back toward them. When Peri saw his face in the dim light of evening, she turned to Dutch and answered, "I did."

Chapter 30

Montpelier, Idaho
October 7, 1896

Sam walked into the kitchen of Dorothea's house with his bright smile and his broad chest puffed out with pride. A silver star glistened on his shirt.

"Deputy?" asked Peri, with a smile.

Sam nodded and looked down at his new badge.

Dorothea gave him a hug. "It's about time," she announced. "You be diligent at that place," she warned. "Sounds like the devil himself lives at that compound."

Sam gave her a reassuring nod. "Are you ready to go?" he asked Peri.

Peri gathered her things and gave Dorothea a hug. "Take care of Dorothea," she directed Cooper, who sat by the hearth, playing with a small wooden horse. "I'll see you later this week."

"Yes. And tell Emma hello," Dorothea answered, as Peri and Sam left the house.

When they arrived at the office, Ben, the marshal, and the other deputies sat discussing their plans. Ben ushered Peri to the center of the group and gave them all a quick background on her and what she had found. Their faces showed the disgust of what they heard.

"There are women and children at that compound and they might be used as shields or diversion," Ben cautioned them.

When the men began to pack their saddlebags and bring their horses around, Peri stood on the front steps and watched as Sam and Ben prepared their packs. She smoothed her blouse. She still wore pants, but instead of her shirt and leather vest, she had on a light blue blouse with a small ruffle at the yoke and collar. A ribbon in her hair replaced her hat. She stood in front of the full length mirror at Dorothea's house waiting for Sam to arrive that morning, contemplating his thoughts. Her worries evaporated when he smiled broadly at the sight of her.

"It feels different," she said, feeling awkward and on display. "Do I look silly?"

Sam shook his head, surprised. "No!" he exclaimed. "You look beautiful."

"You look like a woman," said Dorothea.

Sam shrugged. "I've never mistaken her for anything else. I don't care what you wear, you'll always look like a pretty girl to me."

Peri rolled her eyes, but inside her heart swelled. Now as she stood on the steps, watching him prepare to leave, her heart ached.

Sam sensed her gaze and looked up.

She smiled. Peri was proud and happy for him, but also feared what he was about to face. Part of her wanted to go along. She knew the area and was good with a gun, but she couldn't bear going back there, and now that she was safe and free, the exhaustion of the past several days had set in and she was ready to hand over the task to others.

After the group mounted, Sam went to Peri and from his horse mouthed the words, "I'll be back."

Peri felt her eyes well up and she put her hand to her mouth to hide her trembling lip. She stood and watched until they were gone. She took a deep breath and went to where Chance was waiting. She adjusted the saddlebags, mounted and then turned toward the canyon and the cabin where Emma and baby Paul waited.

She rode through town and then turned Chance toward the trail into the trees. The air was cool, and in spite of the horrible events that still weighed heavy in her mind, she appreciated the beauty in the colors of the leaves and how they fluttered and danced in the breeze.

When she reached the cabin, she called out to Emma, knowing that she was still on edge about being found, even though it had been almost four months she'd been living in the small log home. Peri thought about the story Sam had told her of his father and the tragic intersect of their lives and Ben's. She hoped the cabin would eventually be a place of refuge and renewal for them all.

Emma met her at the door with baby Paul on her hip. His head was still a bit wobbly, but he had gained weight and had a mop of dark hair. His large brown eyes were Emma's and Peri remarked on how perfect he was.

"He is," answered Emma. "But he's getting heavy." She adjusted her weight and held him out, offering him for Peri to hold.

It was not something Peri was comfortable with, but she took the baby and smiled at his cherub face. "He is getting heavy," she remarked. She took a seat at the table and Emma went to the stove and brought them both tea.

They sat for several silent and awkward minutes, and then Peri spoke up. "They'll be fine. They'll come back and you won't have to hide any longer. You'll be safe here."

Emma looked up with apprehensive eyes. She swallowed hard, but didn't speak.

Again Peri tried to make conversation and break up the palpable unrest and worry. "I think Sam and I might take the place with the big barn. The woman who lives there can't keep it up and wants to go back east where her daughter is," Peri said.

"I like Sam," said Emma. "And he loves you."

Peri cocked her head surprised.

Emma laughed. "You know he does. Anyone can see it."

Peri smiled and shrugged. She was happy to see her sister without fear and gloom on her face. "And Ben loves you," she countered back.

Emma smiled and nodded. "And I love him. Oh, Peri, I love him so much I'm almost frightened to admit it," she said.

"I know," Peri said, understanding her fears. She too, knew the risk of loving someone.

Both women sat in thought, until Paul gurgled and made them both lift from their melancholy thoughts and laugh.

The next morning Emma cleared the breakfast dishes, while Peri held the baby.

"I need to go," Peri said, pushing back the chair with her legs and standing. "I'll be back soon. There is something I must do."

"You're leaving me?" asked Emma, worried.

"I'll just be a while. I'm going up to the mesa where that stream spills over the rocks. I'm going to bury those babies in that small patch of grass," she said.

Emma looked at her own baby, cradled in Peri's arms. He kicked and looked around unaware of any of the awful events surrounding his entrance into this life.

"I had to show the bodies to prove what was happening at Cedar Creek, but now I need to lay them to rest. That mesa is the most pretty and peaceful place I know. I want to bury them there." She walked around the table, kissed little Paul on the forehead, and handed him to Emma.

Emma still looked concerned, but agreed with Peri. "That's a wonderful thing to do. They deserve at least that."

"Thank you for letting me borrow your blouse," Peri said, as she folded it across the back of the chair.

"Keep it," said Emma. "It looks better on you anyway."

Peri smiled, "It's the nicest piece of clothing I've ever owned. I'll only wear it when I'm not hunting or riding."

"Or you could buy others," Emma suggested.

Peri gave a knowing shrug.

As Peri gathered her things, Emma walked with her to the door. "I'm glad we're here together," she said. "I feel like this is our family now."

Peri nodded and hugged her. "I'll be back," she said, as she closed the door.

The breeze was still cold, but the sun was bright. Peri looked into the cloudless blue and felt the warmth of angels upon her. She wasn't sure if there was a god or heaven, she only knew she didn't believe anything she had been taught on the compound. It had certainly tainted her toward faith, but that day as she stood free, happy, and in love, she hoped those twelve lost souls, wherever they were, knew that someone had cared for them.

She pointed Chance up the hill at the base of the canyon and followed the small deer trail that led to the stream. Sam had taken her there just days after they had returned to show her the expansive view of the valley below. It was his childhood playground and he loved showing it to Peri and talking about his life before the schoolhouse fire. It was the place he leaned in for their first kiss, and Peri wanted it to be the spot that held the remains of the children who would never know that kind of joy.

When she reached the spot, she pulled the shovel from her pack. She paused and studied it. When she gleaned it from her brother's possessions, she had no idea how it would be used. She hoped this was the last time it would dig a grave.

The grassy flat made for easy digging and in just a few minutes, she had a hole large enough for what she needed. She had found a small wooden chest and placed all twelve of the tiny bodies into it. Still wrapped in their individual white cloths, she took a minute with each one as she laid them in their final home.

Peri placed the box into the hole and then covered it with the rich dark dirt and eventually the grass. She pulled twelve palm sized stones from her packs, and placed them in an orderly pile atop the grave. They were all together, and that gave Peri comfort that they weren't in the cold ground alone. The stones would remind her that each was a life cut short. It was a fitting day for her to give them their final resting place. A day that would bring those who ended their lives to justice.

Chapter 31

Cedar Creek
October 8, 1896

The compound was silent, too silent and Ben knew immediately there was something amiss. They had sneaked in with guns drawn, but now they all surveyed the area with quizzical faces. The corrals were empty, the courtyard deserted. The marshal ordered the men to start searching the houses. At the center of the compound, Ben studied the grounds, the homes, and the chapel. It all seemed so simple, so harmless. From the description Peri gave, Ben looked for the house that was the center of the evil at the compound. There it sat, small, white and unassuming. He walked to it with Sam in tow.

"Is this the place she was talking about?" Sam asked.

"I think so," answered Ben.

They reached the house and turned the knob. It was locked. They walked around to the back of the house, checking windows as they went. The curtains were all drawn and the windows all locked. At the back, Ben saw the broken window that Emma had described in her escape, and knew without a doubt this was the place. A lush bed of brilliant purple flowers waved in the breeze as if telling a story of what they had seen. They looked peculiar with their odd shaped petals and meticulously groomed bed against the horror of what had taken place there. For a moment Ben was mesmerized. He reached out to touch one.

"Don't," Sam urged.

Ben hesitated and looked over.

"Wolfsbane," Sam said. "It's poisonous, even to touch."

Ben pulled his hand back and studied the plants. The area had been cleared and prepared for the plants. A garden of poison? Ben shook his head at how the web of repulsion seemed to grow.

"The back door has been kicked in," said Sam.

Ben snapped to and pulled his gun as they slowly pushed open the door. Inside, the room was the scene of chaos. Mounds of boxes, sheets, tools, and broken medical instruments. They pushed through the piles and into the next room. There they found two women. The bloated bodies lay on a bed. Dark dried blood covered the sheets, and the smell was so foul, both Ben and Sam quickly covered their mouths and noses with bandanas, trying to block out the stench. The women's faces were swollen and a ghastly shade of blackish blue. They looked like they had been dead for weeks. A large shard of blood-covered glass lay on the bed, along with a syringe. Hearing the story Emma told about Launa, he figured one was her, but he had no idea who the other was. The condition of the bodies made it hard to determine their age. Their hair was still braided and they wore white long dresses, stained in blood and other body fluids from decay. He tried to cancel out Grace as one, but having only seen her a couple of times, he couldn't say for sure that it was or wasn't her, and he hoped the length of time the bodies had been there was too long for it to be.

They kept their bandanas close to their faces and walked through each room. They didn't know what they expected to find, but with the grisly discovery, they dreaded each step they took. Fortunately, the other rooms were clear of corpses and looked untouched. Sam and Ben opened the front door and stepped out, relieved to be free of the stench of death.

As if emerging from a fog, they found the other men waiting in the courtyard. They wandered, looking confused and uneasy. They already searched the main buildings and some of the homes and found nothing. No people, no animals, no clothes. It was as if they had all vanished.

"Keep looking," Ben said. "We need to search everything. We found two dead women in there. There may be others."

The men split up and went back to searching. After several hours, nothing had turned up. They stood in the courtyard feeling discontented. Their visions of storming the compound and bringing these vile creatures to justice, were dissolving.

Ben pulled the marshal and Dutch aside. "What now?" he asked. "There's no trace of them or where they went."

"I'd have to say, they saw what was coming and left," Dutch said. "They had to know they'd be found out and be facing a fight with the law." He looked at Sam. "And I'm pretty sure that fire didn't help."

Sam gave him a disagreeable shrug.

"You can't just up and move an entire settlement of people and not leave some idea of where you're going," Ben mused.

The marshal spoke up. "These groups may seem alone, but they have allies in other areas. They have probably found refuge at another compound nearby. They'll gain strength and go back to whatever they were doing."

Dutch nodded. "I agree. Silas Heff isn't going to just lay down and give up. This is his legacy. He'll do whatever it takes to protect it. I bet they've had people watching us this whole time."

"Yep, I wouldn't put it past them," the marshal agreed. "With their money, they have people all over this region willing to help them."

"Help them hurt us?" asked Ben.

"They stick together and they do this stuff in the name of God, so they don't view it the same way we do," the marshal explained. "I've seen them shuffle people around to keep them safe, and also trade women and children like cattle. The idea of killing off their own was a first, but it didn't surprise me. They feel death is the price you pay for going against them. I've seen them hunt down women who've left years later and three states away. Why last year a colony down in southern Utah—"

"Wait," Ben said, cutting him off. "You don't think they've been watching us and waiting for us to leave Montpelier, do you?"

The marshal gave Ben a look as if he hadn't been listening to a word the marshal had said. "Looking at this," he said, motioning to the deserted compound. "I'd say that's exactly what they've done."

Ben's shoulders dropped. "That means they know Emma is there. And alone. I left her alone." He closed his eyes tight and put his head back in frustration. "I left her alone," he said again. The words rang out like a siren in his head. How can this possibly be happening again? he thought as he ran to his horse.

Sam followed, knowing exactly what Ben was thinking. "Peri's with her. She's not alone," he called out.

Ben heard, but his pace only quickened. He began to hear Cooper's mumblings in his head "Emma's in the cabin. Emma's in the cabin." He prayed silently that his intuitions were wrong. He had taken Emma there to protect her, and now he worried he had placed her like bait in a trap.

He relived the conversation as he raced homeward.

When Ben had gone to Dorothea's to take Emma and the baby away to the cabin, Emma had been confused and frightened.

"You told me I was safe here," she said, holding the baby tight against her chest and taking a step back.

"This house is too close to town, and they may come looking here. I want to take you to a place that no one knows about," Ben explained. "It will be harder for them to find."

"Where?" asked Emma.

"It's at the base of the canyon. It's an old cabin," he answered.

"Who lives there?" Ben felt for her, already alone in a strange home and now he expected her to move to yet another unfamiliar location.

"It's empty. It's been empty for a long time, but it's clean and has everything you'll need until we can get things worked out." He put his hand out to her. "I promise it'll be okay."

Emma nodded and took his hand. "I must put things together to take with me."

Ben stood by the door as she placed a few items of clothes and folded blankets for the baby in a borrowed canvas Gladstone bag. She became uneasy as she searched the bed, the table, the floor.

"What is it?" Ben asked.

"The journal. My mother's journal. It's missing," Emma said, perplexed.

"We can look for it later," he said, motioning to the door.

Emma shook her head. "I need it. It's the only thing I have left of my mother."

"No one's been in the room except you and Dorothea, and she wouldn't take it," Ben said. "It'll turn up. I'll look for it later. Please trust me that we need to go. You'll be safe at the cabin."

"I'll be all alone there?" she asked, her eyes wide with fear.

Ben paused and looked down into her brown eyes. "No. I'll be there. As much as you would like and need." He felt his stomach drop at the increasing need he had to be with her.

They had spent days at Dorothea's kitchen table in casual chatter after Emma was well and feeling up to being around other people. Ben was struck by her mature poise and incredible beauty. Though he was fifteen years older she told him she found him young and handsome. She admired his strong hands and muscled forearms. He told her he would protect her and keep her and her baby safe. When Emma agreed to go with him, she placed her life completely in his care.

"Please don't leave," Emma implored, when Ben told her they planned to raid the compound. "I'm afraid to be alone."

Ben kissed her forehead. "Peri will be here. I'll never leave you alone. I promise."

As Ben relived this in his mind, the guilt and worry tore at his gut, and he spurred the horse on even faster.

The other men followed. The thunder of hooves echoed throughout the valley.

Chapter 32

Montpelier, Idaho
October 9, 1896

Peri shook the dirt off the shovel and tied it on her saddlebag. She stood on the edge of the mesa and looked out over the valley, feeling good about putting a close to a painful part of her past. She took a deep and cleansing breath and let the sun warm her face. On the soft grass, she laid down and looked up to the bright sky. Her breath became deep and rhythmic and soon she drifted off to sleep. She dreamed of Sam riding back from the fire. She saw his horse pounding the ground in a full run, nostrils flared and its mane flowing. Peri couldn't see Sam's face. He was bent down low beneath his hat, hidden as the horse coursed toward her.

Soon worry took over the feeling of anticipation. Why did he seem so frantic and distressed? Her heart hammered in her chest as the anxiety turned to dread. And then as the horse was almost upon her, Sam raised his head, and instead she saw

Marty. The vision shocked Peri awake. Her skin was soaked in sweat and her chest heaved from panic.

The relief of realizing it was all a dream came slowly as Peri sized up her situation. Why did she think he'd just go on his way after she had led him so far off the path? Of course he'd be bent on revenge and anger, and the one way to do it well was to partner with those at Cedar Creek. She should have known and should have planned for what was coming, but with everything that had happened since she returned with the evidence against the Kingdom of Glory, she hadn't really considered the backlash she expected from Marty. She sat up and brought her thoughts back to Sam.

"Do you love him?" Sam had asked as they rode back from her rescue from Marty.

Peri shook her head.

"Did you?" His tone wasn't defensive or harsh, in fact it was the voice of someone sincerely hoping it wasn't so.

Peri looked over to him. "I thought I did. But what I felt . . . that wasn't love."

Sam stayed quiet as they rode. Was he angry, or did he only feel relief? Hopefully, he was so grateful Peri was there with him that he couldn't be mad. She had been betrayed and hurt, and she knew he was angry about that, but she also knew that he didn't want her to be punished for hurting him. It wouldn't make him happy or avenged to see her suffer. She was happy that Sam wanted her for his own. He wanted the angry fire he saw in her eyes to fade for good.

I love you, Sam. It is what she wanted to say, what she should have said, but she didn't and now she regretted not saying those three words more than anything. Her heart pounded, wanting to see him and let him know how she felt. She had felt she was alone in the world and without a home for so many years, and now as she pictured Sam's face, all she thought of was home. He was that for her. No cabin, no bricks and mortar, no town or state, simply him.

Peri stood up and readied herself to go back to the cabin with Emma. She looked for Chance, but he was gone. It wasn't odd for him to wander off looking for grass, but this time it felt unsettling. She called for him, and then stood and listened for his rustle in the branches or the blow of his nose and mouth. Nothing.

At the edge of the vista, she looked out over the valley, hoping to see his large red body against the dry dirt and sage, and as she searched, dust clouds and horses caught her attention. Men on horses. She looked closer, trying to identify who they were. Who was racing toward the town in a frantic sprint? Had Sam and the group returned? She wondered how long she had slept. She felt her stomach drop. Did something go wrong? Were they ambushed? Or was this the very nightmare Emma had feared. Were these men on horses from Cedar Creek?

Peri began to run back to the trail and toward the cabin. "Chance!" she called as she ran, stumbling over rocks and branches. Her stomach sank as she thought about Emma and baby Paul alone and unaware. She had promised Ben she wouldn't leave them alone and now she was rushing back, not knowing if she'd find them safe with Ben and the other men having returned, or in the grasp of Silas and his followers. On a steep hill, she stepped on a fallen tree and her ankle bent. She lost her balance and fell, tumbling down the rough ridge and landing hard on the rocks below. For a moment she saw the sun, but it soon began to spin and the pain in her ankle radiated to her foot. She tried to stand but both her head and her ankle left her slumped on the ground.

Peri felt tears of frustration building, but knew it would do nothing but make her situation worse. She pulled herself to sitting, and then dragged herself under the shade of a juniper bush. She knew that even if she was able to run, it wasn't possible to get to the cabin in time to warn Emma, but she couldn't bring herself to just give up. She tried again to stand, but the pain was too much. She felt her ankle beginning to swell, and her boot start to tighten. She knew if she removed the boot, she'd never get it back on, so she gave up trying to see how it looked. She needed a splint or crutch.

Peri surveyed the area for a large branch. Seeing one in the distance, she used her arms to drag herself to it. The rough and rocky terrain grabbed at her skin and clothes, but she managed to reach the branch and use it to brace herself as she stood up. It was sturdy, but she still wondered if it would hold her weight as she made her way down the canyon and to whatever awaited at the cabin below. The top of the branch was ragged and sharp, so she removed her vest and wrapped it around the splintered edge for padding. She put her faith and weight on the branch and took her first painful step. Peri was surprised at how well it worked and took another. Soon she was hobbling slowly through the rows of willows and cottonwood trees, injured, but determined to make it back.

Chapter 33

Emma

October 9, 1896

I was scared and damaged when I came to this town. I wasn't even aware of what this town was or where I'd been until days later and the fever broke. I remembered that Peri had come to Cedar Creek and was the one who led us to freedom. The memories of Silas grabbing me and my determined swing that allowed me to escape were vivid. I remembered feeling scared and being in pain, but once I heard the cry of my son, everything went dark.

When I awoke at Dorothea's home, I was sure Silas was close. It was Ben who reassured me and kept me calm. Even when I learned that I had been left behind, he made me feel I had a place I belonged. Ben protected me and in just a few weeks I knew I loved him, and he loved me. I was a married woman with another man's child and he still wanted me. Ben tried to tell me my marriage to Deon wasn't real, and now that he was dead, I wasn't married at all, but I remember taking those vows and while I regret what I did, it makes it no less real.

My son is healthy and beautiful. I didn't expect him to be that way. I knew about the problems the babies had in Cedar Creek. They blamed it on wickedness, and I felt I was ripe for punishment. These children of sin were often shunned and shuffled away. Like many things at the compound, if it wasn't the image of perfection it was hidden. No one on the compound wanted to admit or acknowledge there was a problem, so it continued. I know now that is why I was brought there. I was new blood. Even Silas himself had the markings of the children of sin. His ears were low and his forehead was large, and the hair on his face, as sparse as it was, covered the deformed jaw that was characteristic of the children. It happened too many times, and the prophet needed perfect heirs to carry on the work.

They preyed on women who were desperate. Widows, the destitute, and especially those with young girls that could eventually be wives. Deon paid off their debts and promised them lives without want. Their children would be fed and clothed and taken care of by an entire community of faithful god-fearing people. Of course, the church's real intent never surfaced until these women were securely locked away and unable to ever get out. Those who couldn't bear children were given jobs or sent away on what the elders called "missions" for the church. Those women who left were never seen again.

My mother was spared because of us. Peri and I were young and even though Peri was mouthy and stubborn, she was viewed as precious because of her potential to bear healthy children. It wasn't until she ran off that the men of the compound realized the risks they took in bringing in those who were not indoctrinated in the teachings of the Kingdom of Glory church from birth.

This was especially obvious to Eliza, who hated the idea of outsiders. Her other sister wives were all cousins or closer and none of them had been successful in producing an heir for Deon. Eliza had borne many, but lost all except Silas, who was her first. She was aware of his imperfections at birth, but it was new to her and she felt God had a plan. After several more children were born misshapen and eventually died, she clung to Silas as her only hope to keep her status as the mother of the future prophet.

When my pregnancy was revealed, I had no idea how precarious that condition was. And now with the blood of Silas, the new prophet of the Kingdom of Glory, the desire to have his only heir would be the quest of the entire community. I would never be completely safe again as long as they were out there believing I had stolen their savior. It would be their promise of a place in heaven to find him and bring him home. My fate was not what mattered. My life stood in the way and would be sacrificed in the name of God for them to fulfill their mission.

I know that the security Ben gave me was part of the reason I loved him so dearly. I knew I was safe with him, and that he would do whatever it took to keep me and Paul unharmed, but when he was away, fears overtook me. I thought as the days passed I would settle and begin to regain my sense of comfort, but I never have. I've seen too much, known too much, and this not only made me a target for Silas and the others, but also kept the horrifying deeds alive in my head.

I paced the hard dirt floors most of the days and rarely left the walls of the cabin. Only when Ben returned for lunch or in the evening did I find solace. I didn't even have the sense of loneliness. I was alone with my thoughts for hours every day, but the only person I wanted to be with was him. I didn't miss the constant soft toned prattle from my sister wives. I didn't miss anything about the compound. I was glad to be free from the rules and constant hovering of everyone from the elders to Eliza. I wondered what she had done when she went to the Spirit Keeper's house and found Launa dead and me gone. Was she angry or relieved? I wondered if she ever believed that what went on in that house was wrong.

It wasn't until Peri returned with the horrifying proof that I put all the strange and evil pieces together. My mother's letters should have been plenty for me to comprehend the real meaning, but her description of treasures wasn't enough for me to grasp what she had really been tasked to do.

It wasn't until I remembered my walks with Eliza and her passion for the purple hooded flowers that I knew their real purpose. Her dedication to their care wasn't because of their rich and deep color, but for the poison they produced and the serum she was able to create that kept the lineage of the Kingdom of Glory from being tarnished with the markings of sin. Those blooms rid them of the shame that her tainted and immoral union created.

My mother took her own life through those blooms. The guilt and anguish she must have felt seeing and doing the tasks of the Spirit Keepers, was more than she could bear. That is what I tell myself. That is what I hope. I pray she knew that what she was doing, what the Kingdom of Glory church was doing was wrong. Taking the lives of those who didn't measure up to their standards, weren't born in the image and likeness of God. Removing those who didn't serve the purpose of the gospel to help in the bringing forth perfect and pure new members of the family. Eliminating the possibility of competition in the taking of young wives. And killing any threat of unseating the prophet, Uncle Deon.

The other men on the compound were referred to as Brother, the exception was the prophet. Everyone called him Uncle. I never questioned the reason, but now I know why. The guilt of

Eliza was well hidden, but the thought of calling Deon who he really was, must have been too much even for her to hear.

They were culling children. My mother believed it was God's work, until at some point she didn't, and then all that was left was a mind haunted with the deeds she had done. She lost her faith and her purpose, and she wanted to go home. I don't know if I will see her again. If the afterlife does exist, and there is a heaven and hell, I wonder where she'll be. I wonder where I'll be.

I find myself clinging to my child. He's the heir to the Kingdom of Glory church, and I hope he will never live to see a day of it. Our life is here now, here in this cabin and in this town that we stumbled upon in our frantic flight. As I sit, I can hear the thunder of hooves approach, and while my heart races, I tell myself to fight the fear, or I'll never be able to live. Where once there was terror, I'm beginning to feel myself ease as time passes on. I don't know if I will ever feel completely safe or stop worrying that he'll find me. I will probably never be able to remove the man who planned to kill me and my child from the center of my nightmares. And even with time, I still dread the sound of footsteps on my stoop. I hope someday I can breathe, knowing that when I open that door, it won't be violence and hate that I face, but until then, all I can do is hope.

The horses have reached the front, and the clank of spurs and boots are on my porch. They are here. I hold my breath and my child close to me, as I go to open that door.

Chapter 34

Montpelier, Idaho
October 9, 1896

When Emma opened the door, a dirty and disheveled Grace stood there. She kept her eyes downcast.

"Grace?" Emma asked surprised. However, her delight in seeing her young friend turned to dread, when Silas, Marty, and two other men appeared.

"I'm sorry," Grace whispered as she was pushed aside and Silas strode into the cabin. His normal sneer was bolder and more prominent than ever.

"Where's my son?" he demanded.

Emma tried to stand tall against him, but her furtive glance, directed Silas to where the baby lay sleeping. Emma rushed to block him from the basket. "Please," she begged.

Silas huffed and shoved her away. He walked to the basket and looked down at where Paul slept, unaware of the horror surrounding him. He picked up the basket by the handles as Emma recovered and rushed at him.

"No," she screamed.

Grace suddenly came to life and burst forward, grasping at the basket. "You said we'd just get the money!"

"Shut her up," Silas ordered Marty.

Marty stepped up and grabbed Grace from behind. She wriggled free, but then Marty backhanded her so hard she fell to the floor. She lay there sprawled and stunned from the blow.

"Please, don't take my baby!" Emma cried.

"Where's the silver?" Silas asked, as though he was looking to bargain.

Emma ran to the hearth, dropped to the floor and began to remove several planks of wood. "It's here. You can have it all," she sobbed as she removed the bags.

Silas smiled and motioned to one of the other men to retrieve them.

Emma shoved the bags toward them, and then stood and turned to Silas. Silas placed the basket on the floor as he examined the bags and their contents. He nodded to the men and they each took several bags and then left the house.

Emma reached for the baby. Silas booted her aside, hurling her back to the floor. As pain seared through her shoulder, she scrambled to her feet. Silas picked up the basket.

"I gave you the silver!" Emma pleaded.

"And I'm taking my son," Silas answered with venom. "You would deny him his place in God's plan? He has been chosen."

"Please!" Emma begged.

"You were once so faithful. Don't deny our son his destiny. You know this is what the Lord wills," Silas said, his face a mockery of pious and righteous indignation.

"No," said Emma. "This is wrong. You can't do this."

Silas raised his chin, huffed and then stalked out of the cabin with the basket. The two other men were already on their horses waiting. Emma followed frantically.

"Keep her away," Silas ordered Marty as he began to strap the basket to the back of his horse.

Marty threw Emma to the floor inside the cabin.

Silas was about to lift the basket onto the horse when a figure appeared from between the trees.

"That's Emma's baby," Cooper said, pointing a rifle at Silas.

Silas placed the basket on the ground and raised his hands. He looked over at the two other men, who sat watching on their horses. Silas smiled and approached Cooper as he tried to reason with him. "This is not Emma's baby. She stole him from me," he said.

Cooper listened, the gun still pointed. He looked scared and unsteady. "It's Emma's baby," Cooper said again. "That's what they say. It's Emma's baby."

Silas was becoming enraged. His protruding forehead had turned red, and sweat had his hair clinging to his face. "Okay, I'll take the baby back inside to Emma," he said, with his hands still up.

Cooper looked skeptical but nodded.

Silas plucked up the basket and began to walk up the stairs of the small porch.

"Cooper, it's a trick!" Grace shouted from behind Marty, who was at the open door. Marty spun around and lunged to punch her, and then he saw the pistol.

Grace stood with it pointed at his heart.

Emma backed away from the window where she had been watching when Cooper entered the clearing. Shocked by Grace's boldness, she backed into a wooden rocker and dropped down onto the seat.

Marty's hand went to his holster but it was empty. He looked up, surprised, and then leered at Grace.

"You'll never hit me again," Grace said. She held the gun steady in both hands.

Marty scoffed and took a step toward her. The shot deafened Emma for a moment, but she watched as his face turned to disbelief when the bullet hit his chest. He staggered backward. The wall broke his fall, and a blood trail smeared it as he sank to the floor.

Hearing the shot, Silas ducked. He dropped the basket and stood to run, but another shot rang out, piercing the thick tension of the air.

Emma stood in the doorway holding the rifle. Silas lay dead, face down in the dirt.

The other men's horses reared at the sound of gunfire, and spun in frantic circles as their riders drew their weapons. One aimed at Emma. She scrambled back into the cabin, out of sight. Another shot went off, and that rider fell to the ground. Cooper had hit his mark. The remaining man kicked his horse and it took off, racing behind the cabin and out of view.

Emma got to her feet and ran to the basket. She pulled the baby to her. He was crying from the noise, but seemed otherwise unhurt. Grace stepped over the body of her brother and stood in the doorway. Cooper crouched down in thought, the gun on the ground beside him. The cool evening air pricked at them as silence fell over the bloody scene.

As Emma comforted the baby, she leaned against Grace and they stood together, stunned, looking at the bodies of those who had haunted them.

"What do we do now?" Grace asked.

Emma took a deep breath and shrugged.

A lone gunshot rang out in the distance. All three looked up to where the noise came from. Neither spoke, and soon the deathly silence returned.

Emma and Grace rolled Marty's body out onto the front porch, then closed the cabin door.

"It's horses," Cooper said. He stood up and grabbed the gun. The sound of hooves on the packed dirt was near. Emma and Grace hurried back into the cabin and took cover.

"No more," said Emma, weakly.

Grace picked up Marty's gun and peered out the crack of the door as Emma watched out the window.

Cooper stood guard on the porch.

When the horses came into view, Emma recognized Ben and Sam, their faces full of fear as they got closer and saw the carnage. They dismounted and approached the cabin. Seeing Cooper settled them a bit, but the sight of bodies, blood and struggle still had them panicked.

When they came through the door. Emma burst into tears. She ran to Ben and melted into his chest.

"Peri?" Sam asked as he followed Ben inside. In the dark of the evening, he scanned the small room. On the floor was a bowl and spoon with food splattered about, the signs of a struggle, and a light blue blouse. *The* light blue blouse. Sam picked it up and held it to his chest.

Emma shook her head. "I don't know," she said. "She went up the hillside . . ." her voice trailed off as she pointed behind the cabin.

Grace shot her a look. Emma was pointing in the very direction of the lone gun shot. Her heart dropped to her stomach.

"What? Where is she?" Sam's face paled.

"She went up the hillside but she never returned," Emma said. Her eyes burned with unshed tears.

"She left you here alone?" Ben asked.

Emma trembled. "She wasn't supposed to be gone long. Oh dear."

~*~

Sam ran back out to his horse, mounted and took off toward the foothills. He pushed the horse and swiftly made his way through the brush and slopes until he saw a body lying in the trail in the distance. He slowed the horse and approached cautiously. Sam hesitated, looked over, and noticed the sorrel gelding standing, saddled but untied, and grazing casually in the willows. It was Peri's horse.

Sam dismounted and pulled his gun. He walked carefully to the body and felt his eyes begin to well in fear. "Please no," he whispered.

With just the light of the sunset, he came closer. He bent down to roll the body over, and heard a voice from behind.

"Drop the gun." It was Peri.

Sam froze, startled, and then elated, to hear her voice. "Peri?" he called back.

"Sam?" she called. "Sam!"

He turned and tried to find her in the dim light.

"I'm here. I can't move," she called back.

He followed her voice to find her lying next to a large willow. Sam scooped her up. She winced at the pain in her ankle, but still clung to him tightly.

"I thought I'd lost you," he said. His tears mixed with hers on his cheeks.

When Sam entered the cabin holding her, Emma gasped in joy. "We heard a shot," she said.

"She got the last of them," said Sam, as he carefully sat her down.

Grace went to Peri and they embraced.

For several minutes Emma and Grace explained what had happened, and Peri sat looking stunned. When they finished, she took a deep breath.

For a moment they all sat in thought, only the crackle from the hearth breaking the silence.

"Is it over?" Emma asked.

Ben pulled her close as they all contemplated the question.

The exhausted and dazed group sat solemnly together and decided what they must do next. As they watched the wisps of smoke and searched each other's eyes for answers, it soon became clear. To move on they'd need to leave the past behind and eliminate all that might bind them to it.

Chapter 35

Emma

October 10, 1896

I watched as bright amber sparks and soft smoke rose slowly into the black sky. It was the old cabin that went up in flames. No one knows how it started, but it was fully engulfed before anyone was able to even try to save it. It was Sam's old home and people in town put a hand on his shoulder to comfort him, knowing the role it had played in his life. Sam graciously accepted their condolences, and knew they would never fully understand the extent of his mourning.

Along with the logs and mortar, the fire cleared away the past secrets and horrors that haunted those he loved. As the ash disappeared in the breeze, so did any trace of the ones who held their lives and dreams captive.

When the flames had waned and the smoke was but a small curling spire, the light of the moon illuminated the hillside where the grave of the lost souls rested. Their lives had been cut short through fanaticism and fear. They would not breathe the air of spring, or feel the bite of winter's cold. They would never know the love of parents or the pain of sorrow. They had been swept away from this life like the dry leaves of fall. No more tears, no more pain, nothing left but what remains buried in a box. There may be no vengeance, justice, or even closure for them now, but even though these treasures were lost, it is my hope that through this they won't be forgotten.

END

BOOKS BY BRENDA STANLEY

FICTION:

The Color of Snow
Like Ravens in Winter
I Am Nuchu

NONFICTION:

That's a Lot of Crock
Everyday Vegetarian
Fast Mama, Slow Cooker
The Dinner Belle
Tales of the Dinner Belle